The Ultimate Price

"A half-day's travel west of here stands a spire of black rock," Shemnara said. "It is called Karoc-Tor and on its top is the broken citadel, an ancient ruin. It is there that Gadion makes his home. All you need to do to meet your destiny is go there."

"You still haven't said why we should do such a fool thing," Elidor said. "You're asking us to risk an awful lot just to save your town. What do we get if we go?"

Davyn smiled to himself. True to Elidor's nature, the elf wanted to know what was in it for him. If Shemnara was offended by such a question, she gave no sign.

"I know your group travels for a reason," Shemnara said. "Each of you seeks the keys to your destiny. One of you seeks the keys to your past. If you return victorious, I will tell Nearra how to recover her identity."

"What about the rest of us?" Elidor asked.

"Each of you who goes will return with something priceless," Shemnara said. "But know this. If you go, someone close to you will die. And two of you will never be the same."

THE NEW
ADVENTURES

SPELLBINDER QUARTET

THE NEW
ADVENTURES
VOLUME
3

THE
DRAGON WELL

DAN WILLIS

COVER & INTERIOR ART
Vinod Rams

**MIRROR
STONE**

Cover and interior art by Vinod Rams
Cartography by Dennis Kauth
First Printing: September 2004
Library of Congress Catalog Card Number: 2004106846

9 8 7 6 5 4 3 2 1

US ISBN: 0-7869-3354-2
UK ISBN: 0-7869-3355-0
620-17662-001-EN

U.S., CANADA,	EUROPEAN HEADQUARTERS
ASIA, PACIFIC, & LATIN AMERICA	Wizards of the Coast, Belgium
Wizards of the Coast, Inc.	T Hofveld 6d
P.O. Box 707	1702 Groot-Bijgaarden
Renton, WA 98057-0707	Belgium
+1-800-324-6496	+322 457 3350

Visit our website at **www.mirrorstonebooks.com**

TO CHERSTINE, WHO BELIEVED IN ME,
TO STAN WHO SUPPORTED ME,
AND TO TRACY WHO SHOWED ME THE WAY.

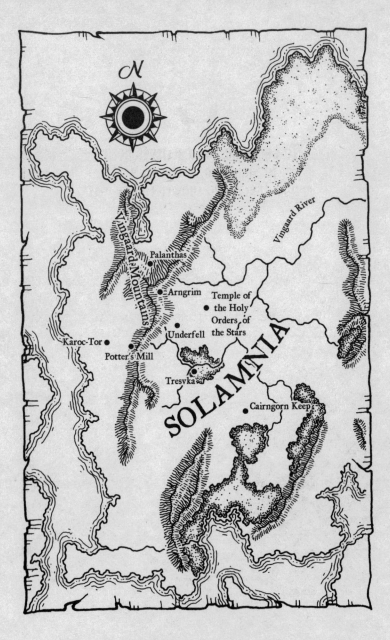

Contents

1   THE REPORT

Cairngorn Keep stood alone on a wooded hillside. Its dull gray towers thrust up from the furry cover of the evergreens like the bones of some impossibly large giant. Yellow lights burned through some of its upper windows, casting round haloes in the foul weather. An early winter storm pelted the unyielding towers and ramparts of the keep with fat raindrops and slushy hail. The wind howled with a vengeance and the pines on the hill creaked and cracked in its fury.

Anyone fool enough to be out on such a night might have seen the wizard. He stood on the main balcony above the gates, as uncaring about the storm as the castle around him. Despite the bone-chilling wind and the heavy downpour, the man was dressed lightly in a robe of fine black silk. Around his waist he had bound his robe with a belt of silver links that gleamed brightly against the blackness of the garment. His hood was thrown back, revealing flowing gray hair and a peppery beard. The rain that soaked the balcony around him seemed to be ignoring the man himself. He stood calmly surveying the valley below, a dry island in a sea of wet.

Maddoc ground his teeth in frustration as he stared off into the gathering darkness. Despite the wizard's powerful magic, his eyes could only see so far and that fact galled him. He knew that somewhere beyond the distant hills the vessel that bore Asvoria's soul struggled to keep that soul at bay. Sooner or later Nearra's strength would fail her, and Asvoria would emerge. When that happened, Maddoc would have his prize. In the meantime, all Maddoc could do was wait, and Maddoc was not a patient man.

A cold, stinging sheet of rain swept over the balcony where Maddoc stood. Normally he wouldn't have been out in such weather, but it had been over a week since he'd last heard from his minion, Oddvar. Nothing irritated Maddoc more than no news so Maddoc had taken to pacing Cairngorn's halls and passages, finally ending up on his favorite balcony. It was as if he felt his watching from the balcony would make news come faster. The more rational part of Maddoc's brain knew that nothing he could do would make Shaera, his familiar, find Oddvar faster. Standing on the balcony in the rain, staring out at the dark countryside, gave Maddoc the satisfaction that he was doing something, so he persisted.

"Your eminence," a raspy voice called from the shelter of the keep.

A brief look of annoyance crossed Maddoc's face and he turned slightly toward the voice.

"What is it, Kaz'un?" he sighed.

"A thoussand pardonss, Lord Maddoc," Kaz'un continued, "but you assked to be informed if there wass any change in the mirror."

"Shaera's found the dwarf, then?" Maddoc asked, turning to face the draconian.

"Sso it would sseem," Kaz'un confirmed, nodding his large reptilian head.

Maddoc swept from the balcony, leaving the dry spot where he'd been standing to be quickly gobbled up by the storm. He pushed past Kaz'un and hurried down the carpeted hallway toward his study.

Maddoc's study occupied the top room in the south tower. It was small and cozy, with curved bookshelves covering most of its walls and provided with comfortable chairs for reading. A fire had been laid in the hearth, and when Maddoc entered he found the room comfortable and snug.

A small, freestanding mirror stood on a low table by one of the chairs. Rather than reflecting the room, the mirror's polished silver surface swirled with colors and strange lights. Maddoc moved quickly to the chair and seated himself in front of the mirror. Eagerly he reached forward but stopped himself before his fingers made contact with the mirror's pulsating surface.

"Leave me," he instructed Kaz'un, who had followed him into the room. "This will take some time," he added as the big draconian turned back to the door. "Tell the cook to prepare my dinner and wait for me in the dining room. I will have instructions for you later."

"Yess, your eminence," Kaz'un hissed, and then he let himself out, shutting the door behind him.

Maddoc took a deep breath and let it out slowly, clearing his mind. He touched the mirror. Instantly, the swirling colors on the silver surface reached out and surrounded Maddoc. The old wizard could feel the miles rushing by him as his consciousness stretched across the land.

"Shaera," he whispered, calling the name of his beloved falcon familiar. "I am here."

Gradually the swirling images in the mirror cleared, revealing snow-covered mountainside bathed in bright afternoon light. Maddoc's eyes were closed but he saw the scene just the same. He felt the familiar union as his mind and thoughts joined with the powerful black falcon so many miles away.

Maddoc looked around through Shaera's eyes and found a short, heavily cloaked figure standing in the snow below.

"Where have you been, dwarf?" Maddoc snapped, perhaps a bit more forcefully than he needed.

"Your forgiveness, master," Oddvar growled from the shadows of his hood. "I'd have reported before this if your bird had found me sooner."

Maddoc's eyes narrowed at the dwarf's impertinence but he chose to let it pass for now. "Where are you?"

The dwarf shrugged. "I'm not sure."

"Oddvar," Maddoc said, menace creeping into his voice, "I'm paying you to know these things."

The dwarf gave a humorless laugh. "Not nearly enough," he said under his breath.

Maddoc's jaw clenched reflexively as he wished Oddvar were there in person so he could use some rather unpleasant spells on the dwarf. He was about to tell Oddvar exactly what would happen to him if he kept up this insolence, but something made him stop. As Shaera looked around, it became plain to the wizard that the dwarf was high up in the mountains, a place where he had no business to be.

"Where are you?" Maddoc asked again, staring hard through the falcon's eyes in an attempt to get his bearings. "Where is the girl?!"

"We're somewhere up in the Vingaard Mountains. It's been snowing for over a week so I'm not sure exactly where."

"What are you still doing there, you fool? You had specific instructions to trail Nearra to Arngrim and use the Scarlet Brethren to force the Emergence."

"I'm afraid your plan was a failure, master. A part of Asvoria emerged in the girl, but when Arngrim was destroyed, she seemed to regain control."

"Then what of Tezrat Junction? Did you not send your little rodent companions to set the next stage of our plan in motion?"

"Yes, but it's pointless now, master. You see . . . " Oddvar gulped. "The girl is headed over the mountains along with those useless friends of hers."

"Over the mountains!" Maddoc's mind raced. Only a fool would travel into the mountains with winter coming on. Davyn knew better, Maddoc was sure. His son would never risk anything so foolish.

"I don't think you're giving those youngsters enough credit," Oddvar continued when Maddoc didn't reply. "They made it out of Arngrim and far into the mountains on their own."

"Stop blaming a group of children for your failures," Maddoc said, cutting off Oddvar's excuse. "You're sure the children went into the mountains?" he asked the dwarf again.

Oddvar nodded, his steamy breath emerging from the folds of his hood.

"Where are they now?" Maddoc asked.

"Well, that's the trouble. Once it started snowing we lost the trail."

"What!" Anger surged through Maddoc. "You're beginning to annoy me, dwarf," he hissed. "You can be replaced."

"You're going to put Drefan in charge? I'd almost pay to see that." Oddvar chuckled.

"And where is that ridiculous goblin?" Maddoc growled, scanning the trees through Shaera's eyes.

"Drefan saw some signs that other goblins were in the area." Oddvar pulled the front of his hood down to keep the glare out of his sensitive eyes. "He's going to convince them to help us through the mountains and find the little brats."

"Good. Find the girl and force the Emergence. If she's come through the mountains, then she and her friends are miles from any settlement. Now is your chance to press them."

"Not to worry, master." Oddvar flashed a devilish smile. "The youngsters aren't properly equipped or provisioned for a trip through the mountains. If they aren't at their wits' end already, they will be soon. Asvoria will emerge when they start freezing to death."

"See that it happens," came Maddoc's reply. "If the cold doesn't do the trick, there's a bandit named Gadion somewhere near there. He owes me a few favors."

"I know the place," Oddvar grumbled.

"I want that sorceress's power and I want it now, Oddvar."

"As you wish, master." Oddvar bowed.

Maddoc took his hand from the mirror and broke the connection. He poured himself a brandy from a decanter on the table and sat back in his chair. Normally he would have enjoyed the fire's warmth, but his mind was troubled.

Oddvar was becoming a problem. Maddoc knew the dwarf was usually sullen and surly, but he must be especially inept to allow a group of wet-behind-the-ears children to keep getting the better of him. Still, Maddoc was forced to wonder if there was something to the dwarf's objections. He knew that Davyn had great potential, but at fifteen the boy was too inexperienced to be much of a threat.

"Sixteen," Maddoc chuckled, breaking the silence of the room. Davyn's birthday had passed just a week ago. "At this rate I'll be a grandfather before Oddvar succeeds."

Still, Maddoc could not help dwelling on Davyn's decision to go over the mountains. There was just no reason to take such a chance. A sudden thought occurred to Maddoc, and he froze in the act of raising his glass to his lips.

What if Davyn went into the mountains to keep the girl away from me? Nearra was pretty for a peasant girl, but could Davyn be so smitten he would openly defy me, his father?

"Impossible," Maddoc scoffed aloud. He took a swig from his cup, but there remained a nagging doubt in the back of his mind. Davyn had shown impertinence in the past, but he had never taken it quite this far. A betrayal of this magnitude would have serious consequences.

Maddoc took another drink. Despite his frustration there was still plenty of time to coax Asvoria's spirit from Nearra's body. Patience, he reminded himself, would yield great rewards once the long-dead sorceress's knowledge was his. The Emergence first. There will be time enough to punish Davyn when his plans are completed. The thought made Maddoc smile.

Quenching the fire with a wave of his hand, Maddoc set down the empty glass and the decanter and went down to dinner.

2 THE DOG HOUSE

Davyn felt the sodden leaves shift under his feet as he led his friends up the trail through the seemingly impassable Vingaard Mountains.

The mountain slope gleamed in the late morning light. At the highest elevations, snow had fallen, blanketing the upper slopes with sheets of white that reflected the rising sun with blinding brilliance. Lower on the mountains the fir trees and the evergreens marched upward, like rank upon rank of fuzzy soldiers. Some of the trees on the hills around them still clung vainly to their leaves. What leaves had fallen pooled on the trail, occasionally rising to dance and play in the passing wind.

Davyn walked quickly with the appearance of a confidence he didn't feel. He knew enough about mountains to suspect that the pass he was aiming for would take him through to the western edge of the continent. But he had no way of knowing how long a journey it was likely to be—or whether they'd make it out alive. Despite the heat generated by his rapid walking, Davyn shivered. The weather had been mild, but Davyn could feel it turning.

Behind him, Davyn could hear Nearra, trudging wearily along the path. Despite her small frame and general lack of stamina, the girl had neither complained nor stopped. She just kept shuffling wearily onward. Farther back were the sounds of Catriona, wheezing under the weight of her heavy armor, and then the voice of Sindri, who was apparently boring the elf with tales of his misspent youth. Elidor walked in silence, bearing the onslaught of conversation from the kender with tremendous patience.

A week had passed since they'd left the cursed land of Arngrim, and Davyn's pace was designed specifically to put as much distance as possible between him and it. Davyn knew Maddoc's plans and he'd had enough of them. What happened in Arngrim was beyond all reason. The only way Nearra had survived was by tapping some of Asvoria's power—and that bothered Davyn immensely. Asvoria's power had been terrible. In those moments beneath Arngrim, Davyn knew Asvoria must never be allowed to emerge. Nearra had to be taken someplace safe.

"Do you mean to conquer the mountain today?" Catriona puffed, lumbering up from behind. "I need to rest."

Davyn turned at the warrior's remark, surprised to hear her voice. He knew the weight of her armor must be exhausting but he was shocked to hear her admit it. Only a few weeks ago, Catriona wouldn't have allowed Davyn to lead the group so far into unknown territory, much less admit she needed a break. But what happened at Arngrim had left her spirit shattered. She had barely spoken since.

Davyn sat down with his back against a tree trunk. A few moments later his weary companions came trudging up, and sank to the ground around him. Only Elidor seemed unaffected by the walk, though Sindri seemed to recover himself fully after only a few minutes rest. All of them were shivering in the cold and the damp. Remnants of snow lingered in places, and their breath steamed in the frigid air.

"So what's your plan?" Elidor asked once everyone had found a seat. "You have to know we can't go over the mountain like this."

The elf held up the hem of his thin wool cloak to emphasize his point.

"We won't have to," Davyn responded, not bothering to keep the irritation out of his voice. "There's a dwarf trading post just up this trail."

"How, exactly, do you know that?" the elf challenged.

Davyn reached over his head and tapped the tree-trunk with his knuckles. Barely visible in the bark was a carved symbol surrounded by three dots.

"Trail marker," Davyn explained. "The symbol is dwarvish for trading post and the dots say how many miles."

"So it's just three miles away?" Sindri said, perking up at the possibility of a new place to explore.

"If we hurry, we'll reach it before dark," Davyn said.

Catriona lifted her head wearily. "You still haven't said why you want to go over the mountains in the first place."

"He wants to hide," Nearra said.

"What does she mean, 'hide'?" Sindri asked.

"We all know what happened back there—in Arngrim," Davyn explained. "You most of all," he added when Catriona lowered her eyes. "That was no accident."

"Maddoc wants us dead," said Nearra.

Davyn felt his cheeks flush at the mention of his father's name. He still hadn't found the strength to admit to his friends who he really was and what he knew of Maddoc's plan. He knew full well that Maddoc didn't want Nearra dead, at least not yet. She was to be the vessel, the final step in his terrible plot to gain control over the powers of an ancient sorceress. But it would never happen, if Davyn could help it.

As soon as we reach the other side of the mountains, he thought. *As soon as Nearra is safe, I'll tell her everything.*

Sindri's voice snapped Davyn out of his reverie. "But how does going over the mountains help us?"

"Because it's the last thing anyone would expect us to do," Davyn explained.

"There's a good reason they wouldn't expect it," Elidor pointed out evenly. "It is clearly insane."

"Winter hasn't set in yet," said Davyn, casting a wary eye at the sky. "With luck, we'll beat the heavy snows through the pass and be on the other side in a few days."

"I like it," Sindri spoke up. "I've never gone straight over a mountain before."

"Let's go then," said Catriona, getting to her feet. "With any luck that trading post will have a good fire going."

Davyn stood and was about to lead the way when Elidor grabbed his shoulder.

"Awfully convenient, you knowing about this trail," the elf observed quietly, so as not to be overheard.

"You're welcome to find your own way," Davyn hissed back. "No one's forcing you to come."

Elidor looked for a moment like he wanted to tell Davyn exactly what to do with the dwarf trading post, but he clamped his mouth shut instead. Not bothering to see whether Elidor would follow, Davyn turned and strode off through the gathering leaves.

When they finally arrived at the trading post, weary and footsore, they found it little more than a cabin standing by itself in a little clearing. The building was old, but its cut-block walls and shingled roof were clean and well maintained. A wooden porch ran along the front, and there was a rail below it for tying up animals. Light shone through cracks in the shutters and beneath the heavy door, and there was smoke coming from the squat, stone chimney. The door and windows seemed smaller than normal, hinting at dwarven construction.

"This is it?" Catriona gasped when she finally caught up.

"It certainly doesn't look like a thriving business," Elidor added.

"Whatever it is, someone's home," Davyn growled, mounting the steps to the porch.

Davyn knocked loudly on the heavy door, then stepped back. There was a moment of shuffling inside the house. Then a small hatch, about chest high on Davyn, opened and a pair of steely eyes looked out.

"Who's there?" a guttural voice called from inside.

"Travelers seeking the trading post," Davyn replied.

There was a strange silence as the dwarf behind the door considered this. Davyn saw the eyes dart around, taking in his companions on the trail behind him.

"How many are you?"

"Five," Davyn said.

The eyes swept the group one more time, and then the little hatch closed. There was a noise of scraping and bumping as the door was unbarred and then, after a long moment, it opened. A sturdy-looking dwarf with a short beard and a short axe stood just inside. He peered out at them for a moment, as if to make sure their numbers had not increased during the time it took him to open the door. Then he stepped back, beckoning Davyn in.

"I'm not used to visitors this late," he said as the group filed in, "especially humans."

"Don't forget me," Sindri piped up, drawing the dwarf's steely gaze over his kender frame. The dwarf made a sour face upon recognizing the kender, but Sindri seemed not to notice.

Inside, the squat building was a model of dwarven efficiency. The main room was large, with a low-slung ceiling and cupboards all around the walls. In the center of the room, a long table with short chairs stood under a massive chandelier made of intricately worked iron. Candles in the chandelier and in sconces along the wall lit the room, augmented by the cozy fire in the stone hearth.

A heavy door blocked the only other opening, leading, no doubt, to storage rooms and the living quarters of the dwarf.

"My name's Dog," the dwarf growled as he shut and bolted the outer door.

"Dog?" everyone asked at once.

"That's right," the dwarf replied, no trace of humor in his voice. "Like the animal you humans are so fond of."

"That's a bit of an unusual name for a dwarf, isn't it?" Elidor asked, barely able to stifle a smirk.

"What if it is, point-ears," the dwarf spat. "What tales are there of your name that make you so worthy to laugh at mine?"

"I'm sure he meant no offense," Davyn interjected, stepping between the axe- bearing dwarf and Elidor. "My name's Davyn," he continued, holding out his hand.

The dwarf held Elidor's gaze with his steely eyes for a long moment, then shifted to look at Davyn.

"Welcome to my home," he said flatly, taking Davyn's offered hand. "Now," he went on, sliding his axe back into his belt sheath and moving to the fire, "what can I be doing for you?"

"We need some supplies," Davyn said.

"You planning on going over the mountain?" Dog asked, a skeptical look on his face.

Catriona sighed. "That seems to be the idea."

"It's a bit late in the season," Dog said, poking the fire. "But the snows haven't hit yet, so you might make it."

"How very reassuring," Elidor grumbled under his breath.

Dog shot him an angry glance, then turned back to Davyn. "You'll need heavier cloaks," Dog said, looking Davyn up and down appraisingly. "And provisions, I assume?"

Davyn nodded, wondering if their meager funds would be sufficient.

"How much have you got to spend?" Dog asked, as if reading Davyn's thoughts.

"Not much," Davyn admitted.

Dog put away his fire poker and strode over to one of the cupboards against the wall. He opened the doors, revealing a series of shelves stocked with boxes and jars of herbs. Below were small barrels, neatly stacked. With a strength beyond his short stature, Dog hoisted one of the kegs onto his shoulder and set it down on the table. He then went to a separate cupboard and opened it. Inside were dozens of pegs with cloaks hanging on them. Dog took one out and brought it over to the table. To Davyn the cloak looked only marginally thicker than the one he had on.

"These should do you if you hurry," Dog said, handing the cloak to Davyn for inspection. "They're the heaviest I've got. You humans usually require thicker ones once the snow starts."

"What about dwarves?" Nearra asked suddenly.

"Dwarves are hearty," Dog replied with a shrug. "We don't need as much protection."

Davyn rubbed the cloak's fabric and looked up. "What's the fastest way over the mountain?"

"You're already on it," Dog replied. "Just follow the trail outside my door. It will take you up through the great saddle and on to the far side."

"Any settlements on the other side?" Elidor asked.

"There are some human towns," Dog admitted, "but personally I've never been."

"If you've never been," Sindri interjected, "how do you know?"

"Because no one builds a road to nowhere, you half-wit," Dog thundered.

"What about provisions?" Davyn cut in, trying to ease the hostile mood in the cabin.

Dog grunted and pulled the lid off the keg. Inside were what appeared to be large, square, white crackers. Dog reached into the mass and scooped some out onto the table.

"Dwarven hardtack," he explained, holding one up for inspection. "It's bread made without yeast. They keep darn near forever and you can live on them indefinitely."

Sindri picked up one of the solid little crackers and tapped it on the table. It thumped loudly against the wood. "How do you eat these things?"

"You soften them up in your mouth or in a broth first," Dog said. "But they aren't bad eating."

"I hope we can carry enough to get us over the mountain," Davyn said.

Dog swept the crackers into two small sacks. "If you put a good foot under you, it only takes a week."

"How much for the cloaks and two weeks' rations?" Davyn asked.

Dog did a few mental calculations and came up with a figure that was more money than they had. Davyn countered, and the bargaining began. After half an hour, Davyn managed to get the cloaks and rations, but it took all but their last few coppers and their existing cloaks in trade. Davyn then counted out their precious few coins while Dog passed out the cloaks and the sacks of hardtack.

"Here," Dog said, putting a small box on the table as Davyn donned his new cloak.

Davyn picked up the box and opened it. It was full of strange roots, the like of which Davyn had never seen. They were fat and brown with yellow meat showing where they'd been cut.

"I was going to try to sell you this, but I doubt your purse will bear any more," Dog chuckled.

"What is it?" Davyn asked, holding up one of the fat roots.

"This is cavern root," Dog explained as he shut his cupboard doors. "Put one root in a pot of water and brew it for an hour. When it's finished, it makes a thick drink we call deep-brew."

"Is that like tea?" Elidor asked.

"Not quite," Dog said. "Deep-brew warms the blood when you drink it. Put a pot on every morning and every night and it'll help keep you warm."

"Does it work on humans?" Nearra asked politely.

Dog smiled and nodded. "I know humans who swear by it," he chuckled. "One fellow comes in once a season and buys whatever I've got on hand."

"Thank you," Davyn said, grateful for the little act of kindness.

"Think nothing of it," Dog scoffed. "You're under my roof and that means you're my responsibility. You're going to need all the help you can get if you're going to make it over the mountains before the first real snow."

Davyn wasn't sure he liked the sound of that but he was determined to go anyway. He stuffed the box of cavern root into his pack and then stood, shouldering the pack under his new cloak. The others, seeing Davyn rise, stood as well.

"Where do you think you're going?" Dog demanded, looking at Davyn as if the boy were crazy.

"We've imposed on you long enough," Davyn said. "We're grateful for your hospitality—"

Dog waved him silent.

"Don't be daft," he said, shaking his head. "I said you're under my roof and I meant it. Till morning, you're my guests."

"Unless that back room is bigger than it looks, I don't think you've got room for us," Nearra said.

"You humans," Dog said. "You never look at anything right."

When Dog was greeted with blank stares, he moved over to the back room door and said, "Where do you think a dwarf would build extra rooms for his house?" He twisted the knob.

The door swung open, revealing a small staircase that descended out of sight, and Davyn suddenly knew why the trading post looked so small. Most of it was underground.

"Now," Dog said, ushering the youth through the door, "I've got a nice joint of mutton on a spit down there and a room with some cots where you can sleep."

"We can't pay you," Nearra said, her voice slightly trembling.

"Not to worry," Dog continued. "A dwarf takes his hospitality seriously. You get some food and some rest, and I'll give you a good breakfast before you go tomorrow. With any luck you'll be up and over the mountain in no time."

"I wish there were some way to repay you," Davyn said after everyone else had gone down the stairs.

"Tell you what," Dog said. "If you make it over, just bring me back a map of the other side."

"It's a deal." Davyn smiled, shaking hands with the dwarf. Then he turned to the stairs and descended toward the wonderful smell of roasting mutton.

3 MOTIVES

It was after midnight when Davyn awoke. It took him a minute to orient himself in the near-total darkness. Then he remembered. He was in Dog's trading post, in the common room the dwarf kept for travelers. Around him, Davyn could hear the rhythmic breathing of his sleeping friends.

Davyn wasn't sure what had awoken him. He sat up on the dwarf-sized cot he'd been using. The remnants of a fire glowed in the hearth, shining a tiny flicker of light into the room. As Davyn looked around, he was instantly aware of what had roused him.

Nearra was gone.

Trying not to worry, Davyn got quietly to his feet. Stooping so as not to hit his head on the low ceiling, Davyn made his way to the door and out into the hallway. At the far end of the carpeted hall was Dog's kitchen. Davyn and his friends had dined there just a few hours ago. A dancing light from the kitchen's massive hearth illuminated the hall. Davyn saw a shadow moving in the kitchen. Davyn released a breath he hadn't even realized he'd been holding. Nearra was safe.

Davyn made his way quietly to the kitchen. He found the girl sitting at the heavy oak dining table nursing a cup of tea.

"Dog said I could help myself," Nearra explained as Davyn entered.

"I was worried about you," Davyn said. "What are you doing up? It's past midnight."

"I couldn't sleep." She tried to cover the blush on her face by taking a drink of her tea.

"Are you still having nightmares?" Davyn asked, taking the seat across from her.

"No, I was just thinking about our journey." Nearra put her cup down and looked Davyn directly in the eye. "I was wondering if it was worth it."

Davyn was surprised. The one constant in their travels had been Nearra's drive to recover her memories and her identity. To hear her doubting it was quite a shock.

"Is this because of what happened in Arngrim?" Davyn asked after a long pause.

Nearra nodded, taking another sip from her steaming cup.

"It was like a door opened in my mind." She shivered.

"That's good then." Davyn forced a smile. The prospect of Asvoria emerging actually sent shivers down Davyn's spine as well, but he couldn't admit that without telling Nearra how he knew.

"I don't think I want to remember any more," Nearra was saying. "In Arngrim, when I could almost remember, it was terrifying—like a waking nightmare. I'm afraid there's something terrible locked up inside me."

Davyn cleared his throat uncomfortably.

"So, you're going to give up?" he asked.

Nearra nodded. "It's for the best. Ever since we left Arngrim, I've been feeling better and better. I'm not having nightmares, and the voice is gone."

"Maybe it was just Arngrim doing that to you."

"No." Nearra shook her head. "The nightmares and voices were there long before Arngrim. I'd felt it ever since you found me in that forest clearing. Whatever it was, it's coming from inside of me—Arngrim just made it stronger. But now . . . " Nearra's eyes shone in the dim light. "I feel almost normal again."

Davyn reached across the table and put his hand on Nearra's.

"You know I'm with you—whatever you want to do," he promised her.

She smiled and put her other hand on top of his. Davyn's heart suddenly beat faster.

"I'm glad you're taking us over the mountains," she confessed. "I feel like I've been given a chance to start my life over with a clean slate. It'll be easier once we're away from the mountains—away from Arngrim."

"What if the dreams come back?" Davyn asked, looking for any excuse to keep Nearra's hand in his.

"I don't want to think about that now," Nearra said. "It'll be fine if you're there with me."

Davyn's heartbeat thundered in his ears. He felt as if his body didn't weigh anything at all. He leaned forward across the table, and Nearra leaned toward him. He could feel her soft breath on his lips. He closed his eyes.

And then a noise came thundering down the darkened hallway. They both jumped apart.

"You kids ought to be getting some rest," Dog's amused voice called down the passageway. "You've got a long trek ahead of you and you're going to need all the energy you've got."

Davyn pushed his chair back. "He's right. We should get some sleep."

Nearra stood up, her eyes barely able to meet his. Together, they shuffled back to the common room, being careful not to walk too close to each other.

Davyn found his cot next to Elidor and lay down quickly. It was a long time, however, before he could get to sleep.

Davyn, Nearra, and their friends had been easy enough to track once the early snow had melted. Despite knowing where they were going, however, Oddvar was not happy. The tracks they found were several days old, maybe as much as a week, and, despite all reason, they were still heading straight into the heart of the mountains. He was glad that he had sent Drefan to gain the assistance of the snow goblins. They may need their assistance after all. But he should have insisted Drefan take the other two along. Fyren and Gifre's idiotic antics were even more unbearable without their leader.

The only bit of good news was the trading post marker the dwarf had found along the trail. Oddvar didn't think Davyn had any money, but he had no way of knowing what the boy might have picked up in Arngrim. If Davyn were able to buy cloaks and supplies he could very well dare the mountain and survive. The more he followed Maddoc's son, the more grudging respect Oddvar gained for the boy.

"They stopped here to rest," Fyren's weaselly voice interrupted Oddvar's thoughts.

"Yes," the dwarf grunted, casting his eyes around the little clearing. "There's a trail marker, too."

Oddvar moved over to the tree where the marker was carved and examined it.

"The trading post is near," he concluded.

"Maybe the children are still there," Fyren observed.

"Not likely," Oddvar contradicted the goblin. "They're moving fast. We're going to have some hard going to catch them."

At this, Fyren and Gifre exchanged unhappy looks.

Oddvar didn't care, however. The goblins were weak, sniveling creatures, unworthy of his company. If their sneak-thieving ways weren't so useful, he'd have lost them long ago.

"Come on," he growled. "Let's find this trading post."

Two hours later, Oddvar and his companions stood in a clearing outside a squat building of cut stone.

"That's far enough, Theiwar," a voice called out from inside the building. "What's your business here?"

"I'm going over the mountain," Oddvar lied. "I need supplies and information."

"What's happening in the lowlands that everyone wants to dare the mountain this time of year?" the strange dwarf asked from the shelter of the trading post.

"There are others going west?" Oddvar called as casually as he could manage.

"Just last week a group of humans went," the dwarf answered.

"I don't know what they want," Oddvar explained. "But I have urgent business on the coast. I need supplies."

"Leave your friends and your weapons," the dwarf in the trading post instructed.

Oddvar dropped his pack and his axe and strolled to the porch of the trading post. Even if the strange dwarf said nothing more, Oddvar had what he needed. The children were indeed heading west, over the mountains, and they had a week's start. Now that he knew where the youngsters were going, Oddvar was confident he could overtake them easily.

But Oddvar still would need supplies. And he wasn't foolish enough to pay for them.

He slid the poisoned dagger out of his boot and pushed the door open.

4 THE LOST ONES

Sometime during the night, snow had begun falling over the western Vingaard range. Huge flakes descended and covered the mountainside with a rapidly deepening blanket of white. If Davyn hadn't been in the process of freezing to death, he would have found it pretty.

It had been over a week since Davyn and his friends had left Dog's snug cottage behind them. They had followed the trail Dog had indicated but, after the first snow, all traces of the path had disappeared. Now Davyn was pretty sure they were hopelessly lost. Their rations were beginning to run low and the mountains just seemed to go on and on with no end. To make matters worse the heavy cloaks that had protected them so well at the lower elevations were no match for the bitter chill of the mountain winds.

A movement on his left reminded Davyn that he wasn't alone. Nearra was pressed tightly against him and when she shivered her hair tickled Davyn's neck. The sensation pulled Davyn's fading mind back to semiconsciousness, and he glanced down. Nearra was wrapped in both her cloaks and his, but even still, Davyn could see that her lips were blue. On his other side, Davyn could feel the kender, Sindri, tucked into a ball beside him. Davyn hadn't felt the kender move in some time.

The remains of the group's fire smoldered a few feet from where they all lay, huddled together. A few glowing coals still shone in the semidarkness. He knew that if he added some wood the coals would start it burning again, giving life-saving heat to his freezing companions. Try as he might, however, he couldn't make himself move.

"Wood," came a hoarse whisper from his chest.

Davyn looked down into Nearra's pale face. She was looking up dazedly at him. Her eyes were unfocused and strangely purple in the silver moonlight. Davyn comprehended what she'd said but he still couldn't move. He could flex his fingers but he had no strength. Even the relatively light weight of Nearra and Sindri had him pinned.

"I got it," came a hoarse voice from Davyn's other side.

To Davyn's great relief he felt Sindri uncoil himself and crawl out from under their cloaks toward the meager woodpile. Apparently kender were made of sterner stuff than Davyn had thought. Sindri's fingers, cracked and bleeding from the cold, grasped an arm-sized log and dropped it on the bed of coals. Davyn knew it would take time for the coals to ignite the log but he imagined he could feel it getting warmer.

Suddenly, as if in answer to Davyn's wishes, the log burst into flames and burned cheerily. A wave of warmth washed over Davyn, and his mind seemed to focus.

"Put another log on," he croaked at Sindri.

The kender was way ahead of Davyn. He threw three more on. They too burst into flame almost immediately, and Davyn could feel their heat penetrating his cloak. His strength was returning and he opened up the front of his cloak to allow the heat in. Nearra shivered briefly, but then snuggled closer as the heat from the fire washed over them. She mumbled something, but when Davyn looked down he found her asleep again.

"Is she all right?" Sindri asked, nodding toward Nearra as he held his frozen hands over the fire.

Davyn nodded, suddenly very aware of the girl's warmth on his chest.

"What about them?" Davyn replied, looking over at Catriona and Elidor, huddled just beyond where Sindri had been.

"They're breathing," the kender observed, tossing yet another log on the fire.

"Save some of that," Davyn said. "It's at least an hour till dawn."

Sindri nodded, scooting closer to the roaring blaze.

"Lucky for us I still had enough magic to restart the fire," he observed, reveling in the heat.

"Mmm," Davyn mumbled. He had been surprised at how quickly the logs had caught fire but he wasn't so addled that he was willing to attribute it to Sindri's so-called wizardry. The kender had Davyn's telekinesis ring, but Davyn knew that couldn't affect fire. As much as Sindri wanted to believe in his own powers, the kender was only a wizard in his own mind.

"You get some sleep," Sindri prattled on, flexing his fingers in front of the blaze. "I'll stay up and keep the fire going."

"Wake me if you get tired," Davyn agreed, pulling his cloak around him once more. "We can't let the fire go out again."

Sindri promised that he would and, cradling Nearra close, Davyn surrendered to sleep again.

It was well past dawn when the rhythmic beat of Catriona's sword dragged Davyn back from the bonds of sleep. He sat up stiffly, rubbing his bleary eyes. The fire was still burning brightly, though the woodpile had dwindled to a few sticks. Sindri, Nearra, and Elidor were sitting close to the fire while Catriona used her short sword to strip the nearby trees of burnable branches. A metal pot sat in a bed of coals to one side of the fire, and Davyn detected a faint aroma coming from it.

"That deep-brew?" he asked, shaking the snow from his cloak and scooting closer to the fire.

"What's left of it," Elidor grinned, as Davyn dug his cup from his pack. "I don't think we could have kept Catriona from drinking the rest of it, if you'd slept much longer."

Davyn held out his cup, and Nearra poured out the contents of the pot into it.

"That's the last of it," the girl sighed. Davyn's cup was only half full.

"Do we have any food left?" Davyn asked, sipping the brew slowly, determined to enjoy every warming drop. He sighed as he began to feel the warming effect of the dwarven drink seep into his half-frozen limbs.

"Sure we do," Sindri replied, holding up their sagging food sack. He reached inside and pulled out a white, cracker-like cake of bread. "There's still some dwarven hardtack."

Davyn shuddered but accepted the cake. It was exactly the consistency of a brick, without any of the flavor. Davyn dipped the solid little cracker in his cup of brew. His teeth clamped down on the cracker, and a tiny portion snapped off into his mouth. Despite what Dog had told them, the method did little to soften the bread.

"Here's some more wood," Catriona said, returning to the fire with an armload of badly hacked branches. She sat down heavily between Davyn and Sindri and took a long pull from her water bag.

"Empty," she pronounced when she was done. "Does anyone else have water?"

"There's plenty of snow," Sindri said, as Elidor passed over his water bag.

"How do you suggest I get it in here?" Catriona snapped, holding up the bag.

Davyn didn't answer but picked up the empty pot they had brewed the cavern root in. He scooped up a mass of snow with it and put it back in the coals.

"Melt as much as we need to fill everybody's water bag," he said, tearing a chunk out of the softened hardtack, "then we'll go."

"And where do you suggest we go?" Catriona said, reddening slightly at not having thought of melting the snow.

Davyn rolled his eyes. Well, at least she wasn't depressed anymore. Catriona was back to her old demanding ways. Davyn was pretty sure he preferred the quieter version.

He scanned the sky. It had been overcast for days and, with no sign of the sun, he had no way to get his bearings. The only real landmark was an exceptionally high mountain whose peak was barely visible in the distance. So far, Davyn had been keeping the peak on their left and hoping for the best.

"We've been going that way," he said finally. "I say we keep on going."

"What, until we freeze to death or starve to death?" Catriona shot back.

"You want to stay here?" Davyn asked, incredulously. "If we don't keep moving we *will* starve to death."

"Sorry," Catriona grumbled, refilling her water bag from the pot. "This is just so frustrating. I hate being cold all the time."

"Well, a good walk will warm you up," Elidor said, filling his water bag and standing up. "The sooner we get started, the sooner we'll get somewhere warm with a ham on the spit."

Nearra groaned, putting her hand to her stomach. "Don't talk like that," she said. "I'm hungry enough as it is."

"There's more hardtack," Sindri offered helpfully, but Nearra waved him away.

"Let's get going," Davyn said, finishing his deep-brew and standing up. "If we find a good spot this afternoon we'll make camp early. Maybe then I can shoot something for dinner."

"You didn't have any luck last night," Catriona said seriously. "Maybe you should give yourself more time."

"Are you saying I'm not a good hunter?" said Davyn, a note of challenge in his voice.

"No, no," Catriona responded, holding up her hands. "I'm just saying that, if we stay here you've got all day to find something."

"We can't risk staying in one place. We're on the run, remember? If Maddoc finds us—"

"Just face it. We're LOST. And we're all starving."

"She's right, Davyn," Nearra said. "It won't do any good to keep wandering when we all need a hot meal and a full night's rest."

"It would give us some time to build a warm shelter and cut some decent firewood," Elidor agreed.

"We should've gotten an axe from Dog," Sindri added. "It takes a long time with the sword."

"All right," Davyn said at last. "We'll rest. But just for today. You cut some wood and see if you can build a shelter. I'll go look for something to eat."

"You want to come?" Davyn asked Elidor.

The elf held up his hands defensively. "Hey, I was raised in the city," he replied. "My idea of hunting is finding a pie someone left on the window to cool."

Davyn laughed, stringing his bow. "Clear a space under the big tree," he told Catriona, slipping the bow over his shoulder. "That's the best place for a shelter. The branches will keep the snow off us."

"I don't know the first thing about building shelters," Catriona said, looking at the broad oak with a skeptical eye.

"We'll figure something out," Nearra said before Davyn could reply.

"Don't go too far," Elidor called as Davyn set out for the trees.

"Why not?" Davyn shot back.

"Because you might never find us again," Catriona said.

"Just make sure you get enough wood for tonight, Mother," Davyn grumbled.

"Why, you little . . . "

Whatever Catriona said was lost as Davyn moved into the trees.

He knew that Catriona's hollers plus the smell of the fire would drive any sensible creature away from their camp but Davyn didn't care. He was determined to enjoy himself anyway. With all day to hunt, he was sure to find something.

Davyn made his way to the rim of the little valley and began skirting it looking for tracks. Before long he found a rabbit run and set up a snare across it. With any luck they'd have rabbit for lunch.

Davyn continued his scouting for the better part of the morning without finding anything suitable. He was a little surprised at the absence of game but with the weather so foul, he decided many of the animals had gone down to lower elevations.

By midday, Davyn still hadn't found any signs of game and he was beginning to get worried. He sat down at the base of an elm tree and choked down a hardtack cracker. The silence of the forest, which was so peaceful at first, now seemed oppressive and eerie. Davyn had almost resolved to go back to camp when movement caught his eye. A little ways from him, through the trees, a white fox prowled cautiously through the underbrush.

Barely daring to breathe, Davyn eased an arrow from his quiver and drew back his bow. He took a deep breath and let it out slowly, releasing the arrow smoothly. With a solid smack the arrow caught the fox in the chest and it slumped to the ground, dead. It wasn't as hearty as Davyn had hoped, but there was enough meat on it to keep them from starving. With any luck he could drop the fox off at camp and go back out in the evening.

On his way back, Davyn checked his snare and found, much to his delight, a fat, white rabbit caught in it. Davyn tied it to the fox. He realized he wasn't bringing a stag back with him but, as hungry as his companions were, he expected a hero's welcome all the same.

Davyn was almost to the campsite when he was greeted by the unmistakable smell of cooking meat. He stopped short, wondering if Elidor had been lying about his hunting abilities. After a moment, strange voices from the camp began to filter through the trees.

The blood in Davyn's veins seemed to freeze and he stood stock still, listening intently. The voices were faint and garbled at this distance, but Davyn could clearly tell that they were not the voices of his friends.

Crouching quickly and dropping his catch, Davyn crept silently forward, straining his vision to see the camp. He worked his way through the densest part of the woods until he was just opposite the enormous oak.

There was now a massive fire of cut logs burning in the center of camp with a deer carcass turning over it on an iron spit. Eight armed men were moving around in the ruddy light. They were clad in heavy fur cloaks and boots, and Davyn could see a mule tied to a tree.

One of the men turning the spit moved and the muscles in Davyn's stomach tightened. His friends were sitting at the base of the big oak with their hands bound behind their backs. Catriona had an ugly bruise on her face, and Sindri appeared to be unconscious. A man who had just finished securing Elidor's bonds stood and walked to the man turning the spit.

"They don't have anything valuable, Dee, except the girl's chain mail," he said, tossing the companions' pouches into a heap beside the fire.

"We can always sell them to a slaver," Dee said, laughing darkly. "If we can find one, that is."

"I don't know," The man said, laughing and moving over to Nearra. "This one's kind of pretty." He grabbed hold of Nearra's hair and jerked her head so Dee could see her face. Nearra whimpered. "I've been meaning to get me a wife. What do you think? Does she look like the next Mrs. Maul?"

Davyn didn't hear Dee's answer. A loud rushing had filled

his ears. He eased his bow off his shoulder and nocked an arrow almost without thinking. His hands trembled with rage as he drew the arrow to his chin. Davyn took a deep breath to quiet his hand and took aim at the center of Maul's chest.

Suddenly, a cold steel blade pressed against his throat.

"I wouldn't do that if I were you."

5   SET-AI

"J ust ease that arrow back down, boy-o," the gravelly voice whispered in Davyn's ear.

Davyn felt the cold steel of the knife at his throat and slowly let the arrow slip. A large hand in a thick, armored leather glove reached into his vision and took the arrow from the bow. Davyn's heart slowed a bit as the knife disappeared from his throat. Davyn turned and found himself confronted by a grizzled man in a heavy cloak made of white rabbit pelts.

"And what were you plannin' to do once you skewered that fella?" the stranger asked quietly, waving the confiscated arrow in Davyn's face. "Do you think you could've shot 'em all before they rushed in here and killed you?"

"Uh," Davyn responded, not sure what to say.

The stranger slipped his broad-bladed hunting knife back into his cloak and Davyn heard it slide home in a hidden sheath. His knife secured, the stranger considered Davyn with piercing blue eyes. The man was at least fifty, with gray hair, bushy eyebrows, and a thick, neatly-trimmed beard. His face, neck, and shoulders were large and powerful-looking, and Davyn got the impression he'd lived roughly for most of his life.

Davyn shivered in the cold as the stranger's gaze swept over him. Finally the man shook his head with a wry smile on his face.

"What's a young pup like you doin' out here anyway?" he asked, disbelief in his voice. "It's a wonder you haven't froze to death."

Davyn opened his mouth to reply, to tell this interloper about the dwarf and about losing the path, but the stranger waved him silent.

"I'm Set-ai," he said by way of introduction. "You just sit here and behave yourself," he said, rising to a crouch. "I'll deal with these lowlifes, then we'll talk."

Without another word, Set-ai stood up and moved away from Davyn. After a dozen yards or so, he stopped, and Davyn saw, for the first time, a donkey tethered to a tree. The animal had been standing there quietly awaiting its master. It was so still Davyn had completely missed seeing it when he'd approached the camp. Without making a sound, Set-ai removed a long staff from the animal's pack, untied the donkey, and began walking toward the camp. After a few paces, he began whistling loudly.

The reaction from the camp was immediate. The armed men stood up and scanned the trees intently, hands on their weapons.

After a moment, Davyn saw Set-ai emerge from the tree line, noisily leading his donkey behind him. With no apparent concern for the ruffians around him, Set-ai walked right up to the fire.

"Well met, stranger," he said, addressing Dee. "Can a humble traveler share your fire?"

Dee, Maul, and another man had gathered around Set-ai. The other men hung back, but their hands were still on their weapons.

"Sure you can," said Dee, smiling pleasantly. "It'll cost you, though."

Set-ai looked around at the armed men.

"Fine," he said, reaching inside his cloak and removing a jingling purse. "I'm tired and I'm hungry and I don't want any trouble."

Set-ai tossed the purse on the ground at Dee's feet.

Smiling greedily, Dee bent to pick up the fat purse. As his hand closed around the little bag, however, Set-ai's staff shot out and smashed Dee square in the face. Before Davyn could even register the blow, Set-ai had brought the other end of the staff around. He slammed it into Maul's unprotected belly. Dee and Maul both went down, Maul gasping for air. The third man started to step in but Set-ai brought the butt of his staff backward and drove it into the man's throat, sending him into a twitching heap.

Before Davyn could even draw his bow to help, the three men around the fire were down, and Set-ai turned to face the remaining five. He stepped up beside his donkey, using the animal to screen his left side.

What happened next was almost too fast for Davyn to follow. A quick flick of Set-ai's staff sent an attacker's shortsword spinning into the woods. Set-ai followed this with savage blows to his opponents' ribs, heads, and groins. Within moments the men were reduced to moaning lumps on the ground.

After surveying the damage for a moment, Set-ai moved to Davyn's companions and bent down to cut Elidor's bonds. Davyn was about to join him when movement caught his eye.

Dee rose up and lunged at Set-ai's back with a jagged knife.

"Set-ai!" Davyn yelled in warning. Without even thinking about it, he drew his bow and fired.

Despite the quickness of the shot, the arrow flew straight across the camp and struck Dee square in the back. With a gurgling cry, Dee staggered and then fell, unmoving, to the ground.

Davyn charged into the camp, another arrow nocked and ready.

"What did you do that for?" Set-ai bellowed.

"He would have killed you," Davyn said.

Set-ai threw open his cloak, revealing a complete suit of leather armor dyed in varying shades of green.

"These are two cross-grained layers of boiled leather, boy-o," he growled, thumping the armor on his chest. "That little pig-poker couldn't get through it."

"I—I didn't know," Davyn stammered, sheepishly.

"I told you not to interfere," he continued, waving his finger in Davyn's face. "Now you killed one of 'em. You made this personal."

Davyn didn't understand what Set-ai was talking about. He didn't see how killing one of the men was any different from beating them senseless.

"Can you tie a good knot?" Set-ai asked.

Davyn nodded, and Set-ai threw him a coil of rope from the pack on his donkey.

"Then start tyin' these lowlifes up before they get their breath back."

Davyn set to work, tying the bandits' hands behind their backs and taking their weapons.

When he was finished, he found that Set-ai had freed his friends and dragged Dee's body into the trees.

"Now," he said, slicing a hunk of venison off the deer on the spit, "why don't you tell me what you lot are doin' this deep in the mountains with no food or gear?"

Davyn and Catriona took turns telling the grizzled man about Dog and their losing the trail. He listened quietly, cutting pieces off the deer and passing them around to the hungry group. When Catriona finished their story, Set-ai shook his head.

"Dwarves," he muttered. "They're not as sensitive to cold as humans. It probably didn't occur to him that you'd need shelters as well as cloaks."

"Do you know where we are?" Sindri asked between mouthfuls of venison.

"O'course I do," Set-ai laughed. "Only a fool would travel these mountains blind."

Catriona shot Davyn a meaningful scowl, which Davyn chose to ignore.

"The nearest town's four, maybe five days," Set-ai continued.

"We'll never make it," Nearra whispered, shivering despite the fire's heat.

Set-ai took off his enormous fur cloak and threw it over the girl's shoulders, and then he turned to Davyn, Elidor, and Catriona.

"It's time to get you pups some survival gear," he said. "Gather up these lowlifes' cloaks while I see what they've got on their horse."

The men that had regained consciousness struggled a bit as Davyn and his friends removed their fur-lined cloaks, but none of them could get free. A few moments later, they had a stack of cloaks, and Set-ai had removed an axe, several shovels, and some sacks of foodstuffs. Much to Davyn's delight, he saw that Set-ai had also found a box of cavern root among the men's gear.

"You kids take off them cloaks of yours," Set-ai said. "Get one of the heavy ones on."

Davyn and the others quickly shed their thin cloaks and donned the bandits' fur-lined ones.

"Now, you lot," Set-ai said, turning to the bound men. "I'm turnin' you loose. You can keep your knives, but we're keepin' your swords. I don't care where you go but you can't stay here, and I better not see any of you again."

"We're not afraid of you," Maul growled menacingly. "You killed Dee, and that means we owe you one. We're called the Highland Rangers and we always repay our debts."

Set-ai chuckled, then knelt in front of Maul.

"My name's Set-ai the Hunter," he said, sneering at Maul. "Better men than you have tried to take me and all they got was dead."

At the mention of Set-ai's name some of the Highland Rangers muttered. None of them made any further challenges.

"Right then," Set-ai continued, cutting Maul's bonds. "Cut your friends free, take your horse and get out."

"Without our cloaks we'll freeze to death," Maul said as he cut his companions free.

Set-ai picked up the light cloaks and the remaining fur ones and tossed the lot to Maul.

"You'll have to take turns wearin' the warm ones," he said. "Now get out of here."

Maul and his companions sullenly donned the cloaks, took their horse and started out of camp. Set-ai watched them until they were out of sight. Then he turned to Elidor.

"Can you move quiet-like, boy?" he asked. Elidor nodded and Set-ai continued, removing a wrapped package from his donkey. "Take your bow and follow them as far as the ridge—"

"I don't have a bow," Elidor interrupted.

Set-ai gave the elf a quizzical look, then retrieved a short bow and a quiver of arrows from the Highland Rangers' gear and handed them to Elidor.

"I've never heard of an elf who didn't have a bow," he said. "Can you shoot?"

"A little," Elidor replied, his eyes not meeting Set-ai's.

"Follow them fellers as far as the ridge," he instructed, passing the wrapped package to Elidor. "Keep back from 'em and don't let 'em see you. Here's some dried meat and cheese in case you get hungry."

Elidor accepted the food and tied it to his belt. He strung the bow rather clumsily, then tied the fur cloak around his slim shoulders.

"Make sure you keep count of 'em," Set-ai advised as the elf turned to leave. "They'll probably figure they're bein' followed and they might try to ambush you. If they stop or turn back, you hustle back here quick, understand?"

Elidor nodded and then disappeared into the trees without a sound.

"What do we do now?" Catriona asked once the elf was gone.

Set-ai grinned and tossed the two shovels he'd taken from the bandits to Catriona and Davyn before answering.

"You've got to make us some shelter," he said enigmatically. "Pile up as much snow as you can over there," he indicated a spot under the big oak, "and make sure you pack it down good."

Set-ai put Nearra and Sindri to work brewing cavern root into deep-brew and cutting up the venison for dinner. After about an hour, Davyn and Catriona had a pile of snow as tall as they were.

"Good work," Set-ai commented, taking a break from chopping firewood.

"What now?" Davyn asked, sweating profusely despite the chill air.

"Now you digs her out," Set-ai explained, tracing a circle in the side of the snow pile. "Not too much, mind you, just enough so three of you can get inside."

Davyn and Catriona carefully cut out the hole Set-ai had traced. Then they took turns shoveling snow back out. Eventually Davyn had to crawl inside, scraping snow from the roof and piling it in the opening where Catriona shoveled it outside.

"Be careful now," Set-ai advised, coming over to check on their progress. "You have to go slow or it'll collapse on you."

The work progressed slowly but steadily. Eventually, Davyn had to take off his new fur cloak because it was too warm.

"We're done over here," Davyn called at last, crawling out of the shelter.

Set-ai crawled inside the shelter, which was no mean feat in his armor. "Not bad," he said, wiggling back out. "Now all you need to do is make another one."

Davyn and Catriona groaned, and began shoveling snow into a pile for the second shelter. By the time they had hollowed out the second mound, Elidor had returned.

"The Rangers went over the ridge," he reported. "I watched until they were out of sight."

"Good work, lad," Set-ai said, slapping the elf on the back. "Your friends are almost finished makin' shelters. I'd say it was time for supper."

Davyn was ready to sleep for a week. He and Catriona collapsed by the fire and tried to catch their breath while Sindri passed out hunks of steaming venison.

"Not a bad job for a bunch of pups," Set-ai commented, surveying the camp. "I might make woodsmen out of you after all."

"Why are you helping us?" Catriona asked after taking a long pull from her water bag.

"'Cause I don't like thievin' bullies," Set-ai answered.

"Thank you," Nearra said with a shy smile. "You saved our lives."

"Not yet I haven't," the woodsman responded with a grin. "You pups have got no idea how to handle yourselves out here in the wilds. Tomorrow I'll teach you a thing or two about that. Right now, you lot need to get some sleep. Be sure to take your cloaks off once you're in them shelters or you'll be too hot."

The group stood up. Catriona and Nearra took one shelter while Elidor, Sindri, and Davyn made for the other one.

"Not you, boy-o," Set-ai said, grabbing Davyn's shoulder. "You've got first watch."

Davyn groaned and pulled his cloak tighter around himself. He started to head back to the fire, but Set-ai had already begun shoveling snow on the flames.

"It's no good watchin' a fire," he said. "You'll ruin your night vision."

The clearing took on an eerie glow in the scant moonlight that managed to make it through the clouds.

"Sit there," Set-ai pointed to a spot in the trees at the edge of camp. He lowered a wooden whistle on a string around Davyn's neck.

"Now don't go blowin' that at just anything," he instructed. "First you make sure you know what you're up against. If you see something, put the whistle in your mouth and nock an arrow. If it's something dangerous, shoot, then blow the whistle while you get your next arrow, understand?"

Davyn nodded, and Set-ai tromped over to where his little tent stood beside the snow shelters.

"I'll take the next watch," he called before entering. "Wake me in an hour or two."

Davyn watched the big woodsman strip off his armor and climb into the meager tent.

Davyn shivered in the bitter cold. The fur-lined cloak was much warmer than his old wool one, but without the fire to help, it was a losing battle. Despite being cold, wet, and exhausted, though, Davyn felt better than ever. He quietly thanked whatever gods had sent the woodsman to them and resolved to learn everything he could from the veteran.

For the first time in months, Davyn finally felt that things were going his way.

6   TRAINING DAYS

Davyn seemed to take a long time to wake up the next morning. Exhausted from the hard labor of the previous day, and warmer than he'd been in weeks, he'd slept soundly. When he finally did open his eyes, the sun was well up. Its penetrating rays illuminated the crystalline roof of the shelter, filling it with light.

The snow shelter had been incredibly warm and much less damp than Davyn had expected. The cramped quarters weren't too bad, though Davyn did have to get up in the middle of the night to push Elidor's knee out of his back. Now he found himself alone in the shelter, Sindri and Elidor having already risen.

Davyn gathered up his cloak and squirmed out of the snow shelter's small opening. The morning was clear for the first time since they'd left Arngrim, and Davyn reveled in the feel of the sunlight on his face. The air was crisp and cold and Davyn threw the fur cloak around his shoulders quickly. A new fire had been built over the ashes of the old, and Sindri was humming happily to himself as he fried what smelled like bacon.

"'Bout time you were up," Set-ai said.

The big woodsman had donned his rabbit-skin cloak and was tying bundles of wood to his donkey.

"I thought I was going to have to send Nearra to get you," he added with a mischievous grin.

Davyn felt himself blushing furiously.

"Where is she?" he asked.

"Scouting. We need to find a river so we know where to go."

Davyn poured himself a cup of deep-brew. "I thought you knew where we were."

"I do," the woodsman said, smiling, "but I'm going to let you kids get yourselves out of this mess you've got into."

Davyn looked up at the sun and noted its position in relation to the big mountain he'd been using to navigate.

"We've been going south," he said with a grimace. "That's why we haven't gotten out of the mountains."

Set-ai popped a piece of bacon into his mouth. "Very good," he said.

"Thanks," Sindri and Davyn said together.

"Why do we need to find a river?" Davyn inquired as he snagged a piece of bacon with his knife. "Why don't we just go west?"

"You need to learn how to find your way around when you can't see the sun," Set-ai said.

Sindri fished the last of the bacon out of his skillet. "How does finding a river do that?" he asked as he added a thick white batter into the greasy pan.

"If you follow a river downstream, you'll eventually find folk," said Set-ai. As Sindri turned back to his pan, the woodsman stole another strip of bacon from the plate.

As Davyn thought about it he realized that most towns and cities were built near water. "I should've thought of that," he admitted.

Sindri turned over a tantalizingly brown griddle-cake.

"Well, I'll make a woodsman of you yet, boy-o," Set-ai said, grinning.

With that, Set-ai moved off to finish packing up his gear. Sindri wrapped his finished griddle-cakes and the remaining bacon in oilcloth pouches to keep them fresh for the others. Davyn pitched in to help him, scraping out the pan.

"Why didn't you tell us you could cook, Sindri?" Davyn asked.

"You never asked," the kender shrugged, tying up one of the food packs. "Magic isn't my only talent, you know."

"You'd learn a lot about these friends of yours if you'd open your eyes, boy-o," said Set-ai. He cinched up the various straps that held the bundles on the donkey's back. "Take that pretty little lass, Nearra, for example. She was the first one to volunteer when I asked for scouts this mornin'," he said. "Looks to me like she wants to prove herself."

Set-ai shot Davyn a wry smile. "A smart man would make sure she gets the chance."

"What if she gets lost?" Davyn asked.

"Not much chance of that," Set-ai chuckled. "You could follow her footprints right to her. Besides," he continued, "how will you ever know what she's capable of if you never let her do anything? Now, if you two are finished with the food, we ought to be goin'. I told the others to wait for us on the ridge once they finished their scouting."

They found the others dutifully waiting for them on the rim of the little valley. Set-ai handed them each an oilcloth sack of food.

"Eat this while we walk," he instructed them.

"We found a river just over there," Elidor reported.

"Very good," Set-ai said. "Nearra, I want you to lead the way."

Nearra looked surprised. "But Davyn usually leads."

"Everybody needs a turn," Set-ai explained.

As the group headed out behind Nearra, Davyn fell in beside Set-ai.

"Are you sure it's wise to put her up front?" he whispered. "She's not as strong as the others."

"That's why she's leading," Set-ai whispered back. "She'll set the pace for everyone else and it'll push her just a bit. The more she leads, the more confident she'll get."

True to Set-ai's word, Nearra kept up a good pace all through the day, leading the way along the little river she'd found while scouting. The food sacks Set-ai had handed out that morning had enough food for lunch, so the group kept on moving with only a few short rest breaks. Despite the strenuous trek through the still-deep snow, Sindri talked incessantly. He seemed to possess boundless inner reserves of energy when confronted by someone whose story he'd never heard.

"So why are you in the mountains?" Sindri pressed.

"I've been in these mountains most of my life," Set-ai said. "I was born way up north of here and my father used to take me hunting when I was barely old enough to walk."

Sindri was hanging on every word. "And why are you down here? Do you have family around here?"

A strange look passed over Set-ai's face. "I used to," he admitted. "Before the war, I sent my wife and son north to live with my father."

"What happened?"

"They never made it," Set-ai said quietly.

Catriona cleared her throat and deftly changed the subject. "Did you fight in the war?"

Set-ai nodded. "My unit spent a lot of time in Solamnia."

"Did you ever see any Draconians?" Sindri asked.

A look of pain and raw, untamed hatred crossed Set-ai's face. It vanished almost immediately. If Davyn hadn't been looking squarely at him he never would have seen it.

"That's enough for today," Set-ai declared with no trace of irritation in his voice. "We'll make camp here."

The group had come out onto a small plateau where the ground was mostly level but there was precious little shelter.

"What about the wind?" Davyn asked.

In response, Set-ai tossed him one of the two short-handled shovels.

"Build another shelter," he grinned, passing the other shovel to Catriona.

"Excuse me," Nearra said, "it's still early and I'm not that tired. We can keep going."

It was the first time she'd spoken during their trip, and Davyn was relieved that she didn't sound exhausted.

"I know you can, lass," Set-ai smiled, clapping her on the shoulder. "But we've come far enough today and I need some time to teach you pups some skills."

"What kind of skills?" Catriona asked, bristling at being called a 'pup.'

"Never you mind, my girl," he replied, pulling his axe from his pack. "You just get those shelters ready."

While the group built the shelters, Set-ai cut four long, straight branches from the aspen groves nearby. When the group finished, they found him sitting by the fire, stripping the bark off of the poles with his knife. Sindri's hoopak and his own, iron-bound staff lay at his feet.

"What are you doing?" Sindri asked, eyes alight with curiosity.

"Time for you kiddies to learn how to defend yourselves," he replied, tossing the kender his hoopak and passing out the remaining poles.

"With these?" Catriona laughed as the woodsman handed her the longest pole. "What are we going to do when someone comes after us with a real weapon?"

Davyn was inclined to agree with Catriona. On the other hand, Davyn hadn't forgotten how easily Set-ai had taken down eight armed men, so he kept his mouth shut.

"Is that what you think?" Set-ai asked as he picked up his staff. "Then let's see how you handle that sword of yours, Cat."

"Don't call me Cat," Catriona growled, throwing aside the pole and drawing her shortsword.

Set-ai leaned easily on his staff. "Then come over here and earn a better name."

Catriona was angry, but, much to Davyn's surprise, she didn't let herself be provoked by the woodsman's challenge. Cautiously, she stalked forward, sword in the guard position. For his part, Set-ai simply stood there leaning on his staff, as if Catriona were approaching him with the cook pot rather than a sword. Catriona took a tentative swing in Set-ai's direction but the woodsman didn't even move as the blow was well short of him.

"How did he know she was faking?" Sindri whispered in Davyn's ear.

Elidor leaned in and answered. "She didn't shift her weight. She'd have to step forward for a proper lunge."

Davyn could see Catriona's cheeks getting red, a sure sign that Set-ai's indifference was getting to her. She stepped in and swung at his unprotected left. Before the blow could connect, however, Set-ai simply leaned his staff into the sword's path. The blow landed soundly on the staff and stopped dead.

"I see we've got a lot of work to do," the big woodsman said, shaking his head.

This time, his taunting hit home. Catriona uttered a curse and lunged at Set-ai with her teeth bared. Obviously expecting just such action, Set-ai stepped back, bringing his staff up to a guard position. Catriona hacked and slashed at the woodsman, raining down blows with all the fury she could muster. Each time her sword darted forward, however, it was met by a parry from the staff.

From his vantage point, Davyn saw that, while Catriona was giving it everything she had, Set-ai was barely trying. The woodsman's moves were slow and precise, easily moving to counter the furious sword blows. After a few minutes of this Catriona began to slow down. Davyn knew you could only swing a heavy sword so long before fatigue took away your edge.

Mercifully, it was then that Set-ai decided to end the match. His slow, lazy motions vanished and his staff suddenly moved with blinding speed. He caught Catriona's sword with an overhand stroke attempting to knock it away. Amazingly, Catriona kept her grip on the weapon though it rang like a bell when the staff hit it. When his first stroke failed to dislodge the sword, Set-ai simply reversed the blow and hit it again. This time the heavy blade went spinning from Catriona's grip and landed at Elidor's feet, making the elf jump.

Before Catriona could recover herself, Set-ai twisted the lower end of his staff behind Catriona's knee and swept the big girl right off her feet. She landed with a thump, the end of Set-ai's staff right in her face. If he'd continued the blow any farther he could have stunned or even killed her.

"Swords are excellent weapons," he said, extending his hand to help Catriona up, "but you have got to learn to crawl before you walk."

Catriona's face flushed with fury and humiliation. She swatted the staff end out of her face and lunged to her feet, attempting to grapple Set-ai with her bare hands.

"Claws in, Cat," Set-ai growled, using his staff as a lever to throw Catriona back into the snow. "You need to learn when you're licked."

Catriona landed with a solid-sounding thump. This time it took her a minute before she was ready to get up.

"If you're finished now," Set-ai grinned at her, "get your sword and we'll continue the lesson."

Catriona glared at the woodsman as she retrieved her sword but said nothing.

"I think you did good, Cat," Sindri whispered as Catriona stalked back to her place in line.

"Don't call me that," she growled back.

"This," Set-ai said, holding up his staff, "is the perfect weapon. It's fast on attack and defense and you can carry one just about anywhere, no questions asked."

"As you've just seen," he continued, tossing Catriona's staff back to her. "If you know how to use it, you can even take on heavily armed opponents."

Set-ai then broke them into groups and began showing them the basics of staff fighting. Davyn found himself paired with Elidor and he had to work hard to overcome the elf's natural grace and balance. After several hours of practice, they were all in high spirits and had bruises to spare.

They settled down around the fire for a dinner of leftover venison.

"That was pretty good," Set-ai admitted between mouthfuls of meat. "A few weeks of that and you'll be competent fighters."

"What about my sword?" Catriona asked, quietly.

"Don't worry, lass," Set-ai said in a fatherly tone. "The staff will teach you how to manage your weight and balance. Those things translate well to the sword."

Elidor nodded. "It's lucky for us you came along."

"Yeah," Sindri said. "You never did say what you are doing this far into the mountains anyway."

"Looking for lost pups," Set-ai chuckled. He looked as if he would stop with the joke but after a moment he continued. "I heard tell of this monstrous beast. They say it kills anyone or anythin' it can find out after dark."

Sindri's eyes were as wide as saucers, and Nearra shivered despite being right in front of the fire. Davyn looked around at the thick cover of trees on the nearby mountainside. His eyes met Elidor's and he could see that the elf was wondering about the wisdom of their position as well.

"Why would you want to go near a thing like that?" Davyn asked, his mouth strangely dry.

"I'm a hunter, o'course," Set-ai said as though that explained everything. "I've come to test my mettle against the creature. I've hunted everything that goes on four legs in these mountains, and some things that go on two. But I've never met my match so I go right on huntin'."

"Could this creature be nearby?" Catriona asked, not nearly as nervous as the rest.

Set-ai shrugged. "Anything's possible."

There was a long moment of silence.

"So," he continued, "who wants the first watch tonight?"

7   GOBLINS, BEASTS, AND DRAGON CLAWS

Oddvar rolled his eyes. For a tribe that had lived in the mountains for years, these goblins simply didn't know how to make a decent fire. He pulled his cloak more tightly around him as the inept goblins attempted to improve their fire by spreading the logs out. This caused the meager flames to sputter and die. Fire building was a critical skill for a dwarf, and Oddvar's father had taken great pride in teaching his son the art. For a brief moment, Oddvar remembered his father and his home with a fond smile. Despite his history with his people, he had to admit there were many good memories there as well. The memory of his humiliation and banishment drove these thoughts from his mind quickly, however.

The cave in which the snow-hunter goblin clan lived was fairly large and provided enough shelter so that their fire-making deficiencies weren't critical.

"At least it's dark," Oddvar grumbled to himself.

Oddvar's eyes were large and pale, designed for seeing in almost total darkness. Aboveground, the brightness of the sun made them sting. Usually keeping his deep hood up was sufficient to protect his eyes. On the snow-covered mountainside, however, the reflection of the sun on the snow was so bright that Oddvar had to bind a cloth over his eyes to protect them. Without the cloth, he could lose his vision to snow blindness in a matter of hours.

The cloth, of course, presented its own set of problems. If it was thin enough to see through, then the sun was still painfully bright; any thicker, however, and the dwarf would have to be led like a blind man. Here, in the semidarkness of the cave, Oddvar was able to rid himself of the cloth and enjoy normal sight.

"What have you found out?" he growled, as Drefan approached.

"Their leader's name is Sek'laar," the goblin reported.

"That's a strange name for a goblin," Oddvar commented absently.

"It means 'Snow Lord,' " Drefan said.

Oddvar chuckled humorlessly. "Where did you find this bunch?" He asked, shaking his head. "They're denser than a room full of anvils."

"It's true," the goblin agreed, his long, pointed nose bobbing up and down. "They are, however, willing to help us."

"What does this 'Snow Lord' want in return?" Oddvar sighed.

"He says he'll help if there's treasure to be had," said Drefan.

Oddvar thought on this for a moment. "Tell him his clan can have the children's weapons and equipment."

"What if the children put up a fight?" Drefan asked, his long fingers flexing eagerly.

"As long as the blond girl and the human boy live, I don't care what happens to the others," Oddvar instructed. "Tell them not to kill them all, though," he added as the goblin turned away. "I may need a few to torture."

Two days had passed since Set-ai's first training session. The group hadn't made very good time traveling, mostly because they were busy with their training. As they traveled, he'd teach them about hunting, tracking, and how to find water and food. Each time they camped they built better shelters and were faster making camp. While they worked, Set-ai told them what gear travelers needed and how to best use and pack it. He taught them how to cut and split the best wood, and how to build a small fire that gave off heat but almost no smoke to avoid being spotted. The lessons everyone craved, however, were in combat.

Davyn and Elidor were now required to shoot fifty shots before and after each session to improve their archery. Sindri and Nearra worked extra time with their staff fighting.

For her part, Catriona, whom everyone was now calling Cat, had extra work too. But she wasn't excited about it at all. Set-ai had her walking her way through complicated sword forms that he swore would prepare her for combat. Sindri said it looked like she was dancing. Catriona threatened to kill Sindri while he slept.

On top of everything, Catriona vehemently objected to being called Cat, a fact that simply encouraged everyone. She took revenge while she practiced her thrusts and slashes by picturing each of them in turn. The more she hacked and slashed, the angrier she got.

"You've got to calm down, girl," Set-ai growled at her as a particularly violent slash pulled Catriona off balance. "Swordplay is all about control."

Catriona didn't reply, swinging even harder. Her stubborn refusal to do as she was told finally got to Set-ai, and the big warrior slapped Catriona's sword right out of her hand with his armored gauntlet.

"What are you doing?" Catriona almost screamed at him.

"Why bother practicing if you aren't goin' to do it right?" Set-ai growled at her. "If you do that in a real fight a single goblin could get the better of you."

Catriona ground her teeth together in fury and stormed over to get her sword. Set-ai put his hand on her shoulder.

"What's the matter with you, lass?" he asked, turning her to face him. "You've been madder than a wet hen these last few days."

"Sindri said this looks like I'm dancing," Catriona fumed.

"Is that all?" Set-ai laughed. "Sword forms are just like dancing. They develop timing and balance. Besides, it doesn't matter what anyone else says. What matters is why you're doing it."

"I suppose," Catriona muttered sullenly.

"Is there somethin' else?" Set-ai pressed.

"Everyone's calling me Cat," she said, hanging her head.

"That's a sign of affection," the big woodsman said, grinning. "True companions always have pet names for each other. In the war, my companions used to call me Whiskers on account o' my beard."

Catriona crossed her arms and gave Set-ai a dark look. "I don't like it."

"Look at it this way," Set-ai said, "at least your friends like you well enough to give you a nickname."

"You think so?" Catriona asked.

"I know so," Set-ai said. "Now get back to your work. You've got six more forms to do before dinner."

Set-ai drifted over to where Davyn and Elidor were practicing their archery. For Davyn, archery practice was the most fun of all. Set-ai had picked out a tree as a target for him, well within the range of Davyn's bow. Davyn hadn't failed to hit the tree yet, and now the broad tree had sprouted so many arrows it looked like a hedgehog.

"I see I made your target too easy," Set-ai commented as Davyn smoothly drew another arrow and shot it into the tree. "You need more of a challenge."

Set-ai paced off one hundred paces and picked a tree at that distance.

"No problem," Davyn called, nocking another arrow.

"Just a minute," Set-ai called. He reached up with his hunting knife and lopped off a low-hanging branch from a nearby tree. He quickly stripped the branch and shoved it into the ground in front of the target tree.

"Hit that," he called, stepping back out of the way.

Davyn drew the arrow to his ear and let his breath out slowly before loosing the arrow. It hit the tree squarely several inches from the stick.

"That's a better challenge," Set-ai called as he walked back to where Davyn stood. "You can quit as soon as you hit the stick three times."

Davyn ground his teeth together, fishing another arrow from his quiver.

"You only get better when you shoot at the hard targets." Set-ai patted Davyn on the shoulder, then went to check on the others.

Davyn continued to shoot at the little stick but without much success. After fifty shots, Davyn had only been able to hit it once. His only real consolation was that Elidor seemed to be having even less fun with his bow.

Despite Elidor's heritage, he was a terrible shot. His short bow had only half the range of Davyn's longbow, but even close targets were safe from Elidor's archery. While Davyn shot at a tiny stick, Elidor was barely managing to hit a tree at twenty paces. Davyn knew every time the elf missed when he heard Elidor swear in his native language.

"You sure you're an elf?" Set-ai wondered, as he stood behind Elidor.

"Yes." Elidor glared at Set-ai.

"No offense meant, pup." Set-ai held his hands up defensively. "You've got the natural speed and grace the bow demands. You just need to develop your skills."

As Davyn drew his bowstring to his ear for another shot, and Elidor grunted something unintelligible, Nearra and Sindri practiced their staff skills nearby. The clicking and clacking of the staffs had a strange rhythmic quality that helped Davyn relax and shoot.

"What in the Abyss are those?" Cat's raised voice interrupted Davyn's concentration, and his shot went off into the trees.

The big woodsman was approaching Catriona carrying two of the strangest weapons she'd ever seen. They were shaped like swords with a curved top and a wicked hook on the bottom. The handle, unlike a sword, was attached to the back of the blade down near the bottom, and a long, pointed spike protruded downward from it. A nasty-looking serrated edge started about two-thirds of the way up the blade and ran the rest of the way to the hook. Catriona had never seen anything like them.

"These are dragon claws," Set-ai explained. "They were made special for me during the war by a gnome."

"A gnome?" Catriona screwed up her face in disgust.

"That's right, Cat," Set-ai responded, putting emphasis on the word *Cat*. "And a far better arms-man than you, rest assured."

"It looks like it was made from a sword blade," Elidor chimed in.

"It was," Set-ai nodded. "These swords belonged to some draconians that were unlucky enough to find us. I broke my sword, so Bloody Bob whipped these up for me."

"Bloody Bob?" Sindri asked, his attention sucked away from his fight by the story. A moment later, Nearra hit him in the stomach.

"The most bloodthirsty gnome I ever knew," Set-ai said as Sindri picked himself off the ground. "Bob was fascinated by war. All he ever did was design weapons."

"Did any ever work?" Catriona asked, her distaste still showing on her face.

"O'course they did," Set-ai growled. "I remember he had this little tube that would spit oil on your foes and then light it with a spark. Ol' Bob burned up hundreds of draconians before it blew up on him."

Sindri's eyes were as wide as saucers, obviously imagining such a thing. Elidor and Davyn, however, still wore expressions of disbelief.

"So, what's so special about these dragon claws?" Nearra asked, leaning on her staff.

Set-ai smiled and held up his hand, indicating that they should wait a moment. He took off his cloak and picked up the strange weapons, one in each hand. In his right hand, Set-ai held the claw point out but in his left hand he held it point down with the spike facing up. With a grand flourish, he held the two blades up end to end so they formed one long blade across his front.

"What do you see?" he asked the group.

"It certainly looks dangerous," Sindri admitted approvingly.

"It looks difficult to wield," Elidor added critically.

"It's a staff," Nearra said, a smile springing suddenly to her face.

"Right you are, my girl," Set-ai beamed. He took a step back and began swinging the claws in an alternating pattern, bringing first one and then the other whizzing in front of him. "The dragon claws can mimic a staff," he said, swinging the weapons easily. "Or you can use them like swords. Both blades can attack and defend. In normal use, you hold one in the attack position and one in the defense position."

"How is that different from using two swords?" Catriona asked.

"With these, you don't have to worry about catching your opponent's blade," Set-ai said, holding up his left arm, showing that the blade covered it. "You just block. On top of that, you can change it around if you're fighting easier or harder opponents."

Set-ai flipped the defensive claw around with a quick toss and suddenly both blades were in the attack position.

Catriona was impressed, her fingers suddenly itching to try the strange weapons. Set-ai shooed everyone else back to their tasks and set to work showing Catriona how to hold the weapons and how to attack and defend. After she dropped the weapons several times while trying to flip them, Set-ai advised her not to change her grip.

Davyn wanted a crack at the dragon claws but, after he and Elidor had practiced their staff fighting, Set-ai sent them both back to archery.

"Focus on your strengths," he told them.

After another horrible shot, however, Elidor threw down his bow, cursing fluently in his native language.

"Trouble?" Set-ai chuckled from where he was cutting firewood.

"This is not one of my strengths," Elidor argued. The elf threw open his cloak and drew one of the short, heavy throwing knives from the baldric he wore over his shoulder. "This is what I'm good with."

To emphasize his point, Elidor took a step and hurtled the knife at the tree he was using as an archery target. Unlike the arrows that littered the ground around the tree, the knife hit dead center and stuck there quivering.

"Very impressive," Set-ai said as he ambled over to the tree for a closer inspection. "Too bad it's useless." When he reached the tree, the big woodsman tapped the knife with the tip of his finger, and it fell free of the tree.

Davyn could see the tiny nick in the tree trunk where the tip of the dagger had penetrated. Set-ai bent down and picked up the fallen knife.

"This weapon is only good at a dozen paces," he said, handing it back to Elidor, "and then only against unarmed opponents."

Elidor mumbled something under his breath that Set-ai chose to ignore.

"This, however," he went on, picking up the discarded short bow, "will stop an armored man at fifty paces."

To emphasize his point, the big woodsman knocked an arrow and shot it into the tree. It hit with a solid-sounding thud and sunk in past the head.

"At least someone can do that," Elidor growled as Set-ai held the bow out to him.

"It's like anything, lad," Set-ai said soothingly, "the more you do it, the easier it gets."

"Trust me, lad," he coaxed when Elidor didn't take the bow. "You hit a man with this, he'll go down and all you'll lose is an arrow. Them knives are nice, but once you throw them, how are you going to defend yourself?"

Finally Elidor took the bow, looking sheepish. He drew an arrow and, after taking a long moment to aim, he shot. The arrow caught the edge of the tree and twisted around at funny angle—but it stuck.

"You see?" Set-ai clapped the elf on the back so hard he almost fell over. "Keep it up."

"Now what about you?" he went on, noticing Davyn had stopped shooting.

Davyn drew an arrow to his chin, regulated his breathing, and shot. There was a loud crack just before the sound of his arrow hitting the tree. As Davyn watched in disbelief, he saw the shaft of his arrow sticking out from the center of the little stick he was shooting at. Somehow he'd hit it dead on.

"Excellent," Set-ai cheered as Davyn ran to confirm his hit. "I think you're ready to get us something to eat."

With that, Set-ai left the others to make snow shelters for the night and led Davyn into the woods in search of game. Davyn's last hunting trip hadn't turned out too well, the fox and the rabbit notwithstanding. This time Set-ai showed Davyn how to find the subtle signs of game, and soon they were on the trail of several deer.

"You're doin' well, laddie," Set-ai hissed under his breath as Davyn correctly tracked the deer through the undergrowth.

A few minutes later, Davyn brought down a young buck with

a single shot. He'd hunted deer before, but the combination of the difficult tracking, the accurate shot, and Set-ai's praise made Davyn feel as though he'd just brought down a dragon.

Davyn's father, Maddoc, wasn't one to hunt and had never taken Davyn into the forests. Here, in the middle of the mountains with Set-ai, Davyn felt more at home than he had in the castle of his own father.

"Hold on, lad," Set-ai interrupted Davyn's reveling just as he was about to begin cleaning the deer. "We'll take him back to camp just as he is."

"Why?" Davyn asked, puzzled. "It will be much easier to do it here."

"True," Set-ai said, "but then your friends won't know how to do it."

Davyn smiled at the thought of Elidor and Nearra cleaning a deer. As it turned out, however, they both handled the messy job better than he expected. After he and Set-ai had hauled the heavy animal back to camp, the others had taken their instruction from Davyn without complaint. Within an hour Davyn's friends had the deer cleaned and skinned and ready for cooking.

Set-ai then showed them how to cut up the meat and cook it on long spits over a bed of glowing coals. While the meat sizzled and cooked, the tantalizing aroma made their mouths water.

"So," Set-ai said as they sat around the fire, "you pups never did tell me why you were roamin' around in the mountains."

There was a long silence. Everyone looked at each other, then Nearra spoke.

"They're here because of me," she said. "I lost my memory—I don't know how—and my friends are trying to help me get it back."

"In the middle of the mountains in winter?" Set-ai pressed.

"There's a wizard named Maddoc," Nearra continued after an uncertain pause. "He wore the white robes, but I don't think he's good."

"We think he's trying to hurt Nearra," Catriona said.

"What would a wizard want with you?" Set-ai asked.

"We're not sure," Nearra admitted. "It has something to do with my memory loss."

Davyn's face went red and he looked down, hoping no one would see.

"Maddoc's been a step ahead of us the whole time we've been together," Catriona picked up the story again. She told Set-ai about their journeys with Jax and Raedon and about the cursed land of Arngrim.

"So," Set-ai said once Catriona finished, "you figured that you'd give him the slip if you crossed the mountains?"

"That's right," Davyn confirmed.

"I've decided to stop trying to regain my memories," Nearra added. "All it's brought us is pain."

"Well, I don't think that's a good idea, lass," Set-ai said. "If this wizard really is after you, your only defense might be knowin' what he wants."

"What if it's something terrible?" Nearra asked in a barely audible voice.

"We're here for you," Sindri said. "Even if it's something really terrible."

Set-ai picked up one of the spits and began pulling sizzling hunks of venison off it with his knife. As he passed the meat around, Set-ai told them a story about his service in the war.

"It were a night like this one," he began as the fire crackled and popped behind him. "My squad and I were camped in this little ravine. We knew there were goblins about but we figured they didn't dare attack us."

"What happened?" Sindri pressed.

"Our lookout fell asleep," Set-ai answered seriously. "We woke up to nigh-on fifty goblins chargin' down at us."

"How many of you were there?" Catriona asked.

"Just me, Bloody Bob, Zack, Bucky, and Serina," Set-ai answered gravely.

"What did you do?" Nearra shivered at the thought of goblins.

"What could we do? We put our backs to the ravine wall and attacked. Now goblins aren't much of a foe," Set-ai conceded, "but fifty of 'em still take a bit of killin'. When it was all over, there were only ten of 'em left and they ran just like the fires of the Abyss was after 'em."

"You won," Sindri gasped.

"Not really," Set-ai admitted. "We lost Bucky that night."

There was a long silence while they all took this in.

"Now I want you to remember that story whenever you're on watch," Set-ai said seriously. "If our lookout hadn't fallen asleep, maybe Bucky would be alive today."

Set-ai looked around at the faces of the youth, then gave them a wink and a smile. The somber mood invoked by his story was dispelled.

"Set-ai?" Nearra spoke up.

"What is it, lassie?"

"How come you weren't afraid when you fought all those goblins?"

"Wasn't afraid?" Set-ai scoffed. "Lassie, I was scared to death. I was sure that night was goin' to be my last."

"Then how did you go on?" Nearra asked in a small voice.

"Bein' scared will only stop you if you let it," Set-ai replied with a smile. "Most folks are scared all the time." He winked at her. "The trick is to admit you're scared and then do what you have to do anyway."

Nearra seemed to think about this for a long moment, then she looked up at Set-ai with her beautiful blue eyes.

"I think I can do that," she admitted, hope in her voice.

"I know you can, lass." The woodsman smiled back.

By the time they'd eaten their fill and packed away the rest for later, Davyn was just about as happy as he'd ever been. Not even having the first watch could dampen his spirits.

The moon was up and near full, bathing the entire mountainside in silvery light. As everyone else made their way to the shelters, Davyn sat with his back to a large oak tree. He tightened his cloak around him and shifted his shoulders, moving out of the way of a particularly sharp knot.

The first hour of a watch usually wasn't too bad. People occasionally moved around in camp, taking care of any last-minute needs before turning in. The surrounding terrain was new and interesting, begging the watcher to inspect it closely. After the first hour, however, boredom began to set in. Everyone in camp was asleep and the countryside became far less interesting after the watcher had seen it a dozen times. It was at this point that Davyn began doing things to keep himself awake. He would count squirrels or owls moving around in the darkness or sharpen his knife or watch the stars.

Davyn was watching a particularly daring squirrel dig for nuts when he heard something that made the hair on the back of his neck stand up. It was a sound that came echoing off the mountainsides, faintly at first but louder as it went on. At first, Davyn thought it was a wolf, howling at the nearly full moon. When the sound came again, however, it seemed to possess an element of size and menace that was unlike any wolf he'd ever heard. Set-ai too had heard it and the grizzled woodsman stuck his head out from his tent flap, listening intently. The sound came a third time, a long gurgling roar that seemed to come from everywhere at once.

Davyn shivered at the sound. Something in that unearthly howl chilled him in a way that sitting in a snow bank never could. Unconsciously, Davyn drew an arrow from his quiver and nocked it into his bow.

8   ON THEIR OWN

"What the Abyss was that?" Catriona asked, sticking her head out of the shelter as the eerie sound finally died away.

Davyn looked to Set-ai for an explanation but the big woodsman held up his hand for silence. He was listening intently, as if he could force the ringing howl to continue by will alone. For a full minute, Set-ai stood still, straining to hear any sound from the forest. Finally he lowered his hand and motioned for Davyn and Catriona to approach.

"What—" Catriona began.

"Get everyone up," Set-ai whispered. "Now."

Davyn was about to argue, but the look on Set-ai's face made him reconsider. As Davyn turned to wake Elidor and Sindri, Set-ai took his bow and stalked off into the trees.

Elidor snapped awake as soon as Davyn crawled into the shelter. Sindri was noticeably harder to wake.

"Is it my watch already?" the kender mumbled groggily once Davyn had succeeded in rousing him.

Davyn quickly told Sindri and Elidor of the strange howl as the pair scrambled into their cloaks.

"What do you think it was?" Elidor asked as he squirmed out 63 into the frigid night.

"I don't know," Davyn admitted, "but it's got Set-ai worried and that scares me."

As if on cue, the woodsman strode out of the nearby trees. He was wearing his armor and carrying a heavy longbow. To Davyn he looked like a warrior from one of the great stories.

"Pack up the camp," Set-ai hissed, as everyone rushed over to him. There was an urgency in his voice that made the hair on the back of Davyn's neck stand up.

"But it's dark," Nearra pointed out.

"Now," Set-ai replied, hurrying over to his gear.

Before anyone could move, the strange, unearthly howl came again. This time it sounded farther away than it had been before, something Davyn was very grateful for.

Set-ai began stuffing gear into his pack.

"It's the creature, isn't it?" Elidor asked. "The one you came to the mountains looking for."

"I don't know," Set-ai admitted. "I never heard anything like it, and that's sayin' something."

Sindri helped Davyn pack up the cooking gear and the food. "It makes your insides go all funny."

"Dragons do that, too," Set-ai said.

Whatever had made that sound had made Set-ai nervous, and Davyn didn't like that at all. The whole time the big woodsman had been with them, Davyn had felt his confidence growing—not just in himself, but in everyone. Now his stomach seemed to have turned to water and a chill fear was crawling up his spine. He wasn't the only one. Elidor and Sindri were packing at a record pace, casting many glances at the treeline. Catriona was helping Set-ai load his donkey, apparently calm, but Davyn could see that she was sweating in the frigid air. Nearra was the worst. She was visibly trembling and she kept very near to where Davyn was working—a fact that made Davyn feel a little braver.

"All right," Set-ai said once the camp was all packed up. "There's a town somewhere south of here. I want you to take charge," he said, turning to Davyn, "follow the river south till morning. Don't go too fast and don't stop except to sleep."

"You're not coming with us?" Nearra asked. "What are you going to do?"

"Don't worry about me, lass," Set-ai said. "I'm goin' to go have a look 'round and see if I can find that critter."

"Wait a minute," Catriona bristled, "why is Davyn in charge?"

"Because he can find his way in the woods." He looked as if he were about to continue, but he stopped and took a deep breath.

"Look," he said, kneeling in the snow. "You kids have come a long way in the last few days, but that was as individuals. Now you've got to learn to function as a team."

"Aren't we a team?" Nearra asked.

"No, lass," Set-ai said gently, "you're not. You've all been doin' what you do best and leavin' the rest up to everyone else. That's fine when you're just travelin', but when your life's at stake you have to be able to depend on each other."

"What do you mean, 'when your life's at stake'?" Elidor asked, a dark look on his face.

"I may not know what made that sound," Set-ai answered, "but I can tell you it's a predator—a big one."

"What happens if it finds us?" Nearra squeaked.

"I'm going to keep that from happenin'," Set-ai told her, putting his hand on the girl's shoulder.

"Now, I want you all to stop thinkin' about yourselves and help each other." Set-ai looked Davyn square in the eyes. "You know most about how to get along in the woods, so it's your job to bring everyone off the mountain safely."

"What about the rest of us?" Catriona asked, softly.

"You're the strongest and the best fighter," Set-ai replied. "You've got to keep the others out of harm's way."

"I want you to follow the river until the sun comes up," he went on. "Sleep during the day and travel at night. Do what Davyn says and stay together."

With that, Set-ai cinched up the harness on his donkey and led the creature to the edge of the trees. He turned back for a moment and tossed a wrapped bundle to Catriona.

"Good luck," he called, then turned and vanished into the trees.

"What's that?" Sindri asked, trying to peek under the cloth.

Catriona pulled back the cloth to reveal two shining blades. "He gave me his dragon claws," she whispered.

It had been a long time since anyone had believed in Cat, Davyn knew. Even their own little group had rejected her leadership. Tears were shining in her eyes as she clutched the bundle to her chest. Davyn suspected Catriona would die before giving them up.

"All right, let's get moving," Davyn said after an uncomfortable silence. "We follow the river. Elidor, I want you on point and stay sharp. I don't want any surprises."

Elidor nodded and nocked an arrow in his bow, despite his still shaky archery, and slipped silently away downstream. The pointman was something else Set-ai had taught them: always have a man scouting the road ahead to look for danger. Davyn knew that with Elidor's infravision, he would see trouble long before trouble saw him.

"Sindri, I want you up front," Davyn said once Elidor was out of sight. "Nearra and I will be right behind, and Cat, you bring up the rear."

Catriona nodded grimly, tucking the wrapped dragon claws into her pack and hefting her staff. Sindri carried his hoopak easily and set off at a good pace. Nearra followed using her staff as a walking stick. Davyn had his bow slung over his shoulder, ready to go, and carried his own staff. He smiled as he realized how right Set-ai had been. Anyone watching them would think them unarmed, and yet they each had a weapon in hand, ready to use.

Davyn was surprised at how easily he'd slipped into the role of leader. Before they'd come over the mountain the others had followed him, but Davyn suspected that had been because no one else knew where to go. Now Davyn felt a confidence in his abilities unlike anything he'd ever felt before. Even with the threat of the unknown predator hanging over them, Davyn felt as if he could handle anything. He realized he was probably giving himself too much credit, but he reveled in the feeling nonetheless.

The night was impossibly cold as the group made their way along the river. The moon was up and its light, reflecting on the snow, lit up the landscape with a ghostly glow. No one felt like talking, so the only sound to be heard was the crunch of snow under their boots. Their breathing left little frost clouds in the frigid air. Elidor returned from time to time to report that the path ahead was clear. Davyn offered to trade point duty with him, but the elf refused, saying that the safety of the group was Davyn's responsibility.

Most elves would have thought themselves the only logical choice for leader, yet Elidor avoided every such opportunity. Davyn was forced to wonder again why the elf had left his own people to live like a human among humans.

The sky was especially dark, and Davyn knew there were only a few hours left before dawn. By his count he'd been up almost a full day and he was beginning to feel the effects of weariness. Whole stretches of countryside went by in a blur as Davyn struggled to focus on following Sindri. Behind him, he could hear Nearra and Catriona trudging along, stumbling occasionally on hidden roots and holes.

When they had reached a small clearing near a stream, Davyn called a halt. It looked safe and there was plenty of snow on the ground to build shelters. Elidor hadn't returned but they were all near exhaustion. Nearra was leaning heavily on her staff, and even Catriona was swaying visibly as she stood in the snow.

"Let's rest here." Davyn let his pack fall heavily to the ground and stretched. He wanted to stop, to sit in the snow and rest, but he knew there was still a lot of work to be done. He reached into his pack and pulled out the pouch of venison meat. Set-ai had left them most of the cooked meat, taking the raw meat with him, presumably as bait.

"Shouldn't we call Elidor back?" Catriona asked as Davyn cut chunks of venison for everyone. "He might go a long way before he realizes we've stopped."

Davyn shook his head in response.

"No, this is a good spot to set up camp. Besides," he went on, "Elidor's due to check in soon anyway."

"You think Set-ai will be all right?" Nearra shivered.

"He can take care of himself," Davyn answered, hoping he spoke the truth.

"What about the creature?" Sindri asked as he chewed. "What if it finds us before Set-ai finds it?"

"It probably won't bother us," Davyn shrugged. "Most things go out of their way to avoid people." Even as he said it, Davyn didn't believe it but he didn't want to scare Nearra.

"What if it's hungry?" Sindri wondered aloud.

Davyn shot the kender a dirty look. They finished their meal in silence.

After he finished eating, Davyn knelt by his discarded pack and began digging around in it. Finally his cold, weary fingers closed around one of the shovels Set-ai had left them.

"I'll start on a shelter," he announced, swaying slightly as he stood back up. "Cat, get your shovel and help me. "

"We might want to wait on that," Elidor said, striding out of the trees.

"What's up?" Catriona said, leaning against a tree.

"There's a fire up ahead," the elf reported.

"Did you get close enough to see who it was?" Davyn asked.

"I was practically in their camp." Elidor smiled mischievously. "It was a group of goblins, about fifteen of them."

"What do we do?" Nearra asked.

"We ignore them," Davyn answered.

"You might want to take a look first," Elidor put in quickly. "They've got a hostage."

"Set-ai?" Catriona asked before Davyn could.

Elidor shook his head. "But he's a human. They seem to be arguing about what to do with him."

"Goblins only take prisoners if they think they can ransom them for steel," Catriona said.

"So they might kill him?" Nearra asked quietly.

Elidor nodded but didn't reply.

"We should do something," Catriona said, a burning intensity in her green eyes.

"We can't just let the goblins kill him," Nearra agreed.

"We've been walking all night with no sleep," Davyn said. "We're in no shape to take on fifteen goblins."

"Set-ai took on eight full grown men for us," Sindri said. "Don't we owe it to him to do the same?"

Davyn's stomach knotted up. Sindri was right.

"This isn't smart," he warned. "There's only five of us. They outnumber us three to one. On top of that, they probably have armor."

"They're camped," Elidor said. "Most of them have their armor off."

Catriona crouched down and brushed a smooth patch of snow with her hand.

"Show me what the camp looks like," she instructed Elidor.

The elf crouched and quickly sketched out a little clearing in the snow. He indicated the position of the fire and the prisoner and then added rough positions for the goblins.

"Excellent," Catriona said after studying the drawing for a few moments. Then she turned to Elidor, indicating a point across the camp from the prisoner. "Is there any cover on this side of their camp?"

Elidor nodded. "There's a clump of fir trees here," he said, drawing a circle on the map.

Catriona turned back to Davyn. "Can you and Elidor get here without being heard?"

Davyn glanced at the elf, who nodded confidently, then nodded to Cat.

"Good," Catriona said, sketching on the map with the tip of the dragon claw. "Sindri, Nearra, and I will hide here, behind the prisoner. Once we're in position, you two start shooting. I'll rush them while Nearra cuts the prisoner free."

"What about me?" Sindri wailed, noting his omission.

"You protect Nearra," Catriona explained.

Davyn was about to protest when he saw Nearra shiver. Suddenly he remembered the girl's fear of goblins.

"Don't look at me like that," Nearra said. "I'll be all right."

"What happens if you freeze out there?" Davyn pressed. "We all know how you feel about goblins."

"I'll be all right," Nearra repeated. "It's like Set-ai said. I'll acknowledge my fear and then do what I have to anyway."

"Fine," Davyn gave in. "But for the record, this isn't the smartest thing we've ever done."

To Davyn's surprise, it was Elidor's chuckle that broke the tension.

"When have we ever chosen the smart path," he said. "It's not in our nature."

With a heavy sigh, Davyn slipped his quiver over his cloak and strung his bow. Elidor led them carefully forward until Davyn could smell cooking meat and hear the guttural undertones of the goblins' foul tongue. A few minutes later they could see the orange light of a massive fire and the black forms of the goblins as they moved around their camp.

Catriona pointed for Davyn and Elidor to circle the camp and get into position opposite the prisoner but, before they could go, Sindri held up his hand.

"They're arguing about whether or not they're allowed to kill the man," he whispered.

"You speak goblin?" Nearra whispered back, her eyebrows raised in surprise.

Sindri nodded, listening, and Catriona rolled her eyes.

"Why didn't you tell us you spoke goblin," she hissed.

"You didn't ask," Sindri replied, as if that was completely obvious. "Some of them think this is the human they've been looking for. Others are saying it's a different human."

"What human are they looking for?" Davyn asked.

"There's supposed to be a group traveling together with a blond human girl and a human boy," Sindri reported. "They're not supposed to kill the girl or the boy, just capture them. Apparently they might be allowed to kill any traveling companions of the boy or the girl." Sindri looked back at his friends. "That group sounds like us."

"It is us." Elidor swore under his breath. "You do realize what this means."

"Maddoc," Davyn whispered. "He's found us."

9   THE GOBLIN RAID

"Y ou still want to do this?" Catriona asked
    Davyn.

Davyn nodded, grim determination on his face. "If the goblins
were sent by Maddoc, it would be better if they never reported
back."

Davyn looked around at the faces of his friends. None of them
raised any objection.

"All right," he said, nocking an arrow. "Let's go."

Davyn and Elidor made their way silently around to the fir trees
on far side of the camp. As Davyn went, he saw the prisoner. He
was a young man, maybe a little older than Davyn. His face was
bloody and he had a black eye. Despite his injuries, he appeared
to be wiggling his bound hands in an effort to free himself. The
goblins had taken his heavy fur cloak and the young man was
shivering in the bitter mountain chill.

When Davyn reached the clump of firs, he knelt behind one of
the larger ones, only a few feet from the camp. Davyn remembered
Set-ai's lecture about never keeping watch near a fire. The bright
fire ruined the goblins' night vision, and they hadn't seen a thing
as Davyn and Elidor moved into position. Most of the goblins were
lazing about their camp, resting or eating. The blackened carcass of

a wild pig hung over the fire, and the aroma made Davyn's stomach grumble alarmingly loud.

"Ready?" Elidor hissed from the other side of the fir clump. Davyn motioned that he would take the goblin tending the fire and he drew the arrow to his cheek.

This attack was a stupid risk. Davyn's hand trembled, and the arrow in the bow wavered. He wanted to believe it was the strain of holding the drawn bow, but the sick feeling in his stomach told him it was fear. Fear for himself, fear for his friends, fear for Nearra. Despite the fear, however, Davyn knew they had no choice. He couldn't risk Maddoc finding him now.

With a silent prayer that his stupidity didn't get Nearra killed, Davyn released his arrow. Elidor had been waiting for Davyn to shoot.

As soon as the arrow left Davyn's string, he heard Elidor throw a knife from his left. Davyn's first arrow struck, impaling the goblin cook square in the chest. Before the unfortunate goblin had a chance to realize he'd been shot, Davyn sent his second arrow on its way.

The goblins yelled and grabbed their swords. At that moment, Catriona leaped into camp from behind the prisoner and began slashing at the nearest goblins with the dragon claws. Nearra and Sindri darted out from the woods behind the prisoner. Sindri stood guard while Nearra began sawing at the young man's bonds.

Davyn didn't have time to worry about Nearra as two goblins charged into the forest right at him. He shot the first one but the second arrived before he could nock another arrow. The creature sliced through Davyn's bowstring with its sword. Davyn hurled the useless bow at the goblin and snatched his staff from the ground beside him. The goblin was coming too fast. Before Davyn could defend himself, the creature stabbed and Davyn cried out as hot pain seared his shoulder. He slammed the goblin in the face with his staff. The goblin stumbled back, and Davyn quickly swung again at its head. With a sickening crunch, the goblin went down in a heap. It didn't get up.

Trembling, Davyn saw the goblin's sword blade reflected in the ruddy light. A bright red stain covered the first inch of the tip, and Davyn's hand went instinctively to his shoulder. When he pulled back his palm, it was covered in blood. The pain wasn't bad, but he was bleeding awfully fast. He balled up the fabric of his tunic and pressed it over the wound, hoping that would hold, then turned his attention back to the battle.

To Davyn's surprise, most of the goblins were down. Catriona was holding her own against three of the little creatures though she was bleeding from several minor wounds to her arms and legs. Sindri had driven a goblin back away from Nearra, and the girl had almost finished cutting the prisoner's bonds. Elidor had nocked an arrow in his bow and was aiming at the goblins facing Catriona but, given his unreliable aim, was holding his fire.

Clutching his shoulder, Davyn picked up his staff and pushed into the camp. To his horror, he saw one of the goblins facing Catriona break off and lunge for Nearra's unprotected back. Without thinking he turned to Elidor.

"Shoot!" he yelled.

The arrow flew from Elidor's bow. The arrow buzzed like an angry bee and caught the goblin in the shoulder, spinning him around. The goblin fell, but not before his sword lashed out and hit Nearra in the back.

Cold fear gripped Davyn's guts. He yelled something incoherent and charged across the camp. The remaining goblins took one look at the charging man and fled shrieking into the woods, their wounded trailing behind them.

Davyn rushed to where Nearra had fallen. "Are you all right?" he called. Before he could roll her over, however, she got up as if nothing was wrong.

"Are you hit?" he croaked, turning her forcefully so he could examine her back.

The sword had hit the cloak, but the dull blade hadn't penetrated the thick layers of fur and hide.

"Thank the gods," Davyn said, releasing Nearra. His heart was beating so hard he thought it might leap out of his chest.

"You're hurt," Nearra said, her face going pale.

"It's nothing," Davyn said, trying to close his cloak.

Nearra would have none of it. "Sindri, finish cutting the prisoner free."

While Catriona checked that the goblins were gone and Sindri freed the prisoner, Nearra bound up Davyn's shoulder. The wound wasn't deep, but Elidor suggested that they have a healer look at it once they reached civilization.

Uncomfortable being the focus of Nearra's mothering, Davyn turned to the goblin's prisoner. He was more of a boy than a man, with disheveled black hair and an infectious grin. Despite just being rescued, he bolted for the fire and began eating as much of the steaming pig as he could get in his mouth.

"The goblins didn't feed him much," Elidor observed.

"Obviously," said Cat.

"Name's Mudd," he said between mouthfuls of wild pig. "Sorry," he said, covering his mouth. "They didn't feed me for two days."

"Where were they taking you?" Elidor asked, cutting himself some pig as well.

"Don't know," Mudd admitted. "I don't speak goblin. They did seem to be in a hurry to get me somewhere, though."

"We'd better not stay here, then," Davyn said. "Let's get some of this meat and anything else they've left behind that's useful and get out of here."

Mudd nodded his agreement and began helping Sindri cut meat. Davyn went back to pick up his bow. Then he began rummaging through the goblins' possessions for anything of value.

In the end he came away with another shovel and a bag full of copper coins.

Nearra busied herself binding everyone's wounds. Catriona had a cut on her leg, and it required bandaging. Not wanting to take any chances, Nearra made a sling for Davyn's arm and insisted he use it.

"So what were you doing out here by yourself?" Sindri asked as he and Mudd finished packing up the pig meat.

"Simple." Mudd flashed a goofy smile. "I was looking for you."

10 MUDD'S STORY

I come from a town southwest of here," Mudd said as he trudged beside Sindri through the ankle-deep snow beside the little river. "We're having a terrible problem and we need your help."

"Our help?" Davyn scoffed. "How did you even know we were out here, let alone able to help you?"

"I'm getting to that," Mudd continued. "You see in Potter's Mill—that's my home—we've been under the control of a war-lord named Gadion for years. He and his gang demand that we pay them a part of our food and goods every year."

"I don't think we can be of any help against a gang of thieves," Elidor observed. "We barely managed the handful of goblins that held you."

"Let me finish." Mudd waved Elidor's objection aside. "When the war came many of our men went to be soldiers. After the war our people came back strong and skilled."

"Sounds like you can handle yourselves," Davyn observed. He wasn't sure where Mudd was going with his story, but it was starting to sound like one of his father's plots. The last couple of encounters with Maddoc's minions had failed miserably to extract Nearra's memories. In Davyn's opinion, all they had done was to place Nearra and the rest of them in exceptional danger. Whatever Mudd's motivation in seeking them out, Davyn had no intention of getting involved if it looked even remotely dangerous.

"Once we had warriors, we refused to pay Gadion or his men," Mudd continued. "They tried raiding the town but we beat them. A lot of them got killed."

"What happened then?" Sindri asked.

Mudd took a drink from his water bag, then continued. "Well, we thought Gadion was beaten, but then about a month ago livestock started getting killed during the night. At first everyone thought it was wolves, but soon people began being killed as well."

"Let me guess," Sindri said, eye alight with excitement. "It was some kind of giant beast."

"You know?" Mudd asked, a look of surprise on his face.

"We heard rumors," Catriona said.

"Well, the attacks have been getting more and more frequent," Mudd explained. "Gadion sent us an ultimatum. He said that as long as we refused to pay, the attacks would continue."

"Do you have any evidence that this Gadion controls the Beast?" Elidor probed.

Mudd nodded. "We captured two of his men. They told Shemnara that Gadion controls the creature with a crystal on a chain that he wears around his neck."

"Who's Shemnara?" Sindri asked.

Mudd's infectious smile faltered a bit, and Davyn suspected he'd said more than he wanted.

"She's the spiritual leader of our town," he answered quickly. "She's the one who sent me to find you."

"So, what is it this woman thinks we can do to help you?" Nearra wondered.

"She didn't tell me," Mudd replied, a little too quickly. "Shemnara wants to talk to you about that once we reach Potter's Mill."

"How much farther is this town of yours?" Davyn asked.

"If we hurry, two days," Mudd answered. "I just hope we're not too late."

"What do you mean, 'too late'?" Davyn pressed.

"Attacks by the Beast are becoming more frequent. Two weeks ago the Beast broke into a house and killed some people. My sister was in there—" Mudd's voice broke a little. "She only escaped by hiding in a broken chimney."

Davyn felt for the young man and the ordeal his sister had endured, but he wasn't ready to commit to helping him. "I don't see what we can do about this Beast," he said. "We aren't professional soldiers."

"This Gadion has no honor. He's just a bully," Catriona interjected before Mudd could respond. "I don't like bullies. If there's something we can do to help you, we'll do it."

Davyn opened his mouth to object but he was cut off by a chorus of agreement from the others.

Nearra put a comforting hand on Mudd's arm. "Don't worry," she said, flashing a dazzling smile, "Davyn and Cat are really smart about things like this. They'll think of something."

Davyn felt a surge of anger wash over him. Grinding his teeth in frustration, all Davyn could do was keep his mouth shut and hope that he could talk some sense into his friends before they reached Potter's Mill.

Oddvar cursed as he crunched through the blinding snow. The powder that still covered the ground reflected the sun's rays and made the landscape torturously bright. The bandage over his eyes was so thick that he could barely see a dozen feet in front of him, and still his eyes burned from the light. Trees loomed around him as if out of a fog. His sense of direction told him he was going the right way, but he had no idea whether he was close or not.

Somewhere behind the dwarf, Drefan, Fyren, and Gifre were wheezing, trying to keep up. Not for the last time, the dwarf marveled at the weakness of surface beings. He'd endured forced marches over hundreds of miles and hadn't complained once; these goblins seemed to be made of nothing but complaints.

"Can't we stop and have a bit of a rest?" Fyren said.

"Yeah," Gifre added. "I bet I could catch us some rabbits."

"We march," Oddvar stated simply, not slowing his pace.

"With all due respect, Oddvar," Drefan spoke up in his oiliest voice. "We've not eaten in two whole days and we don't know how much farther we have to go. Wouldn't it be wise to stop and regather our strength?"

Oddvar ground his teeth together. Fyren and Gifre were idiots, but Drefan had enough brains to make a decent argument. It was true that Oddvar had no way of knowing how close they were to their destination but he felt it was close.

"We'll rest for a quarter of an hour," he said at last, "no longer."

"That's scarce enough time for me to catch a rabbit, let alone cook it," Gifre complained.

"I don't mind raw meat," Drefan said.

Gifre shuffled away, grumbling, to look for some game. Oddvar leaned heavily against a tree and pulled his hood down over his eyes. The semidarkness beneath the hood was wonderful on his aching eyes and he took a moment to enjoy it.

"One of you get up the nearest tree," the dwarf growled after a moment. "Tell me if you see a black hill to the west."

After a brief argument and what sounded like some blows, Fyren scrambled up into the tree and began climbing. Despite his willpower, Oddvar's stomach growled. They hadn't eaten in two days. Sek'laar of the Snow-hunter goblins had been very upset when he learned that the so-called harmless children had killed ten of his warriors. The dirty, ignorant goblins had suddenly pointed their spears at Oddvar. Drefan had managed to talk their way out of being killed only after surrendering most of their gear and provisions.

The sound of cursing, crunching, and falling branches told Oddvar that Fyren must be nearing the top of his tree. A moment later Drefan called out to him.

"Do you see a black hill to the west?"

"No," Fyren answered.

Oddvar's heart sank. He'd felt sure they were getting close.

"You're looking the wrong way, idiot! That way is west," Drefan yelled with an exasperated tone.

"Oh," Fyren called back.

There was more crunching, and a thick branch crashed down near Oddvar's feet. Then Fyren's voice rang out.

"There it is. I see it."

"How far?" Oddvar pressed, pulling his hood up again.

"Not more than a league from here," the goblin called down. "It's just beyond the edge of the forest."

Oddvar stood up as Fyren scrambled back down the tree. He was about to order Drefan to find Gifre when the missing goblin returned with a scrubby-looking rabbit in his hand.

"I got one," he said, just as if he'd returned with a prize buck.

"Eat it on the way," Oddvar growled, setting out to the west. "A good fire and a good meal are a league that way."

Oddvar and the goblins continued their march through the forest. As the sun sank, mercifully, over the horizon, Oddvar could see much better. Soon, he was greeted by an awesome sight. Beyond the forest was a little valley and then, rising from the snow-covered ground stood a massive spire of black rock. Its base was at least a thousand feet around and it thrust up into the sky, towering over the forest and the valley. On its top were the remains of a citadel, made from the same black rock, and Oddvar could see torches and wisps of smoke issuing from the broken walls.

"There she is," the dwarf proclaimed as the three goblins broke through the forest cover, "the Broken Citadel on Karoc-Tor."

"Who lives in such a fearful place?" Gifre asked, apprehension in his sniveling voice.

"That," Oddvar chuckled, "is the residence of Gadion, the bandit king—a thoroughly despicable human who makes his living stealing from his neighbors."

"Why do we seek out such a man?" Drefan wondered.

"Because he owes the master a favor," Oddvar answered.

Oddvar led the goblins across the valley and up to the base of the hill. Once there, they were met by a party of armed ruffians who demanded to know what a dwarf and three goblins were doing in their lands. After Oddvar told them his name, they were escorted up the hill on a steep path carved in the black granite. The path wound around several times before it ended at the ruined gates of the Broken Citadel. More ragged humans manned the gates armed with bows. Their greedy eyes followed Oddvar and the goblins as they were escorted in.

The courtyard beyond the dilapidated walls was paved in white stone, which made it look snow-covered. The humans led their captives across the yard, up a large set of granite steps, and through the ill-patched main doors. A few black corridors later they were ushered into a massive audience chamber. In the center of the room a bonfire was burning, with an enormous stag roasting over it on a spit. Unlike the rest of the citadel, this room was warm and snug. At the far end was a raised dais with a rickety-looking chair on it. In the chair sat a human dressed in a faded green silk shirt and worn leather pants. A flamboyant red sash circled his waist. His face was thin and pointed under a ruff of untidy black hair, and he had a small, short beard covering only his chin. A small table stood next to the chair holding up a bottle of wine and a wooden cup.

"So, you are the dwarf Oddvar," the man spoke once Oddvar and the goblins were before him.

"And you would be Gadion," Oddvar replied, being careful to add a flattering tone to his voice.

"Your master said you'd come," the bandit king said, leaning back in his chair, "but he failed to mention why."

"My master requests a favor of you," Oddvar explained. "In return for all the help he has so generously given."

The man on the makeshift throne snorted contemptuously. "Your master is paid very well for his help." Gadion took a drink from the wooden cup. "I owe him no favors."

"What my master requires is a matter of little consequence to you," Oddvar said. "It will cost you nothing, and you will gain my master's good will."

Gadion looked as though he wanted to respond angrily, but Oddvar cut him off.

"Plus three months' payment forgiven," he said.

At this a slow, greedy smile spread over Gadion's thin face, and he stood up from the dilapidated throne.

"Well, why didn't you say so in the first place," he said, pouring more wine into the cup. "I'd be only too happy to do Maddoc a favor."

Gadion dismissed the soldiers surrounding them then stepped nimbly down the stairs to Oddvar. "First we'll have some food and then we'll have some wine, and then you can tell me all about this favor."

As Gadion led Oddvar over to the fire, he surveyed the goblins as if noticing them for the first time.

"They are housebroken, aren't they?" Gadion handed a wineskin to the dwarf.

Oddvar took a long pull from the skin before tossing it to his companions. "Mostly."

Oddvar was about to cut himself a hunk off the stag when a bell rang somewhere outside. Everyone in the room suddenly tensed, their hands moving to their weapons. Some of Gadion's men showed fear on their faces.

"What is it?" Oddvar asked, his knife frozen in midair.

Gadion reached inside his shirt and pulled out a long silver chain from which a large egg-shaped crystal hung. The crystal pulsated with a sickly green light.

"Your master's pet has returned." Gadion turned toward the hall's main door.

A long minute later, the door to the hall was pushed open and a living nightmare limped into the chamber. It was big, built like a bear but larger and more powerful. Long, sharp bony ridges ran down its massive shoulders onto its back and along its tail. The head was flat and triangular, almost like a snake's. But unlike a snake's, the head was crowned with four massive horns, and the open mouth had rows of dagger-like teeth. Its eyes were red slits under the creature's shaggy brow and seemed to reflect the firelight as if lit from within. The Beast moved on all fours, its blade-like claws scratching deep gouges in the stone of the floor.

The only sign of weakness in the Beast was the pronounced limp, and Oddvar could see a gash in its foreleg. As he watched, the humans drew back from the Beast. Only Gadion seemed to have no fear. Wearing the strange crystal outside his shirt, he approached the monster.

"Did you hunt well, my precious?" he asked, tossing it a hunk of the venison.

The Beast snatched up the meat, and Gadion knelt to examine the wound. Dark blood had dried over the creature's fur, but it didn't seem to be bleeding any more.

"I see you've been playing," Gadion admonished. "I trust whoever did this to you is dead?"

The Beast snorted and Gadion seemed to take this for a yes.

"He loves to play," Gadion explained as two men brought up a roast pig for the creature. Gadion turned back to his guests as the

Beast tore into the pig. "Now, what was it Maddoc wants from me?"

Oddvar smiled, his yellow teeth gleaming in the firelight.

"I just might have some new playmates for your friend," he said.

11 POTTER'S MILL

Davyn and his friends crested a little ridge, and the village of Potter's Mill came into view. Evening had passed into night, and only the few lights twinkling in the town revealed its location. Snow had begun to fall again, obscuring the road and covering the landscape with an unearthly silence. In the still whiteness, the troubled village looked peaceful and serene.

Davyn's growling stomach and frozen limbs told him that there was warmth and food there, but he couldn't help wondering about the mysterious Shemnara and the help she would demand of them. The raid on the goblin camp had been little more than a skirmish, yet it had almost killed several of his friends. Davyn's shoulder seemed to be mending nicely. He had taken off the sling and it nearly felt like it was back to normal again.

Catriona's leg wound, however, had gotten progressively worse, forcing her to accept assistance as she walked. She'd been brave about it, of course, but Davyn could see the pain in her face whenever she put weight on the injured limb.

Her wound had forced Davyn to push hard for Mudd's hometown. On the second day of their march, their food had run out, but Davyn insisted they couldn't spare the time to stop and hunt.

If Catriona's leg developed gangrene she'd lose it, and Davyn didn't want that on his conscience. So they'd kept going over another long day of marching, their stomachs grumbling, in the hope that Mudd's directions were right and that there was a healer in Potter's Mill.

As the tired, hungry group trudged down out of the hills toward the town, Davyn noticed that they were much closer than it had first appeared. The lights that he'd seen from the ridge were lamps hung on poles in the center of town. No other lights were visible. To all outward appearances, the town was deserted.

The streets of Potter's Mill were muddy from the snow and partially frozen in the winter air. Davyn's feet kept breaking through the thin layer of icy mud and sliding on the wet ground beneath. As Davyn struggled to keep his footing on the treacherous ground, he came under the lights of the lanterns in the town square. In the pale lamplight he saw what he had missed before. All the upper windows of the nearby buildings were open to the night, and men armed with crossbows watched the square from the darkened rooms.

"Friendly place," Davyn whispered to Sindri as Mudd led them on through the town.

"They wait for the Beast," Mudd whispered. "We must hurry."

Mudd quickened his pace through the square. Davyn had to stop and help Elidor support Catriona through the slippery central square. As soon as they were clear of the square and the road became firmer, Catriona let go of Elidor.

"I can make it from here," she insisted, leaning heavily on Davyn.

Davyn grunted under the effort of supporting her over the uneven ground by himself. Catriona had insisted on wearing her chainmail shirt instead of letting someone else carry it, and the combined weight was considerable. Davyn planted his feet firmly, got his arm around Cat's waist, and lifted her to a more comfortable position. From there they limped the rest of the way until they finally stopped in front of a large house at the far end of town.

The house had two floors and a sturdy wooden porch running along the front. The windows, like those in the rest of the town, were heavily shuttered. A gleam of firelight escaped from a crack under the door, but there were no other signs of life.

"This is the residence of Shemnara," Mudd said, once everyone had arrived. "Come inside and she'll explain everything." Mudd mounted the steps to the porch and knocked on the heavy door with the butt of his hunting knife. There were a few moments of silence, then Mudd knocked again. This time a small hatch in the center of the door opened, and the silhouette of a man's head could be seen beyond. "It's me," Mudd said.

"Who's that with you?" a gruff voice asked.

"It's all right," Mudd replied. "It's them."

There was a long pause, and then everyone could hear the sound of several bolts being drawn back.

The room beyond the door was warm and well appointed. Soft chairs stood around a large hearth and a bearskin rug adorned the floor. Over the hearth's massive oak mantle there was a polished silver medallion depicting the sign of infinity—the symbol of the goddess Mishakal.

The man who had admitted them was a stark contrast to the room. He was tall and ragged, dressed in leathers and carrying several weapons, including a loaded crossbow. His hair was gray and long and flew wildly about his head, dangling down to mix with his bushy salt-and-pepper beard. One of the man's eyes was missing, and a long, vicious scar ran across his face and under the eye patch he wore.

The grizzled man closed the door behind them and began fastening its several bolts.

"Sit down, everyone," Mudd instructed. "I'll go tell Shemnara that you're here."

"Where is this Shemnara?" Davyn asked as he helped Catriona to one of the chairs by the fire.

"She has a shrine in the house where she receives her visions." Mudd turned to leave but, before he could go, a young, blond girl in a pink dressing gown came charging out of the hallway and flung herself, squealing, into Mudd's arms.

"Big brother, you're alive!" She clutched Mudd tightly around the neck. "Tully thought you were surely dead, but I knew you'd make it."

Mudd untangled himself from his sister and set her down gently on the floor.

"This is Hiera," he said, introducing the girl. "Hiera, these are my friends. They saved me from some goblins."

At the mention of goblins, Hiera's eyes grew wide and she began asking Mudd all sorts of questions faster than he could answer.

"I have an idea," he said once he'd calmed Hiera down. "Why don't you ask my friends all about it while I go see Shemnara?"

Hiera seemed to look for the first time at the strange collection of people in the parlor. After a moment, she turned shyly to Mudd and whispered. "You found them?"

"Just talk to them about the goblins," Mudd said, a nervous look on his face.

Mudd turned to leave, but stopped suddenly. "Tully," he said, addressing the man with the crossbow, "my friends and I haven't eaten recently. See if you can get Marla to bring something in."

Tully grunted, a sour look on his face, and then followed Mudd out. A few minutes later a plump, gray-haired woman entered carrying a tray of food. She placed the tray on the low table in the center of the room and bid everyone to help themselves. As she departed, Tully and his crossbow returned.

The food was basic: some cold chicken, a few baked potatoes, some carrots, cheese, a grainy loaf of bread, and a bottle of cider. To Davyn, it tasted as good as anything he'd ever eaten. His stomach had been empty or nearly empty for so long he'd forgotten what it felt like to eat his fill. By the time they all were done, only a few chicken bones and crumbs remained on the tray. Even Nearra had seconds.

Davyn had just sat back in his chair and was allowing the heat from the fire and his full stomach to lull him to sleep when little Hiera spoke up.

"So tell me about the goblins," she demanded. She had somehow managed to restrain her curiosity while her guests ate and now she was bursting with questions.

Sindri began to tell the tale, almost as eager to tell it as Hiera was to hear it. Davyn felt the irresistible draw of the fire as its soothing heat began to coax him to sleep. As he looked wearily around, he saw that Nearra and Elidor were already dozing peacefully in their chairs.

Davyn was about to join them when something else roused him. From somewhere outside came a creaking noise, as though someone were walking on the porch. What caught Davyn's attention was not so much the sound but Tully's reaction to it. At the first creak, the grizzled man had leaped out of his seat and leveled his crossbow at the door.

Sindri stopped his story in midsentence. The room was quiet. Catriona started to ask what was wrong, but Tully put a finger to his lips, warning her to be silent.

For several long minutes no one moved or spoke as Tully craned his neck, listening intently. Finally the grizzled bowman moved slowly to one of the shuttered windows.

Without making a sound, Tully carefully lifted the thick wooden beam that held the shutters closed and set it aside on a table. With the tip of his loaded crossbow, Tully eased the shutter open a crack and peered outside.

The window exploded in a shower of glass and splintering wood. A massive, hairy claw thrust through the opening. It seized Tully by his leathers. An earsplitting roar erupted from outside the window, then Tully was gone.

For a brief moment no one reacted. Davyn was so stunned by what had happened that he didn't know what to do. He was vaguely aware of Tully's screams and the roar of the creature outside, but his mind didn't seem to be able to comprehend it.

"It's the Beast. After it!"

Cat's shout brought Davyn to his senses.

Instinctively, he reached for his bow. But the weapon was useless with the broken string. "I-I can't!"

Catriona tossed Davyn her short sword. He caught it easily, and felt its comforting weight in his hand. Catriona had the dragon claws, and Elidor nocked an arrow to his bow. Sindri and Nearra leaped up and grabbed their staffs, but Catriona motioned them back as she limped to the door.

"Stay inside in case we have to retreat," she instructed as she helped Davyn open the door's many bolts.

Davyn threw the door open and he, Cat, and Elidor charged onto the porch. What met their eyes was beyond a nightmare. A creature the size of a small horse crouched there over the body of Tully. The Beast's back was to them. It was covered in red fur with horny, black spines growing down its back. Tully was obviously dead.

This time there was no moment of stunned hesitation. Catriona hacked at the Beast's back, bringing both the dragon claws down with all her force. There was a wet thud as the claws tore into the Beast. The creature howled in surprise and pain.

Elidor leaped off the porch and began shooting the Beast from the ground. Catriona pulled the dragon claws from the Beast's back as Davyn swung the sword as hard as he could. The blow hit the creature but bounced harmlessly off one of the bony spines on its shoulders.

With a roar of fury that shook the entire porch, the Beast twisted around to confront Catriona and Davyn. Davyn had to leap back to avoid the creature's pointed horns. He stumbled and fell, Cat's sword clattering away along the porch.

From the street, Elidor kept up his fire, sending arrow after arrow toward the Beast. Even with Elidor's minimal archery skills, a creature the size of the Beast was difficult to miss and most of the elf's shots hit.

As the Beast came around to face them, Catriona took a mighty swipe at its head. With an almost contemptuous flick of its head, the Beast knocked the dragon claw from Cat's hand and sent it spinning over the porch rail. Its mouth opened and Davyn could see rows of yellow teeth inside. Catriona limped back from the monster.

Then one of Elidor's arrows suddenly struck the Beast's neck. None of the previous arrows had penetrated the Beast's thick hide. This one, however, must have hit a soft spot. The Beast yelped in pain and its red eyes turned from Catriona to Elidor. With another deafening roar, the Beast launched itself off the porch, smashing through the wooden handrail.

Davyn watched in horror. For a fleeting moment it appeared that the creature would simply land on the young elf and crush him. But, at the last possible moment, Elidor dived forward, rolled out from under the monster's body, and back to his feet. Davyn snatched his sword and scrambled up as Elidor kept shooting. The Beast wheeled around to face the elf.

"Get back in the house!" Davyn yelled.

Elidor didn't have to be told twice. With all the grace and speed his heritage granted him, he turned and fled. The Beast howled, hungry for the chase, and charged after him. Elidor jumped up onto the porch. Without looking back to see how close the Beast might be, he threw himself sideways. The Beast was so close behind him that it slammed into the house right where the elf had been a moment before. The rafters of the house shook and dust showered down from the roof of the porch.

Catriona darted in to attack. The dazed Beast flung out one of its claws. Her chain armor saved her from the blade-like claws, but Davyn was sure he heard some of her ribs break. Staggering from the blow, Catriona fell back into Davyn's arms. Davyn grabbed Catriona and dragged her in through the open door. Sindri and Nearra were there, looking scared but determined.

"Close the door," Davyn ordered, dumping Catriona unceremoniously on the floor. "Elidor, get in here!"

Dropping his bow, Elidor turned and scrambled through the open door. Before Davyn could close the door, however, the Beast's head shot through the doorway. It grabbed the back of Elidor's tunic with its teeth. Thrashing like a dog trying to dry itself, the Beast shook Elidor around as if he weighed nothing at all.

"Stop that!" Sindri shouted. He brought his hoopak down on the Beast's snout with as much force as he could muster. Clearly the blow didn't hurt the Beast, but the creature yelped in surprise. Elidor went flying onto the chairs beside the fire and they splintered under the impact.

It was only when the Beast turned to face Sindri that he seemed to understand the foolishness of his action. He smiled innocently at the creature and hid his hoopak behind his back. The Beast growled and opened its mouth to swallow Sindri with one gulp.

If Davyn had time to think about it, he probably would have done something else—anything else.

He darted forward and shoved his sword into the Beast's mouth.

With a gagging noise the creature jerked its head back. It focused its malevolent eyes on Davyn. Davyn saw its muscles tighten, preparing to leap and crush him. Davyn braced himself for the killing blow he knew would come.

Then, without warning or explanation, the Beast's eyes went wide. It was almost as if the thing was surprised. The creature's muscles relaxed and its head dipped, submissively. It whined once, then turned and, with a speed impossible for something so big, fled into the night.

12   Aftermath

avyn watched as the Beast disappeared into the night. He had been dead; he knew it. The Beast had him. It could have killed him easily, could have killed them all. The weight of that terrible realization pressed down on Davyn like a millstone. Catriona's sword slid from his numb fingers, and he sagged against the doorframe, utterly exhausted. He felt on the verge of blacking out when his ears began working again and a sudden eruption of noise behind him pulled him back to the present.

The room was in chaos. Elidor lay crumpled in a heap atop a pile of broken furniture, and Catriona was lying on the bearskin rug, holding her ribs. Sindri and Nearra were trying to carefully roll the elf over, and Mudd's little sister was screaming. Davyn made a move to help Catriona, but Nearra waved him away.

"Close the door, you fool," she ordered, her eyes flashing violet in the firelight, "and close the shutters over that hole."

Slightly taken aback by Nearra's strange tone, Davyn still did as he was told.

"Stop screaming," Nearra yelled at Hiera, who choked back her cries. "If you want to help, find your brother."

Davyn closed the heavy door and refastened its many bolts as 95

Hiera fled from the room. Next he moved to the remains of the window and shut the shutters over it, securing them with their thick wooden bar.

When he turned back to the room, he found Nearra peeling Cat's chain mail carefully over the girl's head. Whenever the armor pulled at Cat's left side, she screwed up her face in pain.

"You," Nearra called to Sindri. "Come here and help me."

Together, they managed to ease the rest of the armor off. As soon as she was free, Catriona clutched her left arm to her chest. Nearra immediately began binding the arm in place with a strip of cloth from her pack.

Satisfied that Catriona was in good hands, Davyn moved to Elidor. He didn't seem to be bleeding, but Davyn remembered the cracking sound when the Beast had slammed him into the door frame. He was sure the elf had some broken bones.

Please don't be dead, Davyn thought as he knelt beside Elidor, just don't be dead.

Now that he was close, Davyn could see Elidor's chest rising and falling and he breathed a sigh of relief. Gently, he rolled Elidor off the broken chairs and onto his back. As Davyn moved him, Elidor cried out in pain, though he didn't regain consciousness. Whatever was broken, Davyn knew it must be bad.

"What has happened here?" a shaky voice demanded.

Davyn turned and saw Mudd, leading a stately older woman by the arm. The woman was tall, with long flowing white hair that almost matched the white cloth she had bound around her eyes. Her clothes were simple, just a blue dress with a white leather belt, but she clearly projected an aura of authority.

"What happened?" she repeated.

"The Beast was here," Davyn said after no one else spoke up.

"I know that, dear boy," the woman responded. "But what has happened since? Tully, tell me what has happened."

"Tully's dead, ma'am," Davyn answered quickly.

The woman gasped, covering her mouth with her hand and clinging tightly to Mudd for support. For a moment she swayed as if she might faint. Davyn wished he hadn't been so direct in his report of Tully's death.

"Some of you are wounded," the woman said, after taking a moment to regain her composure. "I can smell the blood. Are any of you slain?"

"No, ma'am," Nearra spoke up, "but our friend here will be if a healer isn't summoned quickly."

"No need for that," the woman said. "I was a disciple of the beloved lady Mishakal in my younger days. She graciously still grants me the healing touch." After taking a deep breath to steady herself, the woman released Mudd's hand. "Help them get their wounded to the healing chamber. I know the way."

With that, the blind woman turned and made her way confidently out of the room.

Davyn, Sindri, and Mudd helped Catriona to her feet and walked her down the narrow hallway. On the far side of the house was a large room with two heavy oak tables in its center. The tables were low and long.

"Put her here," Mudd said, leading them to the first table.

Gingerly, they helped Catriona onto the table.

Marla, the plump woman who had brought them food, hurried in carrying a kettle of water. She lit the room's stove and put the kettle on.

"Go get your other friend," she said, passing them a stretcher. "Shemnara will be here in a minute."

Davyn, Sindri, and Mudd returned to the front room while Nearra offered to help Marla.

"Where were you two when that thing attacked?" Davyn asked Mudd on the way.

"Protecting Shemnara," Mudd replied. "The Beast knows she lives here. When it attacks we stay with Shemnara in her shrine."

Davyn, Sindri, and Mudd tried not to hurt Elidor as they maneuvered his unconscious body onto the stretcher. By the time they got Elidor onto the second table in the healing room, Davyn was sick with worry. Sindri was white as a ghost.

"Everyone will please sit down," the blind woman said as she entered the room.

She had changed into a red dress over which a bloodstained apron had been tied. Davyn suspected that, had the dress been some other color, it would have showed many bloodstains as well. Around the woman's neck hung the silver medallion of Mishakal.

"I am Shemnara," she said, though by now Davyn had guessed that. "I will see to your friends. Marla will take care of your minor wounds."

The plump woman had donned an apron as well and was moving over to examine Sindri's bandaged hand. Davyn sat down with Nearra and Mudd on a plain bench along the far wall. He put his hand to his wounded shoulder. During the fight it had started bleeding again.

Shemnara moved quickly and precisely. Her blindness was no impediment; she seemed to know how bad a wound was simply by touching it.

"What is it you want from us?" Davyn asked as Marla examined his shoulder.

"Hush," Shemnara said, her hands gliding over Cat's ribs. "I have to concentrate. There will be time for questions later."

Marla cleaned and redressed his shoulder, but he hardly noticed. Cat's wounds, while serious, were straightforward. Shemnara chanted the prayers that would ease the pain and knit the broken ribs as her hands moved along the wounds. Finally, after many prayers and much effort on her part, Shemnara pronounced Catriona whole.

"This one will be harder," she declared, turning to Elidor. "His wounds are more serious."

Shemnara's voice broke, and Marla pressed a cup of water into her hands. Davyn noticed how tired Shemnara looked, as if the healing involved more than just the touch.

"You two," she said, waving at Davyn and Mudd, "remove his shirt."

"Carefully," she added as Davyn and Mudd stood up.

Slowly they coaxed Elidor's tunic up his body and over the elf's head. As they raised his arms to free the garment, Elidor cried out in pain and tears pooled in his closed eyes.

"Cut it off," Shemnara admonished.

Blushing for not thinking of that, Davyn drew his hunting knife and sliced the garment free.

"Now leave," Shemnara commanded. "You all need rest, and I must not be distracted. Mudd, help them take the girl to the sick room, then take them up to the loft so they can get some sleep."

Davyn was about to protest, but Mudd ushered him over to the table where Catriona lay. Marla had given her something to make her sleep, and already she was unconscious. While Mudd and Davyn held the stretcher, Sindri eased the sleeping girl onto it. Mudd then directed them to a snug room with several soft beds, where they deposited the still-sleeping Catriona. Mudd leaned the stretcher in the corner, then led the group up a stair to the second floor. All along the way Sindri's eyes kept darting down every hall and side passage, his kender curiosity nearly overwhelming him. From the second floor, Mudd led them up a ladder, through a trap door, and into the attic. Several cots were laid out on the floor along with a small stove.

"We use this when people stay over for healing," Mudd explained, lighting a small fire in the stove. "It's not much but it's warm once the stove heats up."

The ceiling of the loft was so low that Davyn had to stoop. He made his way to one of the cots and flopped down on it. He was tired, but with Elidor's life still hanging in the balance he didn't think he could sleep.

"Marla's helping Shemnara so I'll see if I can get some bread and cheese for you," Mudd offered. He put his lamp down in the middle of the floor, then turned and went nimbly down the ladder.

As Sindri and Nearra made their way to beds of their own, there came a faint cry of pain from the open trap door. Sindri eyed the opening nervously and Nearra shivered.

"I wish I'd asked Mudd to bring some cider," Nearra said, drawing her cloak more tightly about her.

Davyn wondered whether Nearra wanted the cider for the cold or for the cries that were drifting up from the healing room. Before Davyn could move to the trap door and yell for Mudd, Sindri brought out his travel bag.

"Allow me," he said, rummaging around in the sling bag. "I conjured something for just such an occasion. Ah, here it is."

The kender drew out a fat-bottomed bottle that Davyn recognized as the one Marla had brought with their dinner. The bottle was still half full, and Sindri offered it to Nearra with a flourish.

Nearra accepted the cider gratefully and drank straight from the bottle. Sindri's face was beaming with the pride all kender have in making their friends happy. His smile evaporated, however, when another cry of pain issued from below. Instantly the kender's face became a mask of frustration and worry. Davyn knew better than to think that his brush with death had scared the kender, but Elidor's safety was another matter.

"He'll be all right," Nearra said, shivering.

Sindri stood up, pacing back and forth under the ceiling that was barely tall enough for him.

"It's not all right!" he exploded finally. "None of this is right."

"Elidor's tough," Davyn interjected. "He'll pull through."

"That's not what I mean," Sindri protested. "I should have been there for him. My magic drove the Beast away. If I'd been at his side, that thing never could've hurt him."

Davyn wasn't ready to admit that Sindri's magic drove off the Beast, but he knew how Sindri felt. If Shemnara hadn't been a healer, Elidor would be dead, and it would be his fault.

"I'm to blame," Davyn said. "If I'd led this group better we wouldn't be in this cursed town."

Sindri looked as if he wanted to say something in reply but he sunk down on his bed and sulked instead.

"I'm not going to stay behind again," he muttered. "When we go after the Beast, I won't be left behind."

"We're not going after that thing!" Davyn nearly shouted. "If Cat hadn't been wearing her armor it would have cut her in half with one swipe. There isn't enough steel in Ansalon to make me go looking for it on purpose!"

"So, you're just going to abandon these people?" Sindri jumped to his feet, a look of astonishment and outrage on his face. "You're just going to leave them to the Beast?"

"Listen, Sindri." Davyn lowered his voice. "These people had problems long before we got here, and they'll have problems long after we leave—"

"We can't leave!"

"Yes we can. As soon as Cat and Elidor can travel." He waved his finger in Sindri's face.

Sindri slapped Davyn's hand aside and stepped forward so they were nose-to-nose.

"Cat would never abandon them," he said softly.

"I know," Davyn shot back. "Look where that's gotten her."

"Fine," Sindri said, turning away. "You can run away if you want to, but Cat's going to be a great knight one day. You'll have to drag her out of here if you want her to go."

"I suppose that goes for you too?" Davyn asked darkly.

"You bet," Sindri said, throwing out his chest.

"Fine," Davyn growled. He was about to tell Sindri exactly what he could do with his stupid, hero-worshiping loyalty when a sob broke the tension.

Nearra was crying, with her head in her hands. The stove had warmed the room, but she still shivered under her heavy cloak. Sindri's face, which a moment ago had been filled with contempt, bloomed to a show of deep compassion.

"Nearra," he said, gently putting his hand on her shoulder. "What is it?"

Davyn knelt beside her.

"I'm sorry, Nearra," he said in a soothing tone. "We shouldn't be fighting—not with Elidor still hurt."

"You don't understand," she gasped, raising her tearstained face to them. "None of you would be here if it wasn't for me." She sniffed and tried to wipe her red swollen eyes with the palms of her hands. "We've been hunted, and tortured, and starved, and frozen, and almost killed—all because of me. If any of you died, it would be my fault," she sobbed, burying her face again.

"That's not true," Davyn declared, putting his arm around the girl. "All of us are here for our own reasons, even me. Cat's here to reclaim her honor, Sindri's here to help Cat . . . "

At the mention of his name, Sindri nodded his head and smiled.

"Elidor's here because . . . well, he has his own reasons, and I'm . . . " Davyn wasn't sure exactly what to say. The truth would only hurt her. "I'm here to see the world—and to make sure nothing happens to you."

"What about Cat?" Nearra asked, tears streaming down her face. "If she goes after that creature, she'll be k-k-killed for sure."

"Let me worry about that," Davyn said. "Cat's a smart girl, she'll listen to reason."

This seemed to placate Nearra a little. She stopped crying and looked up at them. Davyn could see the emotional exhaustion on her pretty face; it had been a long time since any of them had slept.

"You need some rest," he said, easing Nearra down on her bed. "We all do."

Nearra lay quietly, sniffing occasionally, and was soon fast asleep. There was a long, uncomfortable silence while Davyn and Sindri watched Nearra sleep. Finally Sindri looked up with one of his characteristic smiles.

"You're right," he whispered.

"About what?" Davyn said.

"You are the leader, and you've been doing a pretty good job of it."

Davyn chuckled humorlessly. "Right, like leading us straight through the heart of the mountains and almost freezing to death?"

"At least you were leading us straight," Sindri said, grinning. "Any of the rest of us would probably have gone in circles."

"Paladine help us if I'm the best we've got." Davyn shook his head. "So, what's your point?" he asked Sindri.

"I want to know what we're going to do about Cat," the kender replied. "She's going to want to go after the Beast."

"I know," Davyn muttered.

"That's going to get her killed," Sindri said.

"I know," Davyn repeated.

"So," Sindri said, grinning, "what are we going to do about it, boss?"

Davyn thought for a moment. If he knew Cat at all, he knew that the moment she woke up and had the opportunity, she'd pledge her sword to the defense of the town. The trick was preventing that from happening. In his exhausted state, Davyn had to admit he had no clue what to do.

"The first thing we do is get a good night's sleep," Davyn instructed, pulling off his boots.

"And the second thing, boss?" Sindri asked, following suit.

"The second thing is," Davyn said, pulling his cloak over him and blowing out the lamp, "don't call me 'boss'."

"Yes, boss," Sindri yawned from the darkness.

13   THE SEER OF POTTER'S MILL

It was midmorning by the time Davyn awoke. The fire had gone cold, but the sunlight shining on the roof warmed the loft. Slowly, so as not to wake Sindri or Nearra, Davyn eased himself into a sitting position. If he wanted to get his friends out of town before Cat could swear vengeance on the Beast, he would have to hurry. Quietly, he gathered his gear and slipped down the ladder.

The house below was still, but Davyn moved cautiously just the same. Once downstairs, he could hear Marla busy in the kitchen and the unmistakable sound of hammering from outside. After a quick check of the sick room to make sure Elidor and Catriona were still sleeping, Davyn put on his boots and went out the front door.

It was a cold, clear day outside. The shattered window had been replaced, and Mudd was busy nailing a new railing support on the porch.

"Good morning," Mudd called, hefting another support into place.

"You need a hand?" Davyn asked.

"Sure," Mudd replied. "Grab that end, will you?"

Davyn picked up the end of the new top-rail and helped Mudd hoist it into place.

"Where can I pick up some supplies around here?" Davyn asked.

Mudd nodded in the direction of the center of town. "There's an outfitter in the square. Go on ahead. I'm almost done here."

After Mudd had nailed the rail in place, Davyn made his way into the center of town. Potter's Mill was much more inviting in the light of day, Davyn decided. People walked the streets, children played in the snow, and the shops were open and unshuttered. A few farmers and travelers made their way along the main street in search of goods or taverns. To the casual observer it would seem that the citizens and guests of Potter's Mill hadn't a care in the world. Davyn, however, noticed that the farmers who were loading or unloading their wagons seemed eager to finish their tasks. They didn't hurry, but they didn't stop to rest either.

Davyn found the outfitter without any difficulty. The only money he had left was the copper he'd scavenged from the goblins, but it was enough to buy some travel rations, a new string for his bow, and some arrows to replace the ones Elidor had shot into the Beast. It was more than he wanted to spend, but he knew their only chance to get out of town quietly was to be prepared.

His mission complete, Davyn's thoughts turned to Set-ai. He didn't know if Set-ai would follow them to Potter's Mill. But after seeing the Beast up close, he was worried. No matter how skilled a hunter Set-ai was, Davyn doubted he could take down a monster like the Beast alone.

Davyn made his way to the town's single inn in the hopes of receiving some word about Set-ai. The innkeeper, however, had not seen anyone fitting Set-ai's description.

When Davyn returned to Shemnara's house, he found everyone in the kitchen waiting for him.

"We thought you'd gotten lost," Catriona said, passing a plate of eggs.

"I had a little shopping to do," Davyn replied, tossing the bundle of arrows to Elidor. "How are you two doing?"

"Fine," Catriona replied, smiling. "Good as new."

"You still look a bit stiff," Davyn commented to Elidor.

"I'm just not supposed to move too much until the soreness wears off," Elidor replied.

Davyn was about to ask how soon Catriona thought she'd be able to travel, but Nearra cut him off.

"Any news of Set-ai?" she asked, trying to hide a look of worry.

Davyn shook his head. He opened his mouth to elaborate when Mudd came in.

"Shemnara says she's ready for you."

Davyn silently cursed. He had hoped to delay meeting with Shemnara until he could convince Catriona to leave.

Everyone got up and followed Mudd, Davyn more slowly than the others. Mudd led them to a room on the far side of the kitchen and ushered them inside, closing the door behind them.

The room was small and cozy with chairs around a large couch against the far wall. In the center of the room was a large stone basin held in a wood frame. A round, upholstered board leaned against the basin.

Shemnara, dressed again in blue, sat on the couch, leaning over the basin. Shemnara's eyes were unbound, and Davyn could see that they were milky white. A pale scar, like an acid burn, crossed her face where the bandage covered. The basin was glowing with its own pale light, casting the room in stark shades of blue and white. The old healer was looking down into the basin, as if viewing its contents.

As the group stood transfixed by the sight, two wisps of glowing smoke rose from the basin like tentacles. The smoke writhed and twisted before breaking apart and entering Shemnara's eyes. The old woman's eyes glowed for a moment, then she sighed and sat back.

"Come in. Sit," she prompted, wrapping the white bandage around her eyes again.

Davyn moved to one of the chairs and sat down. As he did, he looked into the basin. It appeared to be filled with a milky-white liquid that sloshed and moved even though the basin was rock steady. Wisps of vapor moved restlessly along its surface, but none rose up as they had done for Shemnara. Before Davyn could get a better look, the old healer picked up the upholstered board and laid it over the basin to make a table.

"I'm sure you have questions," she said once everyone was seated, "and I will answer them in due course. For now, I ask that you just listen."

Davyn wanted to ask several questions, beginning with how she knew they were coming, but he held his tongue. Sindri looked as if he might explode, but he, too, kept quiet.

"You know of the tyranny our town lies under," she stated. "The bandit king, Gadion, ruled this town until we drove out his men. Now he attacks us with a monstrous beast, demanding that we submit to his rule."

As Shemnara spoke, Davyn watched Cat. She had a look of indignant outrage on her face.

"Since we will never again bow to Gadion," Shemnara continued, "the town council asked me to discover a way to destroy the Beast."

"Why you?" Elidor interrupted.

"I am a seer," she explained. "An accident in my youth forever robbed me of normal vision. But in losing my sight, I gained other gifts."

"Is that how you knew we were coming?" Davyn asked.

"Yes," Shemnara said simply. "I saw your coming before you even crossed the mountains. When I felt you near, I sent dear Mudd to find you."

"Why?" Davyn pressed. "Surely you don't expect us to take on the Beast for you."

"What I expect or don't expect is of no matter." Shemnara smiled. "I have seen that you will battle with the Beast and that you will slay it."

"Even if that's true," Elidor said, "won't Gadion just try something else? I don't see how that solves your problem."

"Gadion, too, will fall to your prowess," Shemnara said.

Nearra shook her head. "Begging your pardon, but there's no way we could defeat Gadion and his men, to say nothing of the Beast. They're just too powerful for us."

"She's right," Sindri said. "It's not that we don't want to help you, but what can we do?"

Shemnara shrugged, still smiling. "I don't know."

"I thought you could see the future," Davyn said. "If we're supposed to be able to kill the Beast, why don't you just tell us how we do it?"

"The Sight is a fickle gift," the seer said. "Some things I see with great clarity; others are mere shadows. Most things are still hidden, even from me."

"So," Catriona spoke for the first time, "if we're supposed to do these things, what can you tell us?"

"A half-day's travel west of here stands a spire of black rock," Shemnara said. "It is called Karoc-Tor and on its top is the broken citadel, an ancient ruin. It is there that Gadion makes his home. All you need to do to meet your destiny is go there."

"You still haven't said why we should do such a fool thing," Elidor said. "You're asking us to risk an awful lot just to save your town. What do we get if we go?"

Davyn smiled to himself. True to Elidor's nature, the elf wanted to know what was in it for him. If Shemnara was offended by such a question, she gave no sign.

"I know your group travels for a reason," Shemnara said. "Each of you seeks the keys to your destiny. One of you seeks the keys to your past. If you return victorious, I will tell Nearra how to recover her identity."

"What about the rest of us?" Elidor asked.

"Each of you who goes will return with something priceless," Shemnara said. "But know this. If you go, someone close to you will die. And two of you will never be the same."

14   KAROC-TOR

There was a stunned silence in the room. Finally, Shemnara spoke.

"I expect you will want time to consider the matter. You may use the loft for as long as you wish. I will have Marla send lunch up to you."

With that, she rose, and Davyn knew their interview was over. Now that he'd heard Shemnara's reason for seeking them, he was even less inclined to trust her than before. As he made his way back to the loft, however, the thought of Nearra getting her memory back pulled at him.

"She's blind because she stared into the sun too long," Elidor said, once the trap door was safely shut. "It's addled her brains."

"What about the people in this town?" Catriona asked. "They need our help."

"No," Davyn replied, emphatically. "What they need is a squad of armed knights and a score of hunters. What could we possibly do against Gadion, let alone the Beast?"

"Shemnara said we would win," Catriona said.

"What if she lied?" Elidor asked.

"A cleric of Mishakal wouldn't lie," Catriona spat back.

"An ex-cleric," Elidor pointed out.

Catriona crossed her arms. "If Mishakal had abandoned her, she wouldn't be able to heal."

There was a long silence while everyone considered this. Davyn wasn't quite ready to take Shemnara at her word, but he had to admit Catriona had a good argument.

"I think we should do it," Sindri said. "This Karoc-Tor place sounds exciting."

"There is that promise of something priceless," Elidor mumbled, stroking his chin.

"What about her promise that if we went, someone close to us would die?" Davyn said.

"How many will die in this town if we don't go?" Catriona replied.

"Why do we always have to be the ones to do the right thing?" Davyn fumed. "When is it someone else's turn?"

"We do what we're called on to do," Catriona replied, quietly. "That's all we can do. Do you really want people to say that you didn't do all you could?"

Davyn wanted to respond, he wanted to be angry, but Cat's words pierced him and he was ashamed. Set-ai would never back down from a fight just because it might not go his way.

"I'm convinced," Sindri said, turning to Davyn. "I say we go. What do you say, boss?"

"Boss?" Elidor shot Davyn an amused look.

"Ignore him," Davyn said. "I'm still not convinced this is wise. But it wouldn't hurt to go have a look at this place."

"No," said Nearra.

Everyone stopped. It was the first time in the discussion that Nearra had spoken. Now all eyes turned to her.

"What?" Davyn asked.

"I said, no. Shemnara's offered me a way to restore my memories, but I won't put all of you in danger just for me. You've all been so generous and brave, helping me on my quest, but I can't let you face the Beast again. Not for me, not for anything. I'm not worth your lives."

"You're only one of the reasons we're here, Nearra," Catriona said with a smile. "We want to go and see this place because it's the right thing to do. If it looks too dangerous, we'll just leave."

"You can't blame yourself for everything that happens to us," Davyn pointed out.

"That's right," Sindri spoke up. "Davyn's the boss. If it's anybody's fault, it's his."

"Thanks," Davyn growled. He turned to Nearra. "If Shemnara can tell you how to restore your memories, isn't that worth at least a look?"

After a long moment, Nearra looked up into Davyn's eyes. Davyn could see hope and trust there.

"All right," she said. "Let's go tell Shemnara."

As everyone filed out, Davyn held Catriona back.

"Where did you get all that stuff about doing the right thing?" he asked once everyone was gone.

"I was a poor squire," she admitted sadly, "but I did listen to my mistress when she talked about the measure and the tenets of knighthood."

"She'd be proud of you," Davyn admitted.

A strange look came over Cat's face and then, inexplicably and without warning, she kissed him on the cheek.

"Thanks, boss," she said, and then she disappeared down the ladder.

Since the Beast appeared to be nocturnal, Davyn and his friends had set out from Potter's Mill just before dawn. With luck they would reach Karoc-Tor, have a look around, and be back in town before dusk. Even if they were right about the Beast, Davyn couldn't help but think that sneaking into the bandit king's territory was foolish. As Davyn made his way silently through the snow-covered wood, he wondered how he'd let Catriona talk him into this.

To make matters worse, something about the Beast was really bothering Davyn. Quite apart from the possibility that it might appear and dismember him at any moment, Davyn had the persistent feeling that he'd seen the Beast before. This was ridiculous, of course. Davyn knew he'd never even heard of the Beast until a few days ago, yet still the feeling continued.

Davyn ducked around some low-hanging branches laden with snow. He was supposed to be scouting the land ahead of the main group, and he refocused his mind on that task despite his worries and his complaining stomach. It had been decided that, in the interest of time, they would not stop for meals. That was fine with Davyn, as Marla had provided each of them with a sack full of food, including some kind of bread with meat baked into it. Without slowing, Davyn pulled another piece of the meat-cake from his food sack and chewed it absently. The flavor was wonderful, but Davyn's mind was too preoccupied to enjoy it. The sun was now high in the sky, and he knew that they should be able to see the tor soon.

As if in response to his thoughts, the tree cover suddenly broke and Davyn saw it. Karoc-Tor rose up before him, like some enormous black headstone, jutting skyward. He was surprised at how close it actually was, maybe half a mile off. The thick layer of winter-bare trees and the fluffy evergreens had effectively screened his approach.

With the awesome sight of the black rock before him, Davyn decided to wait for his friends. With any luck, he thought as he ate another piece of the meat-cake, I'll be able to convince Cat that this is a close enough look and we can go back. As he'd expected, there had been no sign of the Beast. But Davyn was sure that the fortress of the bandit king would be guarded by more than his pet monster.

As much as Davyn worried for the safety of his friends, he wanted Nearra to be happy too. If Shemnara were telling the truth and she could help Nearra to recover her memories, then perhaps they could stop wandering. Perhaps Nearra could settle down to a normal life. Perhaps Davyn could convince her to settle down with him.

Davyn's wandering thoughts were brought forcefully back to the present by the soft crunch of footsteps in the snow. He quickly unslung his bow and nocked an arrow. To his relief, a moment later Elidor came trudging into the clearing, leading the others.

"Is something wrong?" the elf whispered.

Davyn shook his head and pointed at the opening where the immense black spire could be seen.

"Wow," Sindri gasped. "It's huge."

"I can see the fortress on top," Elidor said. "There isn't much left of it, just a broken wall and a few buildings."

Catriona shaded her eyes and squinted to try to see better. Her human eyes were no match for Elidor's superior vision. "Do you think we could sneak inside?"

Elidor chuckled. "Not unless you can fly. The only way up looks like a path that runs around the tor itself."

"Maybe there's a back door," Sindri said. "You know, a secret way in."

"If it's secret, we're not likely to find it," Davyn pointed out.

"Not if we don't try," Catriona said.

Davyn shook his head. "Are you crazy? Walking right up to the bandit king's hideout is too dangerous. There's bound to be someone keeping a lookout from up there, not to mention patrols."

"It looks like this forest extends right up to the tor," Elidor said. "We should be able to use it as cover without any trouble."

"Whatever we do, we'd better hurry," Nearra said. "We've got to start back soon if we want to make it before dark."

Davyn sighed. "All right, we'll go have a look. Elidor and I will go out ahead. The rest of you stay close. Follow our footsteps."

"Yes, boss," Sindri called cheerfully.

Davyn rolled his eyes, and turned to follow Elidor into the trees.

It seemed like only a few minutes had passed when the massive base of the tor appeared through the trees like a wall of black granite. As Elidor had predicted, the tree cover had shielded their approach from anyone above.

As they waited for the others to catch up, Davyn began to pace. "I don't like this. I don't see any footprints but ours. Doesn't the bandit king send out patrols?"

"Maybe he feels safe up there," Elidor said. "Anyone who wanted to attack him would have to climb the path. That's probably where they put their lookouts."

Davyn merely grunted in response.

"Maybe he relies on the Beast for protection?"

Davyn felt the hair on the back of his neck go up at the thought of the Beast stalking them out in the open. "Don't say that. You'll have us jumping at shadows."

"Yes, boss." Elidor grinned.

For the next hour Davyn and Elidor led the others quietly around the massive base of the tor. There were many small holes and fissures in the black granite walls, but nothing big enough for a person to pass through.

"All right," Davyn said. "We've fooled around here too long. We've got to get going if we want to make Potter's Mill by dark."

"Then why did we come out here at all?" Catriona hissed. "How will skulking around in the woods help anyone?"

Davyn strained to keep his voice quiet. "Look, this wasn't my idea. Right now the only thing I care about is getting everyone back to town before the Beast wakes up. If we leave now we should be able to get there before it catches up with us."

"You're assuming its lair is somewhere around here," Elidor said. "What if it lives near town?"

Davyn gave him a dirty look.

"I was sure we'd find something," Catriona muttered, more to herself than to anyone. "After what Shemnara said—"

"We can talk to Shemnara when we get back to town," Davyn cut her off. "Let's go."

Davyn was torn between being relieved and worried as they headed out through the forest toward Potter's Mill. He was glad they were putting Karoc-Tor behind them, but Elidor's suggestion that the Beast might live near the town preyed on his mind. The last time they encountered the Beast they barely survived. Davyn didn't like their chances if the creature caught them in open country.

The trip back to Potter's Mill seemed to be taking much longer than Davyn remembered. By the time the light began to fade, Davyn reckoned they were still a couple of miles from the safety of town. He had just crested a small rise and he could see the smoke from Potter's Mill's chimneys in the distance.

Suddenly he glimpsed shadows moving among the trees.

"Look out!" he yelled.

The others reacted instantly, drawing their weapons and standing back to back. Davyn ran the short distance to his friends, glancing about, arrow nocked, seeking any signs of movement.

"Was it the Beast?" Catriona hissed, not taking her eyes off the trees.

"I don't think so," Davyn whispered back. "There were a bunch of them moving around in the trees."

"A bunch of what?" Elidor asked.

"Just shoot anything that moves." Davyn scanned the trees.

"You'd better think twice about that," a familiar voice called out from the gathering darkness.

15 CAPTIVES

Two people stepped out from behind a tree. Davyn recognized both of them. One was Maul, one of the Highland Rangers. The other was Nearra. Davyn stole a quick glance behind him and swore.

Maul must have grabbed Nearra during the initial confusion. Now he was using her as a shield, holding a long-bladed hunting knife at her throat.

"Throw down your weapons," Maul smirked, pressing the blade against the girl's thin skin. Nearra whimpered.

Everyone hesitated, waiting for Davyn to move. Maul was holding Nearra in front of him to keep anyone from shooting him. But at this range, Davyn wasn't likely to miss. Davyn slowly drew his bowstring to his ear.

"I said, drop your weapons," Maul said, a slight tremble to his voice. "You're surrounded."

"Even if one of your friends kills me, I'll still get you," Davyn growled, trying to make his voice as threatening as possible. "The great thing about arrows is that all I have to do is let go."

Maul was definitely worried now. He turned his body sideways behind Nearra to present less of a target for Davyn. At the same time, he pressed the knife deeper into the flesh of Nearra's throat.

"Are you willing to risk her life, boy?" Maul taunted. The tone of power was gone from his voice, however. "If you shoot me, I'm liable to flinch. You wouldn't want my knife to slip and cut this girl's throat to the neck-bone, now would you? It's a very sharp knife."

Davyn watched as a tiny drop of blood seeped out between the knife blade and Nearra's neck and ran down her shoulder. Davyn's confidence wavered and the tip of his arrow dipped.

"Shoot him," Catriona hissed in his ear. "They're going to kill us all anyway."

"Now that's not true. We just want you, boy." Maul nodded at Davyn. "You owe us for Dee. The rest of your friends can go, once they've given us our cloaks back, that is."

There was a rustling sound, and Maul's six companions stepped out from the trees. They were a shoddy lot with piecemeal armor and rusty weapons. Davyn had wondered why no one had taken a shot at him. The answer was clear: none of them had a bow. In the pale light of the rising moon, Maul and his men looked bigger and meaner than Davyn remembered them.

As close as Maul's friends were, it was unlikely Davyn would get off a second shot before they would rush him. That meant that, after Davyn shot Maul, their only defense would be Cat and Sindri, unless Elidor managed to hit one of them. Davyn didn't like those odds one bit. It was clear that Maul was doing the same calculations in his head. An evil smile spread over his rough face, and his grip on the knife tightened.

"All right," Davyn said at last, lowering his bow. "Don't hurt her."

Beside him Elidor lowered his bow as well, and Maul's men rushed in to disarm the rest.

"Tie them up," Maul said, finally pulling the knife away from Nearra's throat.

"You said you only wanted me," Davyn protested. One of the

rangers put a sword point to his chest to keep him from charging Maul.

"I lied." Maul smiled easily, still holding Nearra close. "I suspect we can get a good price for you in the slave markets of the south. All except this one," he went on, indicating Nearra. "I like her."

Davyn knocked the sword of the ranger aside and lunged at Maul. He almost reached him before Maul's friends swarmed him, dragging Davyn to the ground. Davyn struggled until the men began hitting him and kicking him. Finally Davyn allowed his hands to be bound with a thick rope. From there the rangers dragged him over to where his friends were being similarly bound and dumped him unceremoniously on the ground.

"Now," Maul addressed them as one of his men tied Nearra's hands behind her back. "Where is your big friend Set-ai?"

"He's out hunting," Catriona replied, forcing a smile. "If you leave now you might make it out of here before he gets back."

"I'd like to believe you," Maul said easily, "but we've been following you for several days and we haven't seen any of his footprints."

Davyn cursed to himself. Maul and his people were evidently better woodsmen that he'd given them credit for.

"Now why would your protector leave a bunch of children to fend for themselves in the woods?" Maul wondered aloud.

"It's because of the Beast," Sindri piped up.

"What beast?" one of Maul's men asked.

Catriona drove her elbow into the kender's ribs, but he just ignored her.

"There's a monster that hunts at night in these parts," Sindri said. "Set-ai wanted to see if he could kill it."

"Fairy stories," Maul scoffed. "There's no beast in these woods. There's a town just a couple miles from here. If there were a beast, the townspeople would have hunted it down and killed it."

"They can't," Sindri said. "It's bigger than a bear and twice as mean."

"And how would you know?" Maul asked.

Sindri shrugged. "Because I've seen it."

At this a rumble of concern went through Maul's men. None of them would trust a kender as far as they could throw him, but everyone knew that kender didn't actually lie.

"Quiet, you lot." Maul glared at his companions. Maul put on a brave face, but Davyn could tell he was worried.

"Sam, go get the horses," Maul continued. "Maybe it would be best if we got going," he added.

The man called Sam was a short fellow with a permanent sneer plastered on his face. He scurried off into the woods in a manner that suggested he had a bad leg. After a few moments he returned leading four scrubby-looking horses.

"Mount up," Maul instructed his men, swinging into the saddle of the best of the horses. "Sam, Grist, and Hithar, you're with the prisoners."

Sam and two others hauled the companions to their feet and slipped a long rope through their tied hands, effectively binding them together.

"Let's go," Maul called.

Davyn had only taken one step when the forest exploded with noise.

The Beast burst from the trees.

With a tremendous roar, the creature flattened Grist, Hithar, and Sam, and knocked Davyn and his friends to the ground. The horses panicked and leaped forward through the forest, heedless of the rangers desperately clinging to their backs.

Davyn could feel the Beast's hot breath on the back of his neck. He was sure the next moment would be his last. The Beast howled with rage and bounded into the trees after the horses.

In the minutes that followed Davyn lay still, listening. From the sounds, Davyn could tell that the monster had caught at least one of the horses. It didn't linger over its kill, however, and was soon crashing through the night after the rangers. When Davyn was sure it was a safe distance away, he pushed himself to his knees.

"Nearra?" he hissed, fumbling to reach the knife in his boot. "Cat? Is anyone alive?"

"Is it safe to move?" Elidor's voice came from the jumble of bodies.

"As long as the Beast is chasing those horses we should be safe," Davyn guessed, awkwardly sawing through the ropes that bound his wrists.

"I think everyone's all right." Nearra's trembling voice came from behind Davyn.

"Everyone except Grist, Sam, and Hithar," Catriona said. She cocked her head in the direction of the three mens' lifeless bodies.

"What do we do?" Catriona asked as Davyn's knife sliced through the rope at her wrists.

"Run for town," Elidor suggested.

"No," Davyn said. "If the Beast decides to come back for us, we'd never make it."

"We can't stay here," Catriona pointed out.

"We're not going to," Davyn said, cutting the others free. "We're going back the way we came. The Beast is smart," Davyn said, accepting his bow from Elidor. "It will assume we're heading for town." He began walking in the opposite direction from Potter's Mill.

"I don't think he's that smart," Catriona said, jogging to catch up.

"Do you want to risk it?" Davyn asked.

Catriona put up her hands and shook her head.

"After we've put some distance between us and the dead rangers, we'll climb a very big tree," Davyn said.

A distant roar echoed through the forest and Davyn quickened his pace.

"I think we'd better find that tree sooner rather than later," Elidor remarked.

Silently Davyn agreed with him.

Davyn led his friends almost half a mile before ushering them up the biggest trees he could find. Even half a mile from the site of the Beast's attack was too close for comfort, but Davyn couldn't risk the Beast catching them on the ground. After everyone else was safely up a tree, he climbed one himself and set about watching for the Beast. He didn't think he could calm down enough to sleep. So he just watched, straining to hear every sound that might herald the arrival of the Beast. But the Beast didn't come, and eventually Davyn got tired. He'd tied himself to the tree, and some time around midnight, he fell asleep.

In the cheery light of morning, the events of the previous night seemed almost surreal. As he untied himself and carefully climbed down, Davyn wondered what had happened to Maul and his men.

"Is it safe down there?" Sindri's voice floated down as Davyn reached the ground.

Davyn hated to admit it but he wasn't sure. He'd been preoccupied thinking about Maul and his men and hadn't been checking his surroundings. He cast a quick look around for signs of anything out of the ordinary and found something immediately. A cold fear gripped Davyn's heart as he looked down to find the footprint of an enormous creature only feet from where he'd landed. Davyn crouched down, listening intently.

"Well," Catriona called down, "is it safe or not?"

Davyn ignored her, searching the ground. From the prints it was evident that the Beast had been there sometime during the night. It had sniffed out each tree where Davyn and his friends had slept. Then, apparently, it had gone.

"It must have known we were up too high," Davyn said, shaking his head in disbelief.

Catriona dropped to the ground beside him. "Who must've known?"

"The Beast," Davyn said, indicating the massive paw prints.

Catriona muttered and drew one of Set-ai's dragon claws.

"Could it still be around?" she hissed, pressing her back to the tree where she'd slept.

"I hope not."

"What? You mean you don't know?"

"Well, the print is a couple hours old at least," Davyn said. "If it truly is nocturnal it would have headed home before dawn."

"That's a big if, boss." Catriona shuddered.

"Don't call him boss," Sindri said, sliding out of his tree. Davyn was about to thank the kender for giving up on calling him "boss" until Sindri continued. "That's my job, right, boss?"

"Why should you have all the fun?" Catriona grinned.

Davyn groaned and stood up.

"We should get going," he said. "I want to get back to Potter's Mill and get something to eat."

Elidor hopped lightly out of his tree. "I've still got a bit of the meat-cake."

"No, thanks," Davyn said.

"There's still some hardtack left," Sindri pointed out helpfully.

There was a collective groan from the group.

Nearra climbed out of her tree. "What's everybody groaning about?" She had twigs in her hair and dirt on her face, but they couldn't detract from her beauty when she smiled.

"Nothing. Let's get going," Elidor said, adjusting his gear and cinching up his cloak. "The sooner we get to town, the sooner I can sit in front of a fire."

"Yeah," Catriona agreed, "and the next time we get into trouble, no surrendering!"

"You'll get no argument from me," Davyn said as they all began walking in the direction of town. "I'm just glad it worked out."

"Luck," Elidor scoffed. "If the Beast hadn't intervened, who knows where we'd be right now."

"I don't care if it was luck," Nearra said, walking close to Davyn, "I'll take it over the alternative any day."

"Elidor's right," Davyn said out of the blue. "We've got to be more careful. If we'd been paying attention we might have seen Maul and his cronies earlier. All it would have taken to discourage them is for Elidor and I to have shot a couple of their men."

"Speaking of which," Catriona interjected, "shouldn't someone be on point?"

"I'll do it," Elidor said, moving up to the front.

"Keep an eye out and whistle if you see anything," Davyn said.

"And no surrendering," Catriona called.

Davyn was about to reply when he walked into the back of Catriona, who had stopped suddenly. Wondering what the delay was, Davyn looked around her only to be confronted by a dozen scruffy-looking men with crossbows.

"Well, looky here," one of the men said, smirking, "right where Gadion said they'd be."

"Drop those weapons, kids," a tall man in a chain mail shirt instructed, gesturing with his crossbow for emphasis.

Facing a dozen crossbows, Davyn dropped his weapons without a fight. As one of the men took Cat's dragon claws, Davyn saw her muscles tense. Fortunately her common sense overcame her desire to cut the man's throat.

"I thought you agreed to no surrenders," Catriona whispered to

Davyn as the men took Elidor's bow and his knives.

"You want to rush a dozen crossbows, be my guest," Davyn hissed back.

In short order, the group was stripped of their weapons and bound together on another long rope. Davyn sighed as his hands were tied for the second time in less than a day.

"Well, well," the tall man said once they were all bound. "What a sorry lot they are, eh, Sten?"

Sten, a short ugly man, laughed. "Maybe the boss wants 'em to feed the Beast. They won't be much good for anything else."

"The whole lot of them wouldn't quench the Beast's appetite for more than a day," the leader chuckled, nodding. "There must be some other reason he wants them."

"Well, that big fella might be man enough to join us," Sten suggested, pointing to Davyn. Then he looked Catriona over. "Doesn't the boss like big women?"

At this there was a round of general laughter from the men. Cat, pushed past her limit, lashed out with her foot and kicked Sten into the dirt. The little man was too far away for a proper blow so the only thing bruised was his ego. He came up wielding a knife nonetheless.

"Sten," the leader cautioned before the little man could do anything.

"Come on, Wil, just let me cut her a little," Sten growled. "We can tell the boss she put up a fight."

"You think you can take me, little man," Catriona taunted him.

Davyn wondered whether Cat was letting her temper get the better of her or if she thought she could take Sten's knife away with her hands tied.

"Enough," Wil said firmly as Sten tensed. "Sten, get our guests moving."

"You might want to mind your tongue," he advised Cat as they started moving. "I don't know what Gadion wants you for, but if he decides you're no use to him he'll be more than happy to let Sten carve you up nice and slow."

16   THE BANDIT KING

Once the group was moving, Wil discouraged talking. He even walked between Cat and Sten to make sure there were no unexpected problems. Davyn didn't have to wonder where they were going. The mention of Gadion could only mean one thing: the bandit king's pet had told its master where to find them. Now, despite all his efforts to stay away from Karoc-Tor, that's just where they were going.

It took several hours to reach the base of Karoc-Tor. Davyn found that being tied to his companions was incredibly fatiguing. Either Cat, who was bound in front of him, would go too fast, or Nearra behind him would go too slow. By the time the tor came into sight, Davyn's wrists were raw.

Sten led them around the base of the spire until they came to the spot where the narrow path had been cut into the granite wall. The path was wide enough and tall enough for a wagon to go up, but only just.

"Stay against the wall," Sten said as they began to climb. "One bad step here and you'll all be quite a mess."

The narrow strip of stone separating them from the ground below seemed to wind endlessly around the tor. Finally, when they were all panting and wheezing from the effort, the path began to widen, reaching the tor's small, flat top.

The hilltop was almost completely taken up with what had once been an impressive fortress. The remaining walls were high and broad, speaking of glory days when the fortress would have been impenetrable. Now the walls were mere shells of their former selves, their broken blocks littering the ground around the massive foundations. A single tower remained intact, along with random sections of wall, but that was all.

Beyond the broken walls were the remnants of three buildings: a barracks, a stable, and a keep. The barracks appeared to have been burned in the past. Smoke stains rose from the empty windows, and the roof was completely gone. One of the stable's walls had fallen over, taking a good portion of the roof with it, but Davyn could still see horses in the remaining space. Of all the buildings, the keep was in the best shape. Its massive square walls rose up, brick-like, in the afternoon sunlight. Despite the bright light, the black edifice seemed gloomy and forlorn. It had two enormous wooden doors that hung limply from ancient hinges. Both doors had been patched, and there seemed to be a more-or-less permanent opening between them.

As Davyn stepped into the courtyard, he saw more scruffy men with bows atop the ruins of the gate tower. They didn't look impressive, but Davyn counted at least twenty, a formidable force no matter what their looks. Sten led Davyn and the others on across the courtyard and through the gap in the keep's doors. If Davyn thought the black edifice was gloomy from the outside, it was nothing compared to the interior. The hallways were narrow and windowless, and the black stone walls seemed to drink up the torchlight without reflecting anything back.

Finally they were led out into a large, open room. This room was better lit than the others due to a large hole in the roof. An enormous fire burned in its center, on which a pig was roasting. At the far end of the chamber was a raised platform on which a decaying chair had been set. There were several more of the scruffy men in this room, but Wil ignored them all, conducting his captives to the platform at the far end of the hall. As they drew nearer, Davyn saw a thin, less-scruffy man sitting easily on the rickety chair. His hair was unkempt, but his goatee was well trimmed and his clothes were considerably nicer than any of the other men. Davyn realized that this must be Gadion, the infamous bandit king.

"What have you brought me, Wil?" the man asked, digging dirt out of his fingernails with the tip of a long dirk.

"These are the trespassers you wanted," Wil responded. "Found 'em skulkin' around in the woods."

"Ah, yes," Gadion smiled from his seat, putting away the thin-bladed knife. "And just what would the likes of you be doing in my woods?" He directed the question at Davyn.

"We were lost in the mountains," Davyn lied. "We couldn't get our bearings but then we spotted this spire and headed for it."

"Is that so?" the bandit king drawled. "And how did little lambs like you come to be lost in the mountains?"

Davyn was about to reply when Wil interrupted.

"They haven't been lost in the mountains," he said, stepping forward and passing Gadion a sack. "Look what I found on 'em."

Gadion examined the contents of the sack, then drew out a piece of Marla's meat-cake and tasted it.

"Well, well," he said, after having several more bites. "I reckon that'd be your wife's cooking, eh, Sten?"

Sten nodded, still grinning. Davyn wondered if he had any other expression.

"It's been a long time since I tasted dear Marla's cooking," Sten admitted.

"You see," Gadion leaned forward to explain to Davyn, "dear Marla left us to go over to the witch Shemnara. That means you've come from her."

Davyn didn't know how to respond to this so he said nothing.

"I knew Shemnara was seeking fresh warriors," Gadion went on. "Ever since I unleashed the Beast on them, they've been looking for a way to get rid of me. Of course, I never expected her to send me children."

At this the scruffy men laughed.

"And to think, I've been sitting here worrying that the old witch might actually come up with something clever." Gadion laughed.

Davyn felt his face getting hot as the men laughed around him. When Gadion had finally regained his composure, he stepped down off the platform and put his arm around Davyn.

"I don't hold it against you, boy," he said easily. "I'm sure you were pumped up with visions of gold and glory. I was young and foolish myself, once," he went on. "As a matter of fact, I'm grateful to you. If you hadn't come, I'd have never known how weak Shemnara and those fools in Potter's Mill had become."

With a sudden burst of energy, Gadion leaped back onto the platform. He picked up a cup from the table beside his chair and held it aloft, calling for the attention of the room.

"Brothers," he called. "Raise your cups to a noble foe. I give you Shemnara and her pitiful townsfolk."

With a great flourish, Gadion drank from his wooden cup.

"And now that we have drunk a toast to our enemies," he said, putting the cup back down, "Wil, assemble the men. If the best defense Shemnara can offer is a handful of children and a kender, then Potter's Mill should be easy pickings. Tomorrow, when the sun rises, take the town. Kill anyone who resists. But bring the witch to me."

Sten's grin widened even more than Davyn thought possible.

"I'll send the Beast along, too," Gadion said absently. "He needs a bit of sport."

Wil turned and marched out with the bulk of his men.

"What do we do with this lot?" Sten asked.

"Throw them in the cells," Gadion replied. "We can't have them running loose. They might try to warn the old witch."

Sten tugged on the rope, and Davyn turned to follow.

Catriona leaped forward. She kicked Sten in the knee and he went down hard. Not stopping, Catriona launched herself at Gadion. Before she could reach him, however, she was stopped short by the rope. The remaining guards had seized it. One held it tight while the others moved to restrain Cat. It took two of them, but they finally held Catriona tight between them.

"You murdering scum," Catriona spat at Gadion as he regarded her coolly from his chair. Despite Cat's attack the bandit king had not flinched.

"Maybe I see why Shemnara thought you were up to the job. I do wonder what you would have done if you'd reached me, though?" He indicated Cat's tied hands.

"You're nothing but a sniveling coward, just another bully, trying to live from other people's labor."

Gadion rose and slapped Catriona across the face, hard. Cat's head snapped back, lip bloodied. She spat on Gadion's silk shirt.

"You sound like a Solamnic." He sighed, wiping the bloody spittle from his shirt. "Such romantic notions as peace and fair play have no place in the real world. There is no such thing as nobility where power is concerned. Those who have power, use it. Those who do not, covet it." He moved close to Catriona as his guards held her tight. "Quite simply, young lady, I do what I do because I can, just like everyone else."

"You're more than a weakling and a coward," Catriona shot back. "You're a fool."

"And you are an idealistic youth, unlearned in the lessons of life." Gadion took Catriona's chin in one hand, and his fingertips brushed her cheek. "You need to learn that the strong can take what they want."

Davyn's muscles tensed. He guessed if he pulled back hard enough on the rope he could free Catriona from the guard's grip. Apparently one of the other guards had the same thought, because at that moment a knife was pressed against Davyn's ribs.

Catriona jerked out of the bandit's grip. "You'd better make sure they tie me tight. I assure you, I can kill you without my hands."

"You really are a hopeless case." Gadion sighed. "You're full of romantic notions of order and justice. Very well."

Without warning Gadion suddenly lunged forward, driving a short dirk into Cat's stomach. Caught completely by surprise, Catriona grunted and gasped, slouching over as Gadion pulled out the bloody, thin-bladed knife.

"I grant you the rest of your life to think about your foolish notions," he said, wiping the dirk on his red sash.

"Throw her in the cells with her friends," he commanded Sten. "Let them watch her die a noble death."

17   Oddvar's Gambit

Oddvar was furious. It was the first time in weeks he'd had a chance for a decent sleep during the brightness of the day, and everything had gone straight to the Abyss. To make matters worse, it had been hours before anyone had told him the news.

Muttering curses under his breath, the dwarf followed the smell of roast pig through the keep's narrow corridors. Finally, he emerged from the hall into a snug, round room with a fire burning cheerily in a black stone hearth. In the center of the room was a round table laden with food at which Gadion and his lieutenant, Wil, were eating.

"Here you are," Oddvar growled, stomping into the room.

"Ah, Oddvar," Gadion called, his mouth full of pork. "Come and join me in this excellent meal." The bandit king indicated an empty chair beside him with a wine bottle, before using it to wash down his food.

"Are you insane?" Oddvar raged.

"What?" Gadion asked, genuinely confused. "Is pig against the dwarf creed or something?"

Oddvar wanted to scream but he clenched his fists until the feeling had passed.

"I'm not talking about the pig," the dwarf fumed, slicing a piece of meat with his knife. "I'm talking about you stabbing that girl."

"Regrettable, to be sure," Gadion said, helping himself to some bread. "But she really wasn't much good for anything else. Too many noble principles."

"Did it ever occur to you," Oddvar asked, "that those children might be the same children I've been looking for?"

"Of course it did," Gadion replied, leaning back in his chair. "Wil told your goblin friends about it the moment they were brought in."

Wil nodded for emphasis, his mouth full of food.

Oddvar ground his teeth again. He had to remember to beat Drefan within an inch of his life.

"That still doesn't explain why you stabbed one of them. Didn't you wonder if you were stabbing the girl I need?"

"Of course not," Gadion scoffed, drinking from his wine bottle again. "You said the girl you want had blond hair. The girl I stabbed had red hair and obviously had her memory intact."

"You've never heard of people disguising themselves?" Oddvar grunted, cutting more pig for himself.

Gadion considered this for a moment, then shrugged. "I suppose that could've happened," he admitted. "Fortunately it all worked out for the best."

"Just how do you figure that?" Oddvar challenged.

"Watching her friend die will make your young problem more responsive," Gadion explained. "She won't want to risk putting the rest of her friends in danger."

"How, exactly, does that help me?" Oddvar wondered.

"Simple," Gadion replied. "You said that stressful situations will force her memories back. What could be more stressful than watching a friend bleed to death?"

"And if that doesn't work?" the dwarf said.

"It'll work." Gadion smiled. "Stomach wounds are a bad way to go. It could take days. And if that doesn't do the trick, we'll just torture a few more of her friends. She'll crack sooner or later."

Oddvar chewed his pig in silence as Gadion helped himself to more bread. Gadion's arguments made sense, and that worried him.

"I wonder," Wil spoke for the first time, "if our dwarf friend isn't worried that you'll get results so fast it'll make him look bad."

Gadion let out a short bark of a laugh at the idea. Then he grinned as he considered what Wil had said.

"Now that I think about it," he said, stroking his beard, "it wouldn't bode well for you if I were to force out the girl's memories in a mere day or two. How long has it taken you?" Gadion laughed.

Oddvar favored Gadion with a sneer but didn't respond.

"Yes," Gadion said, his grin widening. "I think we'll have to start torturing them as soon as the other girl dies. We'll break the little girl in less than a week."

Oddvar clenched his fists but kept his temper. The idea that this human knew his business better than Oddvar did was insulting—worse still, Oddvar was sure that Gadion was right.

For a moment, Oddvar thought of warning Gadion about Asvoria and the very real possibility that she would wreak vengeance upon anyone daring to torture her. That would delay Gadion and perhaps save Oddvar's reputation. But if Gadion knew about Asvoria, he might try to control the girl himself.

"I'd better go see these children for myself," Oddvar said, standing up. "No sense getting worked up if it's the wrong group."

"Any of my men can direct you to the cells," Gadion called after him.

Once Oddvar was back in the darkness of the black citadel's corridors, he paused, listening outside the room where Gadion and Wil were eating.

"He didn't seem happy," Wil said.

"No," Gadion agreed, thoughtfully. "He didn't. Perhaps there's more to this situation than our dwarf friend is telling us?"

"What do you mean?"

"There obviously are important things locked away in this girl's mind. Things our esteemed wizard Maddoc finds very valuable."

"What kinds of things?"

"We'll just have to break the girl and find out. As soon as we're done here, have one of your men kill the dwarf. I'll deliver the girl and her secrets to Maddoc myself." Gadion laughed. "Once he agrees to the right price."

There was a round of ugly laughter in the room, and the humans went back to their meal. Oddvar's mind churned all the way back to the great hall.

He wasn't worried about Gadion's plan to kill him. Oddvar had dealt with death threats before, and Gadion's men were no match for his poisoned dagger. No, he was more angry at the thought of Gadion extracting Asvoria and taking all the credit.

Oddvar had been on Asvoria's trail for months. If Gadion managed to find a way to force the Emergence, it would make him look incompetent to Maddoc. Oddvar doubted that Maddoc was the kind of person who would pay him if Gadion got to Asvoria first.

"If it wasn't for me, those kids would've disappeared over the mountains," he said to himself. "It'd be just like that wizard to reward Gadion for all my hard work."

Oddvar's anger built into a towering fury. Maddoc had been increasingly short with him, despite all his good work, and now this human thief would get his reward.

As Oddvar entered the great hall, he made a decision. He had to do something to stop Gadion—and he had to do it fast.

"Drefan," he shouted.

The goblin looked up from the pile of rags where he'd been sleeping. He scurried over to Oddvar.

"What is it?" he asked, his pointed nose quivering.

"I want you to find the weapons and gear those prisoners had when they were brought in," Oddvar instructed.

"What shall I do with them?" the goblin asked.

"Wrap them in a bundle and bring them to me," Oddvar continued. "Go quickly. We may not have much time."

Catriona was coughing up blood. It wasn't much, but Davyn knew enough about wounds to know that it was a very bad sign. They'd rolled up their cloaks to prop Catriona up and make her as comfortable as possible, but the stone cell offered precious few comforts. They were somewhere below the keep, Davyn knew, but the sputtering torch that had been left by the guard revealed little of their surroundings. The cell itself was a simple stone room with walls of cut block and a grill of iron bars across the opening.

Davyn watched Nearra minister to Catriona as best she could. He had surrendered his shirt, which Nearra had torn into strips and used to bind Cat's wound. All the while, Catriona was flexing her hands in pain. Davyn knew that stomach wounds were extremely painful; he also knew that a person could take a long time to die from them.

Nearra wiped the blood from Catriona's face, prompting another coughing fit. "She needs water."

Sindri raced to the bars. "Guard," he yelled, "we need some water down here."

Tears streamed openly down the kender's face as he pounded on the bars in frustration.

"Here," Elidor said, unhooking a water bag from a loop on his belt. "There's a little left." Even the hardened elf appeared shaken up by the sudden violence Gadion had visited upon his friend.

Nearra pressed the mouth of the bag to Cat's lips, and she drank gratefully.

"Thanks," she gasped, her face screwed up in pain. She turned to look at Davyn, standing just beyond Nearra. "I'm sorry," she whispered. "I should've listened to you."

"It's my fault," Davyn said, fiercely. "I knew this was a bad idea and I led you here anyway."

Catriona was about to argue, but Nearra shushed her.

"It's no one's fault," she said firmly. "What matters now is, how do we get Cat out of here?"

Nearra looked squarely at Davyn, hope in her eyes. Davyn had a sick, sinking feeling as he realized he had no answer for her.

"If I had a good wire, I could pick the lock," Elidor suggested, pressing his eye to the cell's keyhole.

"What about—" Sindri suddenly stopped. He cocked his head to the side and then quickly motioned everyone back from the door. "Someone's coming," he hissed.

"Everyone stay alert," Davyn whispered as the sound of a door opening echoed down the stone hall. "Maybe we can grab the guard."

The sound of footsteps could be heard and then a light appeared, bobbing in the darkness. After a tense minute, two figures came out of the darkness. One was the guard who had locked them in the cell. The sight of the other made Davyn's stomach tighten: it was Oddvar, his father's agent.

As Davyn watched, the dwarf put a bundle he'd been carrying on a little table outside the cell. Davyn noticed the unmistakable shape of Set-ai's dragon claws sticking out of the back of the bundle, along with his bow and Sindri's hoopak.

"Open the door," Oddvar grunted.

The guard didn't respond but removed a ring from his belt on which hung a single brass key. After a moment's fiddling with the lock, the guard pushed the door open and raised his crossbow.

"We need some water," Sindri demanded as the dwarf entered the cell.

"Get them some water," Oddvar instructed the guard.

"I'll have to lock the door," the guard replied.

"What are you waiting for?" the dwarf growled in answer.

The guard grunted and re-locked the cell door. Oddvar waited until he'd shuffled away to speak.

"What are you doing here?" Elidor said. "Is this another of Maddoc's games?"

"Stay quiet and listen," Oddvar hissed. "I only have time to tell you this once. I'm here to help you. That bundle I put down out there has your weapons and gear in it. Getting it's up to you."

"What about her?" Sindri demanded, pointing to Cat.

"I'm getting to that," the dwarf said.

"Why should we trust you?" Davyn said.

Oddvar laughed. "It's not like you have a lot of choices. You can take my help, or you can stay here and watch your friend die."

"Getting our weapons back won't help Cat," Nearra said. "She needs a healer now."

"You can save her," Oddvar said, turning to Nearra.

"I don't know what you're talking about," Nearra said in a weak voice.

"Examine that pendant your friend got in Arngrim," Oddvar replied, backing away from them as the guard came back. "I'm finished here," he said to the man outside the cell.

"What are you playing at?" Davyn whispered to Oddvar as the guard opened the cell.

"Just do as you're told," the dwarf sneered. Then he left the cell as the guard brought in a bucket of water.

"Here's your water," the guard said, dropping the bucket on the floor so that water sloshed out of it.

As the guard turned to leave, Sindri suddenly jumped on him. Without even looking, the guard slammed his crossbow into the side of the kender's head, sending him spinning into the cell wall.

"Anyone else?" The guard grinned, leveling his crossbow at Elidor and Davyn.

When no one moved, the guard laughed and closed the cell door, locking it with a quick twist of his key.

CHAPTER

18   THE GREAT ESCAPE

As the guard's steps receded down the corridor, Davyn and Elidor rushed to Sindri's prone form. Sindri wasn't seriously hurt. His hard kender head enabled him to shake off the blow quickly.

"I almost had him," he muttered, rubbing his head.

Davyn clenched his fists. Just beyond the bars, Oddvar had left all their weapons and gear. Elidor had tools that would get them out of their cell in a heartbeat, and overcoming one guard once they were armed again would be easy. The trick was getting their gear.

Catriona coughed noisily and groaned with the pain it caused. Nearra winced in sympathy.

"You don't think Oddvar was telling the truth about that pendant, do you?" Elidor said, fixing Davyn with a suspicious look.

"I don't know." Davyn cleared his throat nervously. Elidor knew that Davyn and the dwarf had dealings in the past.

"I say we try it," Sindri said. "What's the worst that could happen?"

"I'll remember you asked that," Elidor said with no trace of a smile.

"No. It's too risky. Why would Oddvar tell us the truth?" Davyn said. "He's just toying with us."

Elidor nodded. He turned to lean against the bars of their cell, staring intently at the torch mounted to the wall just beyond.

"Hey," Elidor said. "Take a look at this."

"What is it?" Davyn asked.

"The smoke," Elidor said, as if that explained everything.

"What about it?" Sindri asked.

"It's moving."

"Smoke always moves around," Davyn said.

"No, it doesn't," Elidor said. "Smoke rises, but it only moves if there are air currents pushing it."

Davyn looked at the smoke and saw what Elidor meant. The smoke was drifting lazily from the torch into the cell through the open bars.

"Where's it going?" Sindri asked, after they'd all watched the smoke for a minute.

"There must be a vent somewhere," Elidor concluded, "something that's open to the outside. It's drawing the smoke like a chimney."

"Let's find it," Davyn said, stepping back from the cell bars. As soon as he moved, the smoke swirled and twisted in the air.

"Hold still," Elidor said, "you're disrupting it."

Moving slowly and cautiously, the three crept through the cell. Occasionally their passing would cause the smoke to shift, but mostly it made a straight line for the rear wall of the cell, where it disappeared.

"Here it is," Sindri said, pointing at a small crack in the mortar between two stones. "The smoke's getting out here."

Elidor moved to the wall and prodded the crack with his finger. A shower of mortar fragments fell out of the crack, and the smoke seemed to be drawn into the crack more forcefully. The elf pressed his eye up to the little hole he'd created.

"There must be a passage behind this wall."

"Can we get the bricks out?" Davyn crouched beside Elidor.

The elf shook his head after prodding the crack again with his finger. "This crack is weak, but the rest of the mortar is solid. We'd need something strong and sharp to dig it out."

"Will a dagger do?" Sindri asked.

Both Davyn and Elidor turned to face the kender.

"Do you have one?" Davyn asked.

"I think I can conjure something," Sindri answered.

Davyn and Elidor looked at each other, rolling their eyes. Before they could turn back to the wall, however, the kender reached into one of his many pockets and withdrew a battered dagger. Davyn realized it bore a striking resemblance to the one the guard had carried in his belt, but didn't mention it.

"Here you go." He handed the dagger to Davyn.

"Good work, Sindri," Davyn smiled, relief flooding through him. "Get to work on the wall," he said, passing the dagger to Elidor. "I'll get the girls ready to move."

"Sindri," Elidor said as he began to chip the mortar from the wall, "I take back everything I've ever said about you."

"Thanks," Sindri beamed, totally oblivious to Elidor's dig.

Nearra was sitting beside Cat, staring at the warrior as she slept fretfully. Davyn knelt down and put his arm around Nearra.

"How is she doing?"

"I think we're losing her." Nearra had tears in her blue eyes.

"It'll be all right," Davyn assured her. "Elidor's found us a way out."

Nearra looked over to where Sindri and the elf were chipping away at the wall, then back to Davyn. "Shemnara's too far from here," she said. "Cat will never make it."

Davyn shook his head. "We'll just have to hurry."

"What about that pendant?" Nearra asked. "Maybe Oddvar was telling the truth. Maybe I can use it to save her."

"Are you sure? We have no idea what effect that could have on her." Davyn looked Nearra in the eye. "Or on you."

"If we don't try something Cat's going to die. She would do it for us."

Davyn hung his head. "You're right."

Nearra put her hand on Catriona's shoulder and gently shook her awake. "Cat, wake up. Where's the pendant you got from Alric?"

Catriona's eyes flickered open and her hand fluttered to her chest. Nearra reached beneath Catriona's tunic and pulled out a heavy silver chain. From the end dangled a silver pendant in the shape of a lion's head.

Nearra peered closely at the pendant. She shivered, then looked Davyn in the eyes.

"I can feel something inside it," she confessed. "It's like before, in Arngrim."

A cold chill gripped Davyn as he looked at the sapphire crystal set in the pendant's center. He had suspected Oddvar was making a bid to restore Asvoria; now he knew how. The pendant was magical and its power was calling to Asvoria.

"The last time I felt something like this, I nearly died," Nearra whispered.

Davyn knew it was possible that Asvoria's magic could save Catriona and help them all escape. But only if Nearra could control her power, and keep the Emergence from coming on. Davyn knew what Asvoria was capable of and he was afraid for Nearra to take the risk. On the other hand, if she didn't, Cat would surely die.

"You don't have to do this," Davyn said, pulling her close.

"I know. But I want to do it." Nearra took a deep breath. "I think I can control it. Cat's life depends on it."

Reluctantly Davyn released her. She picked up the silver pendant and touched the blue crystal at its center. For a long minute nothing happened. Then Nearra's eyes suddenly opened wide. Davyn was looking right at her and what he saw made him recoil in shock. Nearra's deep blue eyes had changed. Now they were a vibrant violet color.

Nearra stood and backed away from Davyn, regarding him quizzically.

"Nearra?" Davyn said.

Nearra didn't answer, looking intently around the room. She quickly moved to Catriona and carefully unpacked the wound.

"I will require water," she said. "I think there is still time."

Davyn filled Elidor's water bag in the bucket the guard had brought. When he came back, he found Nearra carefully prying the crystal out of the pendant.

"Fetch me a brick," Nearra ordered.

Davyn retrieved a heavy brick that Elidor and Sindri had just pried from the wall, putting it down in front of Nearra. The girl held the blue crystal in the palm of her open hand and mumbled something over it. A second later the crystal began to glow with a vibrant blue light. With a smile of triumph, Nearra placed it carefully on the black brick.

"The water must be in a cup," she said as Davyn handed her the water bag.

"I have a cup in my bag," Davyn said, pointing through the bars, "but it's out there."

Nearra turned and looked at the cell door. Without pause, Nearra raised her hand and intoned something at the cell door. In response, the lock sprang open with a ringing clang.

"Hurry," she said, turning to Davyn.

Wondering whether the sound would bring the guard, Davyn scrambled out of the cell and grabbed the bundle Oddvar had left. He ran back in the cell and tore open the bundle, digging through the gear until he found his travel bag. He extracted his little wooden cup and passed it to Nearra.

Without waiting for water, Nearra used the bottom of the cup to crush the crystal against the brick. With a few deft strokes, she ground the fragments into a powder, then carefully swept them off the brick and into the cup.

"Quickly, fill it with water," she said, holding up the cup.

Davyn poured water from his bag into the cup until Nearra whispered for him to stop. As Davyn watched, the liquid in the cup began to glow blue.

"Wake her," Nearra instructed, carrying the cup to Catriona's sleeping form. "She has to drink it all, and quickly."

"What is it?" Davyn asked as he gently shook Catriona awake.

"An ancient magic," Nearra answered, holding the cup to Cat's lips. "Drink," she instructed the wounded girl. "The gem has been blessed by Mishakal. Warriors wear them as a last defense against death. They have powerful healing properties."

"Will she be all right?" Sindri asked. Nearra's activities had attracted the attention of the kender and the elf, and they had abandoned the sizable hole in the wall to watch.

"Silence," Nearra chastened. "It will only take a few minutes." Nearra tipped the cup up so Catriona could drain it.

Catriona coughed and spluttered but she got down most of the glowing liquid. A moment later a look of calm and peace came over her face and the expression of pain faded away.

"I think it's working," she croaked, breathing a bit more easily.

Nearra pulled the bandage away from Catriona's stomach. The blood on her abdomen had a strange blue color to it, and the ragged wound had stopped bleeding. As they watched, the tear in her flesh began to shrink, folding in on itself until it was gone. The blood remained, but now there was no sign of the wound.

Sindri reached out and held Cat's hand, relief on his face and tears in his eyes. Even Elidor was smiling. Davyn felt an enormous weight lift from his shoulders. Now that Catriona seemed safe, however, another worry began to grow in Davyn's mind. He'd seen the change in Nearra with his own eyes. Her eyes and her demeanor were different. Clearly some part of Asvoria had taken over. Davyn could feel his heart beating fast as he wondered if Nearra could regain control.

"Shouldn't you be digging?" Catriona smiled weakly at Sindri, her breathing more regular.

Sindri smiled and he and Elidor returned to their work removing blocks. Once the first brick had come out, the work had gone much faster. Now there was a wide hole in the wall and Davyn could see a black opening beyond. A few more minutes' work and they'd be able to escape.

"There's definitely a passage back here," Elidor announced, sticking his head through the hole. "Judging by the dust, no one's been back here for years," he continued. "It looks like it was bricked up a long time ago. Gadion and his thugs probably don't know it exists."

"Do you think it leads to a way out?" Davyn asked.

"There must be an opening somewhere," the elf observed, pulling his head back into the room, "otherwise the smoke wouldn't be drawn to it."

Now that the hole was big enough, Davyn could clearly see the smoke from the torch moving across the cell and into the space beyond.

Elidor continued chipping away at the wall with the dagger. "Just give us a few more minutes," he said, "and we'll have a big enough hole to escape."

As Elidor and Sindri worked to free more bricks, Davyn knelt to sort through the bundle of their gear.

"Davyn," Nearra said, touching him on the shoulder.

Davyn turned to find Nearra regarding him with her violet eyes. She stepped close to him, looking in to his eyes.

"I . . ."

Nearra's eyes suddenly rolled back in her head and she staggered against him. He grabbed her around her shoulders, pulling her against him.

"Nearra." He shook her gently.

Nearra's eyes snapped open, blue as ever.

"Are you all right?" Davyn asked, relief flowing through him.

"I think so." She blinked a few times. "It was like watching myself from somewhere else. Like I was someone else."

Davyn pulled her close. She was trembling.

"Don't let me do that again," she said, burying her face in Davyn's shoulder. "I don't ever want to do that again."

As he felt the warmth of Nearra's trembling body against him, Davyn felt shame burning on his face. He knew what embracing the power would do to Nearra, but he'd let her do it anyway. She seemed to be all right. They were lucky this time. But what would have happened if Nearra hadn't been able to regain control? Would Nearra ever be able to escape Maddoc's grip? Would he?

"Hey!"

The sudden yell startled Davyn back to the present. The guard had come to check on them and had seen the open cell door. He raised his crossbow as Davyn pushed Nearra away. The shot went wide, sliding by Davyn's ear close enough for him to feel the wind, and shattered on the wall beyond. Cursing, the guard drew his sword and charged into the cell.

Davyn didn't have time to dig through the open bundle for his sword. As the guard rushed in with his sword aloft, Davyn stepped forward, grabbing the guard's sword arm before he could strike. Davyn grappled with the guard, but the man was bigger and stronger. The guard forced his sword slowly toward Davyn's neck. Just when Davyn didn't think he could hold the guard's arm any longer, the man's grip suddenly relaxed and he slumped to the floor. Catriona stood over his inert body holding the black brick she'd used to brain him.

"Thanks," Davyn gasped, catching his breath.

"It's nice to be back," Catriona grinned, tossing the brick on the unconscious man's body.

149

"If you're quite finished playing," Elidor drawled from the back of the cell, "I think we can leave now."

Davyn turned and found that the elf and the kender had opened a wide hole in the wall. Beyond it, an inky black opening yawned invitingly.

"Let's get our gear on before we meet another guard," Davyn said, digging through the bundle for his bow.

Catriona slipped on her chain mail shirt and strapped her sword over it. Sindri found his travel bag and his hoopak while Elidor and Davyn buckled on their quivers. After a few minutes, they were ready to go.

As everyone finished checking their gear, Davyn lit his lantern and Elidor grabbed the torch from the wall. Carrying the lantern in front of him, Davyn crossed the cell and held the torch through the opening. As the light passed through the hole, it illuminated a narrow passage beyond. A few feet down the passage, Davyn could see the top of a staircase, heading down into complete blackness.

Davyn drew his bow. Catriona drew Set-ai's dragon claws from her belt as Elidor drew a knife as well.

"All right," Davyn said, taking a deep breath. "Let's go."

19   The Dragon Well

The passage beyond the cell quickly turned into stairs, winding down and around the inside of the tor in a steep spiral. Catriona shivered in the damp chill of the narrow passage. The wound in her stomach was completely healed, she knew. But she could still feel the white-hot sting of the dagger as it slid easily into her gut. She could still feel the shock, the stunned disbelief—even as she'd seen her own blood on the dagger, she hadn't believed it. The thing that made it so surreal was the look on Gadion's face. As he'd stabbed her, his face kept that same look of bored detachment. There was no malice or hatred in his eyes, nothing more than the look one might have when smashing a bug. Here, Catriona realized, was a man without compassion, a man with no conscience. Gadion was obviously the kind of man who'd kill anyone—man, woman, or child—to get what he wanted. Gadion was a man who had to be stopped.

"Do you see anything yet?" Sindri's whisper echoed in the silence of the stone stairway.

"No," Elidor whispered back from his position at the front. His elf vision was better in the dark than any of theirs, so Davyn had asked him to lead.

"Hush," Davyn said, barely audible. "If there is something at the bottom of these stairs we don't want it to know we're coming."

"Nonsense," Catriona whispered back. "The dust is an inch deep; nothing's been here in years."

"Elidor says there's an opening to the outside," Davyn said. "Maybe there is something down there but it's too big to get up the stair."

The idea that something that big could live right under Gadion's nose seemed absurd to Catriona. As she thought about it, however, she realized that they didn't know where the Beast lived. It would certainly have a tough time squeezing up the narrow stair.

"I see something," Elidor hissed urgently.

Both he and Davyn had their bows out. Catriona carried the torch. She hurried forward to give the elf more light.

"What is it?" Davyn whispered.

"You're right about no one being here in a long time," Elidor said.

Everyone pressed forward. Finally, the light of the torch fell upon some debris littering the stair. At first, Catriona couldn't see why Elidor took a pile of garbage to be a sign that no one had been there—then she saw the skull. As she drew closer, she saw that the pile of debris was actually the remains of an armored man. His skeletal hand was stretched out in front of him, as if he was attempting to climb the stair. The remains of two thick arrows protruded from the back of his shirt.

"What is this?" Nearra stepped closer to Davyn.

"Nothing to worry about," Davyn said, not bothering to whisper. "He's been dead a long time."

Sindri prodded the body with his hoopak. "I wonder who killed him?"

"Maybe whoever walled off this passage," Catriona said with a shrug. "Maybe they sealed it up to hide his body."

"It doesn't matter," Davyn said, moving past the body.

"If he was trying to get out, it might," Catriona said.

"What do you mean?" Nearra asked. Catriona noticed that Nearra spoke most when she was defending Davyn.

"I mean that, if there's a way out down there," Catriona said, "why is he crawling up?"

"Maybe the opening down there's too small to get through," Sindri offered.

"Let's hope not," Davyn growled. "In any case, standing here and worrying about it just gives Gadion's men more time to get to Potter's Mill."

With that Davyn turned and started down. He had barely gone a dozen steps when Elidor's voice called out of the darkness again.

"Here's another one," the elf announced.

When Catriona's light fell over the place where Elidor was standing, it revealed another armored corpse. Like the one before, this one was riddled with arrows.

The hairs on the back of Catriona's neck were beginning to rise. The sight of the skeletons, along with the unnatural quiet of the dark stair, was making her uneasy. She gripped the dragon claw in her right hand and felt its comforting weight.

"Let's keep going," Davyn whispered. The sight of the second body was getting to him as well.

They continued past the corpse and moved farther down. Catriona reasoned that they must be deep below the citadel by now. The spiraling passage just seemed to go on and on, ever downward.

"Uh-oh," Elidor whispered from somewhere beyond the torchlight.

"Another body?" Davyn hissed.

"You'd better take a look at this."

Davyn hurried forward and Catriona was hard pressed to keep up. When they reached the elf, she almost ran into Davyn. In the warm circle of the torchlight, she could see dozens of bodies, littering the steps. Some were shot with arrows like the ones above, others still clutched rusting weapons in their long-dead fingers. It was a chilling sight, and Catriona felt the cold hand of fear around her heart. She gripped the dragon claw tighter and tried to shrug the feeling off.

"What happened here?" Nearra squeaked, taking in the decades-old carnage.

"Some great battle." Elidor stepped carefully over the dead. "There's more, too," he continued. "I see a light shining just up ahead."

"Torches?" Catriona whispered.

Elidor shook his head. "No, it's a strange, pale light."

"Some kind of magic?" Sindri said.

"Could be." Elidor shrugged. "I'll go check it out."

"No," Davyn said as the elf turned to go. "This time we all go together. Cat, when that light gets bright enough to see, put the torch out."

He didn't have to tell everyone to ready a weapon. Even Nearra clutched her staff tightly, ready for battle. Careful not to disturb the desiccated bodies littering the stair, the group made their way down. At first Catriona couldn't see the light Elidor mentioned, but gradually, she became aware of a silvery radiance illuminating the bodies on the stair. As they approached the spot where the light appeared to shine brightest, Catriona realized that the narrow passage opened up. The light seemed to be coming from somewhere below the stairs, hinting at a vast chamber beyond.

When they were only a few steps from where the wall fell away, Davyn motioned for everyone to stop. He moved forward, nodding for Elidor to follow him. The pair stalked to the edge of the wall then, in one quick motion, turned and drew their arrows, aiming into the chamber beyond. After a moment, they both lowered their bows.

Everyone rushed forward. "What is it?" Sindri demanded.

The chamber from which the light emanated was vast and round. The spiral stair ran around its sides, finally ending on a black granite floor fifty feet below. In the center of the chamber stood the source of the eerie light—an enormous stone basin of white marble supported atop the statues of six different dragons. The rickety remains of a wooden platform ran around the basin, with a decaying ramp leading up to it. A pale, milky liquid moved and sloshed inside the basin, emitting a bluish, silvery light that cast the chamber in stark relief. Mist seemed to rise and fall over the surface of the liquid, moving of its own accord.

"By the gods," Davyn whispered, his bow hanging in his limp hands.

Heaped all around the basin in scattered disarray were the remains of at least a hundred men. Their armored bodies clutched weapons; their bare jawbones slacked open as if echoing their war-cries. The scene of carnage covered the floor and ran up the stairs all the way to where Catriona stood. What had happened here to cause such carnage she could only guess, but the results were plain to see.

"What cursed place is this?" Elidor whispered.

"It is a dragon well," Nearra answered. The cold edge Catriona had noticed in her voice when she'd healed her belly wound was back.

Catriona wasn't the only one who noticed either. On hearing her, Davyn turned and looked her full in the face. What he was looking for, Catriona could only guess.

"What do you mean, 'a dragon well'?" Sindri asked, taking a step downward, toward the basin.

"It is an ancient ritual," Nearra continued. "Powerful wizards would enslave a dragon, then bleed it slowly. A dragon's blood is linked to its life-force."

"So that's dragon blood?" Catriona asked, indicating the liquid in the well.

"Not entirely," Nearra continued. "The blood was mixed with other things and mighty spells were cast over it."

"Why would they want to do that?" Sindri asked.

"Anyone bathing in a dragon well would receive great magical powers—or so the legend goes," Nearra explained. "More often than not the poor fool who tried would die a horrible death. The liquid in a dragon well is highly corrosive."

"How do you know all this?" Catriona looked Nearra directly in the eye.

"I don't know," she said, turning away quickly. "I just know."

Catriona noticed that the hard edge was gone from Nearra's voice, and the girl suddenly looked much smaller and frightened.

"Does the dragon well remind you of anything?" Sindri asked.

"The basin in Shemnara's room." Davyn nodded, a grim look on his face. "Could this be what blinded her and gave her the ability to see the future?"

Catriona remembered the sight of the seer without her blindfold, how there was a white mark across her face, as if she'd been burned by acid.

"It's possible," Nearra admitted, shivering in the dank air.

"Let's get out of here," Davyn said, noticing Nearra's chill.

"I don't see any way out." Catriona cast her eyes around the chamber. Apart from the dragon well and the corpses, the room was entirely empty. A large, ornate seal was carved in the wall behind the well, but there were no signs of doors or windows.

"I can feel the air moving," Elidor said, making his way carefully down the stairs. "Follow me."

Only a few dozen steps separated them from the bottom, but making their way through the maze of bodies was difficult. Rusting weapons and armor littered the floor along with the bones of men, their hands grasping at each other even in death. Catriona had once been to the catacombs under a Solamnic stronghold. The reverently laid out dead she'd seen there were a stark contrast to the masses of bodies in the well chamber, scattered where they'd succumbed to battle. A sick feeling was spreading in her gut. She knew that whoever had sealed off the stairs so long ago had done so for a good reason.

"It's here," Elidor announced, interrupting Catriona's thoughts. "There's a crack in the wall."

Catriona looked where the elf was pointing and saw a wide crack, nearly ten feet high, cutting down the wall near the bottom of the stair.

"It looks like there's a cave beyond it," he announced after squeezing his head into the crack for a look. "I think I can make it through."

Elidor handed his bow to Davyn and set down his gear.

"Let Sindri go," Davyn said. "He's smaller."

Catriona looked around for the kender, but found him gone from the stair. A quick scan of the chamber revealed him making his way cautiously up the wooden platform to the top of the dragon well.

"Sindri," Catriona shouted. "No!"

"I just want a look," the kender said, a guilty look on his face.

"Go get him," Davyn muttered. "Elidor, see if you can get through."

Catriona bounded down the rest of the stairs, knocking body parts and bits of metal everywhere in her haste. Sindri paid her no mind, climbing up to the wide stone rim of the basin and staring down at the glowing liquid. Catriona put a tentative foot on the platform's rickety ramp, and it groaned under her weight. Not knowing if it would support her, Catriona took a deep breath and climbed the ramp to stand beside Sindri.

"It's beautiful," he whispered, staring at the undulating liquid and the moving mist.

"We should get down." Catriona placed a firm hand on the kender's shoulder. "This may be how Shemnara was blinded."

Even as Catriona spoke, a creeping tendril of mist rose from the basin and moved along the stone toward them.

"I don't think it would hurt a wizard," Sindri said, eyeing the mist eagerly.

"Wizards made this thing," Catriona reminded him, pulling him back onto the platform. "It may not like wizards very much at all."

Catriona propelled the kender down the ramp in front of her. Sindri had his eyes on the liquid in the well until he was too low to see it. Even as Catriona went down after him, she found herself strangely drawn to the pearly liquid. She began to understand why so many had died here and why someone had ultimately sealed the room off.

"Elidor's through," Davyn called when they stepped off the ramp.

Sindri hurried over to see what the elf had found. Catriona followed after, still thinking about the well. From the looks of the chamber, over a hundred men had given their lives to have it, to control its power. What kind of power could compel such a sacrifice?

"There's a cave out here," Elidor's voice came through the crack as Catriona approached. "It leads out to the side of the tor, about fifty feet off the ground."

"Can we get out, then?" Davyn asked.

"I think so," Elidor reported. "There are trees close by. We can jump into their branches and climb down."

"All right, let's go," Davyn said, smiling for the first time since they'd been captured.

"Not yet," Catriona replied, grimly folding her arms.

"What do you mean, 'not yet'?" The smile faded from Davyn's face.

"We can't leave the dragon well for Gadion to find," Catriona explained. "As soon as someone comes to relieve that guard, they'll find the hole in the wall and that will lead them right down here."

"So?" Davyn shrugged. "Nearra said that most people who use it die. If that thing ate up Gadion, I wouldn't be sorry."

"And what if it doesn't kill him?" Catriona said. "What if it grants him some terrible power?"

"We don't even know if that's possible."

"Look around," Catriona said, indicating the body-strewn floor. "These men didn't fight and die here for nothing. They wanted the well. They wanted the power it might give them. Can we risk letting it fall into Gadion's hands?"

Davyn sighed and looked away for a moment.

"We've got to get out and warn Shemnara about the attack," he said without turning. "If we go now, we might just make town by morning."

Davyn turned back to look Catriona in the eyes. Catriona nodded agreement.

"You go," she said. "I'll stay here and destroy the well."

"You'll need help," Sindri said, his face as grim as a kender is capable of. "I'll stay with you."

Catriona bent down and picked up a stone-headed war hammer from one of the corpses.

"I think I can break the basin," she explained, turning to Nearra. "Will that destroy the well's magic?"

Nearra nodded. "The basin and the statues are part of the magic. Breaking it might cause it to explode."

Catriona considered it for a moment, but the image of Gadion's bored expression when he stabbed her rose in her mind.

"I'll risk it," she said. "Gadion must not be allowed to possess the well."

Davyn was removing his gear, passing it to Elidor in the

cave beyond. When he was finished, he handed his lantern to Catriona.

"As soon as we're out, we'll run for town," he said. "Do what you have to, but do it quickly. There's no telling when Gadion's men will discover that we're gone."

Catriona hefted the hammer and turned to the dragon well with its dragons and massive basin.

"I'll stay with Cat." Nearra's voice caused Catriona to turn back to the crack. "She's right. The well must not fall into Gadion's hands. Besides, I'm too tired to run all the way to town."

"All right," Davyn conceded, "but as soon as Cat's done, you all get the Abyss out of here."

Davyn turned and pushed himself into the crack. As Catriona made her way down to the basin, she heard a great deal of grunting and swearing from the crack. Considering that she was bigger than Davyn, both in height and in the shoulders, Catriona was not looking forward to her trip through the narrow opening.

"They're gone," Nearra reported, picking her way across the floor to where Catriona stood by the well.

"Good. You two get back against the wall," Catriona instructed. "I don't want you getting splashed when the liquid drains out."

"What about you?" Sindri asked.

"If I don't make it," Catriona said, hefting the stone hammer over her shoulder, "you get Nearra out of here and make for town."

With that Catriona swung the war hammer with all her strength against the side of the stone basin. There was a thunderous boom. A long clean scar marked the basin where the war hammer had scraped away years of grime, but otherwise the basin was unharmed. Undaunted, Catriona swung the hammer again with the same result.

"This might take some time," Catriona admitted.

"Most unfortunate," a new voice called down from above, "since time is something you've run out of."

Catriona whirled, dropping the heavy hammer and drawing Set-ai's dragon claws in one smooth motion. Up where the stairs entered the chamber stood Gadion and four of his men. All of them had their swords out, and while Gadion leered down on them, his thugs moved down the winding stairs.

20 MUDD, SET-AI, AND THE BEAST

Davyn clenched his jaw as the jagged rock removed several layers of skin from his hip. Elidor had made it through the crack and into the cave beyond with only minimal trouble. But, Davyn reminded himself, he was much larger than the small-boned elf. With a grunt and a mighty shove, Davyn levered his shoulders out of the crack and freed his arms.

"How did you make that look easy?" Davyn gasped, getting his breath back before pulling his hips free.

Elidor grinned. "Elves have flexible bones."

"Cat's never going to make that," Davyn grunted, wrenching his hips free in a shower of rocky debris.

"I don't know." Elidor helped Davyn brush dirt and rock from his shirt. "It looks like you widened it for her."

"Funny."

"You're not going to die," Elidor smirked, handing Davyn his quiver.

Davyn shot the elf a dirty look and began putting on his gear. Now that they were free of the citadel, they had to get down to the ground and run all the way to Potter's Mill before Gadion's troops arrived.

"Why didn't you do that before?" Elidor asked as Davyn emptied his pack of heavy gear like torches and extra food.

Davyn gave the elf a sour look.

"Let's go," he said, swinging the much lighter bag onto his back.

The cave beyond the crack in the well room wall was smooth and damp. Almost no light filtered in from outside or from the dragon well. Davyn put his hand on Elidor's shoulder, allowing his friend to guide him. The dull sound of a hammer hitting stone announced that Catriona had begun her quest to destroy the dragon well.

"What's going to happen when that basin shatters and that glowing acid comes spilling out?" Elidor asked, turning to follow the cave.

"Catriona knows what she's doing," Davyn said. "She'll get out of the way."

Elidor grunted, but didn't sound convinced. A moment later, the cave opened up and Davyn saw stars glittering in the night sky.

"Can you see yet?" Elidor asked, stopping at the edge of the cave's mouth.

"Yes," Davyn said, releasing Elidor's shoulder and looking down. The mouth of the cave was a narrow crack that ran down the steep side of the tor. Davyn leaned out to look at the ground fifty feet below. He knew fifty feet wasn't that much, but it sure looked far.

Just as Elidor had said, large trees grew a dozen feet from the entrance, their bare branches reaching out to them in the pale starlight.

Davyn scanned the sky. "It's close to midnight," he said. "We don't have much time."

Elidor tossed his bow, quiver, pack, and finally his cloak down, leaving him shivering in his clothes.

"Follow me," he instructed.

The elf took two quick steps and leaped at one of the nearby trees, landing heavily among the branches.

"Easy," he said, once he'd pulled himself up to a solid branch.

Davyn dropped his gear after Elidor's. Then, taking a running jump, he leaped into the next tree over. A network of brittle branches tore at his skin as viciously as any of the rocks in the narrow crack.

"Easy," Davyn gasped, sliding down to the tree's lower branches.

On the ground, Davyn scrambled back into his gear. After what seemed like forever, he threw his fur cloak over his trembling shoulders.

"You ready?" Elidor asked, shivering beneath his cloak.

Davyn nodded and Elidor turned, trotting off around the tor.

"Where are you going?" Davyn hissed before the elf got too far.

Elidor shot Davyn a quizzical look, and Davyn pointed off in the other direction.

"Potter's Mill is that way," Davyn said.

"Sorry, boss," Elidor grinned, jogging back.

"Don't call me boss," Davyn growled, falling in beside Elidor.

"Yes, boss," the elf muttered before breaking into a run.

Davyn had to scramble to keep up. As a child, Davyn had chased game in the woods around Maddoc's keep, so he was used to running. His ability, however, was nothing like Elidor's. True to his heritage, the elf possessed a natural grace and endurance that made his running seem effortless.

The miles slipped by as the pair puffed and wheezed through the countryside. There weren't any established roads so they ran among the trees, slowing occasionally to go around denser knots of undergrowth. From the brief glimpses Davyn got of the open sky, he guessed they were making good time. But he had no way of knowing if they'd reach Potter's Mill by sunrise.

"Hold up," Davyn gasped, finally, after about an hour. "I've got to rest a minute."

Elidor stopped, breathing just as hard as Davyn. He leaned against a tree.

"I'm glad you called a halt," he admitted, gulping air. "I didn't want to be the first one to stop."

"I'm not proud," Davyn puffed. "Where'd . . . you learn . . . to run like that?"

"Cutting purses . . . when I was a kid," Elidor admitted, wheezing. "People have a tendency . . . to chase you . . . if they find you've . . . robbed them. The fact that they want to hang you . . . if they catch you . . . provides excellent motivation."

"I see." Davyn smiled.

"What about you?" Elidor asked. "I've never met anyone who could keep up with me."

"I used to hunt a lot," Davyn explained. "Once you shoot a deer, you have to chase it down. Sometimes they can go for miles before they die."

"If they're going to die, why chase them?" Elidor wondered.

"Wounded deer can be hard to find," Davyn said, his breathing returning to normal. "You have to stay close or you'll lose them."

Elidor nodded, closing his eyes and slowing his breathing. Then he changed the subject.

"It's probably a good thing we didn't bring Catriona with us," he said. "She'd probably outrun both of us."

"Or die trying," Davyn said, grinning.

"You ready to go?" Elidor asked, pushing off the tree and moving a few paces off.

"I am," Davyn nodded, rising, "but the town is that way."

Elidor cursed and changed direction, jogging off through the snow.

"Don't take this the wrong way," Davyn said, falling in beside Elidor, "but you're not a very good elf."

"No offense taken," Elidor admitted, smiling. "My mother's Silvanesti family thinks I'm an aberration because my father was Kagonesti. I became a thief just to annoy them. From my perspective, being called a bad elf is high praise."

Davyn knew Elidor had friction with his family, but he'd never heard the reason before.

"You mean they don't like you just because of who your father was related to?" Davyn asked, disbelieving.

Elidor nodded. "That's about it."

"That stinks," Davyn said, jogging along beside Elidor.

"Tell me about it." Elidor smiled grimly.

"Do you have any brothers or sisters?" Davyn asked.

Elidor nodded. "A half-sister. She's pure Silvanesti so the family dotes on her. They've taught her that I'm less than scum, so she doesn't like me."

"Well, you are an unprincipled thief." Davyn grinned.

Elidor gave Davyn a sideways glance. "You're one to talk."

Davyn stopped running, panting. His heart thundered in his ears. This was it. He would have to tell Elidor the truth.

"But you know," Elidor continued, "you're not as bad as I thought. Back in Arngrim, I thought I had you pegged as that wizard's stooge. But you've saved my life on more than one occasion now. You've saved all of our lives." Elidor smiled. "It's quite apparent to me now that you're just as mixed up in all of this as the rest of us."

Relief washed over Davyn. "You've got me there." He extended his hand. "Friends?"

Elidor shook his head. "There's this thing the Kagonesti do. It's usually done when someone saves your life or something and you want to adopt them into your house."

Davyn shrugged. "I'm game."

Elidor drew out one of his throwing daggers. With a quick move he drew the blade across the palm of his hand, just enough to make a shallow cut.

"Now you," he said, handing the knife to Davyn.

Davyn gave him a wary glance, then repeated the process, leaving a bleeding cut on his hand.

"Now we clasp hands," Elidor said, holding out his bleeding hand.

Davyn took the elf's hand and held it there for a moment, not knowing if there was anything else he was supposed to do.

"Now we're bound," Elidor said, still holding Davyn's hand. "Blood for blood we are brothers."

Elidor released Davyn's hand, and they each bound their wounds with a leftover piece of the shirt Nearra had used on Cat.

"I won't let you down, brother," Davyn said.

"Thanks," Elidor said. "No one ever cared enough about me to want to be my kin."

"Anytime," Davyn said grinning. "And now, my brother, we should get going."

Davyn took a step, but Elidor's arm shot out to block him. Davyn looked quizzically at the elf. But Elidor put his finger in front of his lips, warning Davyn to be silent. Davyn listened intently for a moment, then shrugged when he heard nothing.

Elidor listened for another moment, then, still warning Davyn to be silent, motioned for the boy to follow him. Silently the pair moved over the frozen forest floor.

After a moment, Davyn heard what Elidor's sharp elf hearing had detected. Raised voices were drifting through the bare trees, and as Davyn got closer he began to hear what they were saying.

"Maybe we should just kill him," a rough voice was saying.

"We have to find out what he knows first," a second man said with an evil laugh.

"Oh, if that's all," a third voice chimed in, "I'm sure I can get him to talk."

"I was just looking for chestnuts," a familiar voice squeaked, "honest."

As Davyn moved forward the trees thinned and he saw three of Gadion's toughs menacing a young man. It was Mudd.

"What's he doing out here?" Elidor whispered.

"I don't know," Davyn said, nocking an arrow. "If we don't do something fast it won't matter."

"Hold him tight," the man with the knife growled, flicking the blade ever closer to Mudd's face.

"I'll take him," Davyn said. "Can you get Mudd away from the other two?"

"Leave it to me," Elidor nodded, drawing one of his throwing knives from his shirt.

Davyn aimed at the man threatening Mudd with the knife. He let his breath out slowly, steadying his aim, then let the arrow slip. The arrow sped, straight from the string, and landed dead center in the ruffian's back, right between the shoulder blades. He cried out, and the man's knife slid from his hand as he sunk to the ground. At the same moment, Elidor rushed from hiding and slammed into the man on Mudd's left.

As Elidor struggled with the first bandit, Mudd pulled free from the second man. Davyn drew a second arrow and shot. The arrow went wide. The bandit drew his sword and raised it to kill the undefended Mudd.

Davyn drew another arrow, but Elidor beat him. The elf rolled to his feet and flung his knife, striking the man in the side. Stunned by the knife blow, the man stopped long enough for Davyn to put an arrow right into his heart. His sword falling from his numb hands, the bandit fell to the snow-covered earth without a sound.

"Elidor," Mudd gasped, recognizing the elf. "Thank Paladine you found me."

"We always seem to be getting you out of trouble," Davyn said, stepping into the clearing.

Elidor bent to retrieve his knife. "You need to learn to walk quietly."

"Where are the others?" Mudd asked, looking around.

"They had to stay behind and take care of something," Davyn said, evasively. "What matters now is that we warn Potter's Mill."

Mudd looked puzzled.

"Gadion's going to send his forces against the town at dawn," Elidor explained.

"Can the townsfolk handle an attack?" Davyn asked before Mudd could express outrage.

"We can take care of ourselves," Mudd said. "Because of the Beast, most buildings in town are fortified and have balconies for shooting things below."

"Good, let's go," Davyn said.

"How far are we from town?" Elidor asked, as the three young men jogged through the night.

"About five miles," Mudd answered, keeping pace with the older boys. "When you didn't come back, I got worried about you," Mudd panted. "Shemnara said you'd be all right, but I wanted to come look for you anyway."

"I'll bet you didn't tell Shemnara about your plan, did you?" Elidor asked with a raised eyebrow and an amused look.

Mudd gaped, a look of amazement on his face.

Then an ear-splitting roar filled the woods. Elidor and Davyn fell flat on the snow-covered ground, dragging Mudd after them.

"It's the Beast," Elidor whispered as the sound died away.

"You think?" Davyn growled as another cry split the air.

"Where is it?" Mudd hissed in the silence that followed the second howl.

Elidor pointed off to their left. Now that his ears had stopped ringing, Davyn could hear the sound of trees creaking and cracking and the growls and snarls of the Beast.

"We've got to get past it," Mudd said. "We've got to warn Shemnara."

"Take it easy," Davyn put his hand on Mudd's shoulder. "Let's try to go around it."

Before any of them could move, however, the Beast howled again. This time, when the cry died, they could hear the unmistakable sound of the Beast moving away at a run.

"Let's go," Davyn said, springing to his feet.

"Hadn't we better see what it was up to?" Elidor asked as Mudd climbed out of the snow.

Davyn nodded and led them through the trees in the direction of the Beast's cries. A moment later they emerged from the wood onto a forest path. The snow all around was churned and bloody, and the trees on the far side had been uprooted and torn away. Great jagged gashes stood open on the larger trees and it looked as if the Beast had tried to push them over as well.

"Merciful Paladine," Mudd swore, "what happened here?"

"The Beast fought something," Davyn said.

"Whatever it was must have put up quite a struggle," Elidor said, looking around at the devastation.

"Look," Davyn said, indicating a spot farther up the path. A large smear of bright blood was easily visible against the whiteness of the snow.

"I say we go before the Beast comes back," Elidor said.

Davyn had turned to lead the others off toward town when the sound of a twig snapping froze the blood in his veins. Davyn nocked an arrow.

"In there," Elidor whispered, pointing to the torn-up trees.

Davyn stepped quietly off the path and into the trees. Before he could take another step, however, he heard the unmistakable sound of a crossbow being cocked.

"Just stay right where you are," a muffled voice called out. "I've got you covered."

Davyn's heart jumped as he recognized the voice.

"Set-ai?" he called, not daring to hope.

"Boy-o!" the voice called out, full of relief. "Is that you?"

Davyn dropped his bow and pushed through the young trees. Beyond, in a sheltered area, lay Set-ai, his green armor stained with blood and his cloak shredded. His crossbow was raised, but not enough to hit anyone, as if the old hunter didn't have the strength to hold it up. Davyn noticed that Set-ai was clutching his side.

"You're a sight for sore eyes, boy-o, I can tell you that," Set-ai said as Davyn rushed to his side.

"You're hurt," Davyn observed needlessly. "Let me help."

"No," Set-ai shook his head, pushing Davyn's hands away. "You've got to get your friends away from here."

Set-ai looked around as Mudd and Elidor pushed through the trees, the latter carrying Davyn's bow.

"Where's the rest of them?" the woodsman asked, some distress in his voice. "You didn't go and let Nearra, Cat, and Sindri get eat up by the Beast?"

"They're safe," Davyn assured him. Davyn hoped he was telling Set-ai the truth.

Up close, Set-ai's armor was just as shredded as his cloak. Deep gashes were torn in the stiff leather and blood leaked from a dozen places, though none of them looked serious. The wound in the old woodsman's chest was another matter. It wasn't bleeding much, but there was a wheezing rattle in Set-ai's breath, and blood stained his beard where it had leaked from his mouth.

"We've got to get you to Potter's Mill," Davyn declared, digging into his bag for a spare shirt to rip into bandages.

"Do you have a shirt?" Davyn demanded of Elidor. "Nearra used my last one on Cat."

"I'll never make it, lad," Set-ai confessed, putting his hand on Davyn's to stop the boy's frantic action. "I wounded the Beast," he explained once Davyn met his eyes, "wounded him bad. His masters keep callin' him away, but he keeps comin' back. It's only a matter of time till he breaks through them trees to get me."

"We'll take you out of here," Elidor said, kneeling beside Davyn. "When the Beast comes back, we'll be long gone."

Set-ai shook his head, chuckling softly.

"That won't do it, lad," he said. "The Beast is half mad with pain and rage but it can still smell. If I'm not here when it returns, it'll chase us down and kill us long before we can get to that town."

"We'll stay here with you then," Davyn declared, starting to feel real panic. "We won't let the Beast take you."

"What about the attack?" Mudd protested. "We have to warn Shemnara about the bandit attack."

"Who's your friend?" Set-ai pointed at Mudd.

"This is Mudd," Davyn said. "He's from Potter's Mill." Davyn turned to Mudd before continuing. "Do you think you can manage to make it to town?"

After a moment, Mudd nodded.

"I can get there before dawn," he said. "But what about the Beast?"

"The Beast wants me." Set-ai coughed. "It won't bother with the likes of you."

Davyn stood up and shook Mudd's hand.

"We're counting on you to warn the town," he said.

Mudd nodded, then turned and pushed his way through the tight mass of trees.

"Stay in the woods," Set-ai called out. "The Beast is too big to maneuver through the trees."

"And don't get caught again," Elidor yelled after him, but Mudd was already gone.

"You should'a gone with him," Set-ai said, grimacing. "There's nothin' you can do here."

"You said you wounded the Beast," Elidor said, crouching down. "How?"

"It's got a short upper body," Set-ai explained, "like a barrel. That means its heart is high up in its chest, right behind the head."

"I shot it in the neck, right above the shoulder," Elidor interrupted, remembering the fight in Potter's Mill. "It reacted to that."

Set-ai nodded, a wolfish smile on his face.

"Its neck is the only place its hide is thin. I stabbed it with a spear. I was aimin' for the spot right below the chin, but the spear glanced off one of the infernal thing's horns and hit it in the shoulder. It went in deep but it didn't kill."

"Maybe it'll be weaker now that it's wounded," Elidor said.

"Don't you get it?" Set-ai chastised. "There ain't nothin' more dangerous than a wounded animal."

"Maybe I can shoot it in the neck with an arrow," Davyn suggested.

Set-ai shook his head. "You'd have to be right in front of it. And you'd have to hit it right in the heart on the first shot. At that range, you wouldn't get another shot if the first one missed."

"Don't worry," Davyn declared with more bravery than he felt. "The last time I faced the Beast, it ran away from me."

"Well, whatever affinity it may have had for you, it's gone now," Set-ai said. "That thing's mad. It'll kill anything that gets between it and me."

"I'm not afraid of the Beast," Davyn blustered.

With a roar that shook the ground, the Beast hurtled itself against the barrier of trees. The sound of splintering wood and tearing claws filled the air, and both Davyn and Elidor leaped to their feet, hearts pounding.

21   The King Returns

Catriona's mind whirled as Gadion's four thugs made their way down the winding spiral stair. The stair was long enough that if Davyn and Elidor had been there, they could have shot the bandits long before they reached the floor. As it was, however, Catriona had only Sindri and Nearra to help her take on Gadion and his men.

As she gripped the dragon claws, Catriona could hear Sindri and Nearra coming up behind her.

"Wait," she called out. Reflexively, the men on the stairs stopped just above the level of the dragon well. "Chances are that anyone who goes in the well will die."

"Hold," Gadion instructed his men. "I know all about the dragon well, my dear," he said calmly, descending the stairs as he spoke. "We were listening to your conversation while you argued down here. It was most convenient of your friends with the bows to go and leave the rest of you for us."

"If you were listening, then you know I speak the truth," Catriona pointed out, desperately trying to buy some time.

"I say we give it to him," Nearra spoke up from behind Catriona.

"What?" Sindri and Catriona said at once.

"If he wants the dragon well so badly," she explained, "we should give it to him."

"You think it will destroy me?" Gadion smirked, stopping where his bandits waited on the stairs. "Perhaps you're right. Perhaps we need someone else to test the dragon well first." Gadion turned to his soldiers. "Put her in," he said, pointing at Catriona on the floor below.

A chill ran down Catriona's spine at the ease with which Gadion sentenced her to almost certain death. The image of his face when he stabbed her flashed into her mind. He had that same amused, almost bored look now.

The soldiers started down the steps but halted quickly when the man nearest the bottom suddenly stopped.

"Wait a minute," he growled up at Gadion. "If we put her in there and it doesn't kill her, doesn't that mean she'll get some kind of weird powers?"

Gadion nodded. "An excellent point, Manclair. This needs some more thought."

Catriona drew a shaky breath, looking around, desperately seeking a way to escape. The crack where Davyn and Elidor had gone was easily wide enough for Sindri to get through, but she and Nearra would have to squeeze. There was no time to get out that way. Maybe if she led the others up to the scaffold once the guards were on the floor, they could jump to the stairs and race back to the cell. That might work, but the distance from the edge of the scaffolding to the stairs was at least fifteen feet. She doubted Sindri could make it.

"I know," Gadion said, cutting through Catriona's thoughts. "What we need is someone to test the well who isn't smart enough to be a danger if the well . . . does its thing."

Gadion put his arm around the nearest bandit, a dirty fellow with a crooked nose. "Don't you agree, Sandus?"

"Huh?" the crooked-nosed bandit replied.

"Exactly." Gadion smiled, and then he pushed the hapless bandit off the stair with a mighty shove.

The bandit flew out and fell with a scream into the center of the well. Milky white, glowing liquid splashed out of the stone basin and rained down on the floor below.

Catriona covered her face with her arm and turned away as she heard the liquid spatter down all around her. There was a gurgling cry and the sounds of splashing from the dragon well. Catriona and the others moved back to avoid being hit by flying drops of the pearlescent goo. Above them, on the stairs, Gadion and the bandits were staring down into the well with looks of horror on their faces.

The thrashing and screams from the well became more intense. Then a hand emerged and gripped the edge of the stone basin.

Catriona gasped. The hand was huge and deformed, the skin writhing and moving as if the flesh beneath it were made of water. After the hand came the rest of the bandit's body. His skin was a strange red color and he appeared to be growing in size. His head was as twisted as his crooked nose, and now great tusks and horns were growing from his jaw and forehead.

The transforming bandit screamed in agony as his body twisted and grew. Catriona could hear his bones cracking and popping as they moved to accommodate his increasing size. With a mighty spasm, the now-giant bandit rolled off the basin, falling through part of the rickety scaffolding to the stone floor below.

Catriona was so transfixed by the horrible scene that she barely noticed Sindri pulling hard on her arm.

"Catriona!" he shouted, using her full name. "Look."

Catriona broke her attention away from the writhing bandit to see what had so agitated the kender. All around the hall where the liquid from the dragon well had splashed them, the bodies of the dead were rising from the floor. As if waking from a long sleep, the warriors' skeletal remains pushed themselves slowly to their feet. Dust fell from their creaking joints as they hoisted their long-unused weapons, ready to renew their fight. Catriona watched in horror as they cast their empty eye sockets vacantly around the hall, finally coming to rest on the living beings in their midst.

"Oh, no," Catriona muttered, a cold fear gripping her stomach. "Get up on the scaffolding."

"Not that way," Nearra cried, grabbing Catriona's arm.

Catriona turned to look and saw the crooked-nosed bandit, or what was left of him, levering his way to his feet. The bandit was still basically human, but now his body was at least ten feet tall and massive. Knotted muscles rippled across his arms and chest, and fire burned in his eyes. The creature still had the bandit's crooked nose, but the look of mean stupidity was gone, replaced by an expression of unrestrained anger and hatred. The creature tipped its head back and let out a roar that shook dust from the roof of the chamber.

Some of the skeletal warriors who had been creaking their way toward Catriona and her friends turned at the roar and made for the creature. The nearest skeleton picked up the hammer Catriona had been using to smash the basin. It swung the big weapon directly at the monster's thigh. The creature howled in rage and pain and unceremoniously stepped on the skeleton, smashing it to splinters.

Almost as an afterthought, the creature bent down and picked up the discarded hammer. He considered it for a moment before a look of insane glee spread across his vast face. With a roar of triumph, the monster with the crooked nose raised the hammer and brought it smashing down on the scaffolding around the well, tearing away a large chunk of the wooden frame.

"Kill that thing before he destroys the well," Gadion screamed, urging his men down the stairs.

Whether or not they went, Catriona couldn't see. Only a small group of the skeletons had turned aside to attack the monstrous bandit. The rest closed around her. Sindri and Nearra stood shoulder to shoulder with Catriona, presenting a united front as a dozen or more of the creaking warriors advanced on them. Sindri and Nearra had their staffs and struck out with their longer reach as the skeletons moved to attack. Sindri easily tripped one of the bony warriors with his hoopak, tearing its leg free in the process. Nearra landed a solid downward blow, shattering the skull of the nearest skeleton. To Catriona's horror, the headless body kept coming.

Catriona parried a sword blow as two of the nightmare creatures lurched toward her. With two vicious downward chops, she shattered them both, sending bones flying in all directions. She hacked and slashed as the dead warriors closed in on her, tearing off bony arms, legs, and heads, but the unfeeling warriors just kept coming. Catriona felt a sword hit her side and slide off her chain mail and she turned to find Sindri trying desperately to parry three sword-wielding skeletons at once.

"Follow me," she yelled, charging into the skeletons and smashing them with multiple blows. Beyond the warriors, there was a gap and Catriona ran for it, hoping Sindri and Nearra were following.

"What now?" Sindri gasped, when Catriona stopped.

The skeletons they'd just evaded were turning slowly to pursue them with their awkward, creaking gait.

"They're slow," Catriona said. "Keep falling back as you smash them. Make them come to us."

It was a good plan, but just as the three friends raised their weapons to defend themselves, one of Gadion's bandits was suddenly hurled into the oncoming skeletons. They shattered under the impact like dry twigs. Catriona looked up just in time to see the crooked-nosed creature standing over them, its weapon raised.

"Run!" she shrieked as the hammer came crashing down.

They all scattered in different directions. Nearra dived between the dragon statues supporting the stone basin. Catriona ran back across the room, leaping over the body of a second bandit who appeared to have been smashed.

Sindri circled the well, keeping the bulk of the stone edifice between him and the creature. It would have worked if the kender hadn't run headlong into the remaining bandit, who was doing the same thing. The bandit yelled and swiped at Sindri with his sword, but the wily kender scampered up the ramp onto what remained of the scaffolding. This brought Sindri face to face with the creature.

Seeing a target, the crooked-nosed monster grinned, raising its hammer to strike. With tremendous force, the creature brought the hammer down on the fragile scaffolding. Only Sindri's natural agility saved him. He leaped to the side as the blow tore away the scaffolding where he'd been standing.

Infuriated, the monster raised his hammer for another blow. This time Sindri was forced to jump to the stone lip of the basin as the remains of the scaffolding crumbled beneath the massive blow.

Seeing that Sindri had nowhere to go this time, the monster's grin widened. Slowly he raised his maul, preparing to crush the kender like a bug. Catriona realized too late that she had to do something. As she got up to run, the blow fell. It hit the basin with the force of a thunderbolt. Catriona saw Sindri leap from the basin at the last possible moment, his body soaring through the air to land in a heap on the stone floor below.

The shock of the monster's blow knocked Catriona to her knees. There was a rending, cracking sound that made Catriona look up. The blow had cracked the stone basin. As Catriona watched, the well split open, spilling the glowing liquid over Nearra, who still crouched between the dragon statues below.

179

Catriona screamed. With an anger and fury she hadn't known since the death of her aunt, Catriona launched herself at the monster's unprotected back. Leaping over the spreading pool of glowing liquid on the floor, Catriona landed behind the monstrous ex-bandit. With a swipe of the hooked dragon claws, Catriona slashed the back of the creature's legs.

With a cry of rage and surprise, the monster fell backward, the severed tendons in its legs no longer able to support its weight. Catriona darted away, passing the remaining bandit, who was trying to stay ahead of the glowing liquid on the floor. By the time the bandit looked up, it was too late. The crooked-nosed creature came down on him like an avalanche. The crooked-nose bandit was crushed, but even in death he did his last full measure. The creature fell on the bandit's upraised sword, and the impact with the floor drove the weapon through the creature's back and into his heart—killing him instantly.

"Nearra," Catriona gasped in the unearthly silence that followed the monster's death.

"Don't touch me," the girl ordered, waving her friend away.

"Are you all right?" Catriona asked desperately.

Nearra didn't look like she was transforming as the bandit had, but there was a strangeness in her eyes, as if they kept changing color. The slimy liquid from the well clung to the girl's skin, hair, and clothing. As Catriona watched in horror, the liquid began to disappear, soaking into Nearra's flesh. A quick look around revealed the liquid on the floor disappearing into the flagstones in the same eerie manner.

Nearra doubled over in pain and Catriona moved forward to help.

"Stay back," Nearra gasped, clutching her sides.

"What can I do?" Catriona cried. "What's happening to you?"

"I can see," Nearra growled, teeth clenched, "visions in my head—other places, other people."

"Your past?" Catriona probed.

"No," she gasped. "They're memories—but they're not mine."

Nearra's eyes suddenly looked past her and grew wide. There wasn't time to think; instinct drove Catriona forward. She dived to the side, rolled, and came up, dragon claws ready. A sword hit the floor in the spot where Catriona had stood only moments before.

"You've cost me a lot, girl," Gadion growled, raising his sword. "Normally I'd make you pay in pain, watching your friends die slow deaths until it's your turn. Under the circumstances, however, I think I'll just kill you."

The bandit king came at Catriona with a fury of blows. It was all Catriona could do to defend herself. Despite having two weapons to Gadion's one, Catriona could barely keep up with the darting sword of the bandit king. Catriona began giving ground, her feet moving with ease in the "dancing" sword form Set-ai had drummed into her head. She backed around the circular room, determined to find some weakness in Gadion's attack.

Gadion was a far superior swordsman, and he knew it. He rained blows down on Catriona in rapid succession, always pressing her back, never giving her a chance to think. Finally, after a massive exchange of blows, the bandit king backed off. Both he and Catriona were panting from the exertion.

"You could be great," Gadion complimented her. "Too bad you're such a goody-goody."

"I'll take my life over yours any day," Catriona spat back.

"On the contrary," Gadion replied, "it is I who will take your life. I don't know what happened to your little friend, but I'm sure that, given enough time and . . . persuasion, I can coax it out of her."

Catriona felt her stomach churn in anger but she choked it down. Despite Gadion's easy posture, she was sure he was ready for her to lunge at him. He was trying to goad her into making a mistake, and she wasn't going to fall for it.

THE DRAGON WELL

181

"Of course, there's your kender friend," Gadion continued. "If he's still alive, I'll let the men cook him for dinner."

Catriona smiled but did nothing. Seeing that provoking Catriona wouldn't work, the easy look evaporated from Gadion's face.

"So be it," he growled and lunged at Catriona.

Back on the defensive, Catriona was barely managing to keep the bandit king's sword from hitting her. She knew one mistake was all he was waiting for and then he'd finish her off, kill Sindri, and do worse to Nearra. She had to end this.

Catriona leaped back from Gadion, disengaging from him temporarily.

"Why don't you give up?" Gadion asked, approaching her cautiously. "I'm not such a bad fellow. I'll even let you live if you swear on your honor to work for me. You can even keep the kender as a pet if you want to."

Catriona knew Gadion was lying. He was just waiting for her to relax so he could strike. That thought gave Catriona an idea. Almost imperceptibly, she let her guard slip. It was just a little opening, on the left side, but Gadion saw it. With a look of glee, he lunged, driving his sword toward Catriona's throat. The second Gadion reacted, Catriona closed up her guard. It would be too late, she knew that, but the blow wouldn't hit her throat.

White hot fire seared into Catriona's shoulder as Gadion's blow landed. She grit her teeth against the pain. This was her chance. Gadion's body was extended and his sword was trapped in Catriona's shoulder. Catriona brought up her free dragon claw with all her force. It hit Gadion in the belly with a wet thud, and the bandit king's eyes opened in shock.

Catriona wanted to say something witty, like the heroes always did in the famous songs. But, as Gadion slumped slowly to the floor, nothing came to her mind. As the bandit king died, his hand clenched down on the hilt of his sword and it was jerked from Catriona's shoulder.

Catriona screamed in pain, the noise echoing in the walls and ceiling of the well chamber. She grasped the wound, pressing her cloak into it to stop the bleeding. Clenching her jaw, Catriona staggered over to where Nearra still crouched beneath the shattered basin.

"Nearra," she said, shaking the girl.

When Nearra looked up, Catriona gasped. The color in her eyes was swirling like a vortex, with streaks of violet and blue churning around and around.

"Cat," Nearra said, as if just recognizing her. "Whatever happens, promise me . . . "

"What?" Catriona pressed when Nearra didn't continue.

"Promise me you won't let me become a monster," Nearra said. "You know what I mean."

Catriona knew, but she didn't know if she could bring herself to kill a friend.

"Promise," Nearra hissed, her strange eyes rolling back in her head.

"Nearra," Catriona called as the girl went limp.

"What's going on?" Sindri asked, so close to Catriona's ear that she jumped.

"The liquid from the basin poured all over her," Catriona answered, lifting the small girl with her good arm.

"No," Nearra shouted, though her eyes were still closed. "I won't let you."

Catriona and Sindri exchanged confused looks, then turned back to Nearra.

"He's mine!" she ranted. "They're my friends—you can't have them!"

"What is she talking about?" Sindri wondered.

"She said she was seeing someone else's memories," Catriona answered.

"Wow," the kender said. "How exciting."

Nearra's eyes snapped open and she sat up, trembling.

"I . . . am . . . stronger . . . than . . . you," she gasped, then her eyes fluttered shut and she collapsed back into Catriona's arms.

22 A DEATH IN THE FAMILY

The Beast thrashed and tore at the trees, straining to force its bulk between the narrow gaps. Davyn leaned forward reflexively, protecting Set-ai as the wounded warrior rested against a tree. Finally, the Beast tired and it panted, stalking back and forth in the bloody snow.

"It's getting tired," Davyn observed, clutching his bow so hard his knuckles were white. "Maybe it will give up."

"Don't bet your life on it, boy-o." Set-ai coughed as Elidor tightened the makeshift bandages over the woodsman's many wounds. "It's just catchin' its breath," he said. "As soon as it gets its wind back, it'll come at us again. You should go while you have the chance."

"If I distract it," Elidor said, fear in his voice, "would you be able to get a good shot?"

Davyn hesitated.

"It's impossible," Set-ai said. "It'd have to be chargin' right at you."

"Maybe we can arrange that," Davyn said, determination evident in his voice. He turned to Elidor. "Do you think you can lead it away from here, just for a few minutes?"

"As fast as that thing moves, I doubt I could stay ahead of it," the elf answered.

"Lead it off the path and into the trees," Davyn said. "It'll have trouble chasing you and it'll slow down."

"So what do I do, after a few minutes have passed?" Elidor pressed.

"You circle around and lead it back here," Davyn said. "As soon as you're gone, I'll go down the path to that big tree." Davyn pointed to a fallen tree that was partially blocking the path. "Bring the Beast straight down the path, then duck in here with Set-ai as you pass. I should have at least three good shots straight at the Beast."

"Don't shoot until I'm clear," Elidor said.

Davyn was about to reply, but Set-ai interrupted.

"For the last time, will you lads just get outta here?" he said. "There's no need, you gettin' yourselves killed on my account. I'm old. Just leave me be and the Beast won't follow you."

"You saved our lives when we were freezing to death in the mountains." Davyn looked the old woodsman straight in the eyes. "You're part of our family now, and we take care of family."

"That we do, brother," Elidor agreed, winking at Davyn. "If we're going to do this, we'd better go," he continued. "I don't want to be out there after that thing gets its breath back."

Elidor stripped off his cloak and quiver and made his way to the edge of the stand of trees. Davyn checked that his bowstring was tight and that his arrows were loose in his quiver before following.

"Keep to the trees, lad," Set-ai called to Elidor. "That'll slow the brute down. And you," he turned to Davyn, "you're only goin' to get half a dozen shots at most—they'd better all hit the mark."

"Yes, sir." Davyn grinned, then moved to join Elidor. "Are you ready for this?" he asked the elf when they were both at the edge of the sheltering trees.

"Ask me again in five minutes," Elidor replied. Then, without any sign or warning, the elf sprinted out of the trees and down the trail, away from the Beast. It took the Beast a second to realize what had happened, and even then it hesitated. The creature knew its prey was still in the shelter of the trees and wounded, but the lure of an easy kill was too great. With a barking howl, the Beast tore off down the trail after Elidor.

Once Davyn was sure that Elidor and the Beast were gone, he darted from the trees and ran for the shelter of the fallen log. Safely behind it, Davyn took ten arrows out of his quiver and stuck them in the ground in front of him. With any luck he'd get them all off before the Beast found him.

With nothing to do but wait, Davyn nocked an arrow and nervously tested the pull of his bow. The minutes crawled by agonizingly slowly. Davyn knew that no one could run like Elidor, but he also knew that the Beast was faster. If Elidor hadn't kept to the trees, the Beast could still catch him. It was a sobering thought.

About a dozen yards along the trail from Set-ai's shelter, Elidor suddenly burst from the forest. It took the elf a second to realize he was on the trail. Then he turned and sprinted directly at Davyn's hiding place.

Elidor had only hesitated for the briefest of moments, but that hesitation almost cost him his life. No sooner had he turned down the path than the Beast erupted from the undergrowth and slammed into the trees on the far side.

The Beast was as big and as terrifying as Davyn remembered, more so now that it turned and leaped after Elidor. It was foaming at the mouth, and dry twigs and brush clung to its many horns and spikes. One of the horns on its head had snapped off somewhere in its pursuit of Elidor, but the Beast didn't seem to care. The only thing that seemed out of place was the broken shaft of a spear protruding from the creature's shoulder where Set-ai had wounded it. Blood ran freely from the wound and stained the ground with the Beast's every step.

As Elidor ran, Davyn drew an arrow to his chin. He aimed carefully, right for the center of Elidor's chest. If this was to work, he had to release the arrow at just the right moment. Elidor was only two steps away from his destination, but the Beast seemed poised to catch him in its dagger-like teeth. In the last possible instant, just as the Beast extended its neck to grab Elidor, Davyn shot. At the same moment, Elidor dived aside, rolling to his feet and vaulting off a tree trunk onto a low-hanging limb. If Davyn had been looking, he would have been amazed by the elf's grace.

Davyn watched as his arrow sped to its target. The first arrow hit with a solid-sounding smack. It sunk to the feathers in the Beast's neck.

"Bull's-eye," Davyn whispered as he nocked another arrow.

As the second shaft struck the Beast, it roared in pain. This shot was not as perfect as the first, but it did its job. Maddened by the loss of its prey and this new attack, the Beast started howling and turning, seeking the source of the stinging arrows.

Davyn fired twice more, each arrow striking the Beast in the shoulder, just left of the neck. As Davyn was nocking his fifth arrow, the Beast saw him. With a roar of triumph, it hurled itself at him in a great leap. Davyn shot, point-blank, as the monster smashed down on the fallen log, shattering it. The arrow sunk deep into the monster's neck but it missed the heart.

Davyn scrambled for another arrow, but the Beast bowled him over, pinning him to the ground with a massive paw. The Beast hovered over Davyn, spittle dripping from its gaping mouth. Davyn closed his eyes.

But the blow didn't come.

Cautiously, Davyn opened his eyes, and found the Beast staring at him. Davyn slipped his hand down to his belt and grabbed the bone handle of his hunting knife.

"Hold on, brother." Elidor leaped from the shelter of his tree, knife in hand. He flung the weapon through the air. It landed in the Beast's side, just under its right foreleg. Elidor had aimed for the heart, but his knife missed as well.

With a cry of rage, the Beast lashed out with one of its hind legs. The blow caught Elidor squarely in the chest and with a sickening crack the elf was hurled into a nearby tree. Still pinned by the monster, Davyn couldn't see, but he heard Elidor hit the tree and slide slowly down into the snow.

Davyn gripped his hunting knife tighter. The Beast's attention had been distracted only for a second by Elidor's attack, but it was enough.

Davyn lunged upward, driving the knife into the Beast's chest. The Beast howled, a wailing cry of despair, and then, it collapsed on top of Davyn.

As warm blood from the wounded creature trickled over him, Davyn struggled to free himself. The Beast weighed easily as much as a draft horse, and that weight was slowly crushing the breath from Davyn's lungs.

"Elidor," he gasped as purple spots began dancing before his eyes, but the elf was still unconscious.

Davyn began to see a dark ring around his vision, slowly closing in on him.

So this is death, he thought. I hope Nearra's all right.

As the image of Nearra's face swam up out of the darkness, Davyn suddenly had the feeling that the incredible weight was being lifted off him. It wasn't until he heard himself gulping for air that he realized he could breathe again.

With a gasp, Davyn sat up.

His vision swam for a moment before everything came into focus. Elidor lay at the base of the tree where he'd fallen. There was a nasty bruise on his head, and Davyn suspected he broke some ribs, but he could see the elf's breath steaming in the frigid air. There was no sign of the Beast, only the bloody body of a man that was now lying across Davyn's legs. Startled, Davyn reached to move the body, but the man's hand suddenly grabbed his wrist.

"Davyn," the strange man gasped. "Is that you?"

Davyn was too startled to rip his hand away. Who was this man who knew his name, and where had the Beast gone? Davyn looked closely at the man before answering. He was dressed in green leathers, much the same as Set-ai's, and just like Set-ai, his armor was torn to shreds and he was bleeding from dozens of wounds. His hair was gray and brown and he had a short gray beard.

"Who are you?" Davyn asked, pulling his hand free of the dying man's grasp.

The strange man tried to reply, but he coughed violently. His breath was coming in ragged gasps and there was a whistling noise when he breathed.

"Listen closely," he gasped at last, "I don't have much time. I was once a servant of the wizard Maddoc—"

"No, you weren't," Davyn interrupted. He glanced at Elidor to make sure he was still unconcious. "I've lived with Maddoc all my life and I've never seen you."

The man coughed, a look of pain on his face. "My wife and I served him for many years until our first child was born— a son."

"Why are you telling me this?" Davyn asked. "Where is the Beast?"

"Listen," the man implored. "We knew Maddoc was an evil man and when our son arrived, we decided not to expose him to the wizard."

"What happened?" Davyn prodded as the stranger struggled for breath.

"We fled," he croaked, "but the service of the wizard Maddoc is not easily abandoned. He followed us and caught us as we were preparing to sail to the southland. I tried to fight him, but he transformed me into the Beast, a mindless creature driven only by instinct."

"What happened to your family?" Davyn asked, afraid of the answer.

"Maddoc forced me to kill my wife," the man sobbed. "I knew what I was doing, but I couldn't stop myself."

Davyn's stomach tightened. Ever since the affair with Nearra began, he'd been more and more distrustful of his father's motives. Now there seemed little doubt that Maddoc was using them all in some grander game.

"What happened to your son?" Davyn pressed, unable to help himself.

"Maddoc ordered me to kill him as well," the man began, "but something in me snapped. I couldn't kill my own son."

The man began coughing again. Davyn noticed that his breathing was shallow and his skin was deadly pale.

"I'll go get some water," Davyn said, trying to rise.

"No," the man insisted. "You must hear the rest. When the Beast wouldn't obey his orders, Maddoc took it as a sign that the boy had some destiny laid on him."

"You don't mean . . . " Davyn began, a horrible thought entering his mind.

"Yes," the man confirmed with a weak nod. "My name is Senwyr, and you, Davyn, are my son."

"That's not possible," Davyn insisted. "Maddoc is my father. My mother died the night I was born."

"No, look at me." Senwyr shook his head. "Can you see my face and deny that you are my son?"

Davyn looked Senwyr in the face. He'd seen that face before—whenever he looked in the mirror. It was older and more worn, certainly, but it was his own face. Davyn could only stare as the awful realization dawned on him.

"Maddoc kept me as his pet," Senwyr explained, his voice getting weak. "Whenever you were in the keep, he'd lock me in the dungeon. He didn't want you ever to see me. He'd hire me out to anyone with gold who needed to intimidate their neighbors. I barely had any thought as the Beast, just animal drive to hunt and destroy."

"I'll kill him," Davyn spat, a cold fury burning in his chest. "I'll kill Maddoc and avenge you."

"No," Senwyr croaked. "Maddoc is a powerful wizard. You can't fight him."

"He has to pay for what he did to you," Davyn growled, "for what he did to me."

"Vengeance is hollow, my son," Senwyr said, sadness in his voice. "Even if you succeed, how many years will you waste chasing your revenge? Maddoc is far away, you have a chance to escape from him. Take it."

"One of Maddoc's agents knows where I am," Davyn admitted.

"The dark dwarf," Senwyr nodded. "I smelled him in the castle on the black rock."

A violent fit of coughing wracked Senwyr and he spat out more blood.

"The dwarf is Maddoc's eyes and ears," Senwyr gasped, straining to speak. "Once he's out of the way, you can escape to the south."

"Won't Maddoc find us?" Davyn asked, cradling his father's head in his lap.

"Maddoc is powerful," Senwyr admitted. "But the world is very big. Promise me . . . "

Senwyr shuddered and grabbed Davyn's shoulder so hard it hurt.

"Promise me you'll flee this place," he managed at last. "Promise me you'll live free."

"Father, I . . ." Davyn began.

"Promise me," his father implored, looking up into Davyn's eyes.

"I swear, Father," Davyn said at last. "I'll leave this land and go to the coast. I'll take the first ship I can find and I won't look back."

Senwyr eyes seemed to fade and a smile crept across his lips. Before Davyn even realized it, Senwyr was dead.

Tears streaming from his eyes, Davyn clutched the body of his father. Great sobs wracked his body as he wept for the father he'd never known.

"Pull yourself together, lad," Set-ai's soft voice broke through Davyn's grief. "There's nothin' you can do for him now, and the elf needs your help."

"You don't understand," Davyn sobbed, clutching Senwyr's body tighter.

"Aye, I do," Set-ai said, sinking heavily into the snow and leaning on a tree for support. "I came after you when I heard the Beast go down. I saw it change into this man. I heard what he told you."

"Then you know I killed my own father!" Davyn screamed, hot tears of rage and frustration burning in his eyes.

"No, you didn't," Set-ai said firmly, placing his hand on Davyn's shoulder. "After all these years, you finally set him free."

"Look at his face, lad," Set-ai went on when Davyn didn't respond. "All those years of misery and pain are over."

Davyn looked into Senwyr's face and saw the faint smile still frozen on his lips. Set-ai was right. His father was dead, but he had died happy.

"If anyone's responsible for his death, it's that wizard," Set-ai added.

"Maddoc," Davyn said numbly. "He's the reason Nearra and I are out here—the reason we're all here."

Davyn started slowly, telling Set-ai about Maddoc's failed spell stealing Nearra's memories. Then faster and faster the words tumbled out, all the hardship, the danger—and his part in all of it. While Davyn talked, he tended to Elidor, rolling the elf over and covering him with a blanket.

"Your father was right," Set-ai said when at last Davyn was finished. "You've got to get away from Maddoc."

"What am I going to tell my friends?" Davyn asked softly.

"In my experience," Set-ai sighed, "a man can only be truly free if he tells the truth."

Elidor moaned and stirred. Davyn pressed Set-ai's water bag to the unconscious elf's lips.

"What if he won't speak to me again?" Davyn asked, remembering Elidor's suspicions of Davyn's motives.

"It's a risk," Set-ai admitted, wearily. "But are you really his friend if you lie to him?"

Davyn was about to answer when Elidor groaned and gingerly sat up.

"What happened?" he asked, clutching his ribs.

Davyn smiled weakly. "We won."

23 THEORAN

Catriona sat shivering on the stone of the well chamber cradling Nearra's unconscious form in her arms. Nearra's fur cloak alone would have been enough to keep Nearra warm if she had not been lying directly on the icy stone.

At least, Catriona thought to herself, I can keep Nearra from freezing to death.

Sindri picked among the bones of the dead. Occasionally he would hold up a corroded belt buckle or the rusted hilt of a sword for Catriona's inspection. But she paid him little mind. When the liquid in the well had finally seeped away into the stones of the floor, the eerie light that had filled the well chamber disappeared. Now all Catriona could see was the dim circle of floor illuminated by Davyn's lantern and the bright glow of Sindri's torch in the distance.

Catriona took out her water bag and pressed it carefully to Nearra's lips. The unconscious girl would swallow the water, but she didn't wake.

"Any luck?" Sindri asked, picking his way back across the bone-littered floor.

"No." Catriona felt like crying.

195

"She'd better wake up soon," Sindri observed. "Someone's bound to start wondering where Gadion went before too long. Are you sure we can't just pull her through the crack?" he asked for the tenth time.

Catriona shook her head. "It's just too small. She can make it if she's awake to help, but like this we can't pull her through. Come on, Nearra," Catriona urged, gently shaking the girl. "You've got to wake up."

"Is she going to be all right?" Sindri asked.

Catriona just hung her head. "I don't know."

"Look what I found," Sindri brightened up, changing the subject. He held up several gold buttons and a brass baldric buckle stained black with tarnish. "Pretty good, eh?"

"Terrific," Catriona said, humoring him. "Why don't you see if Gadion or his goons had anything valuable on them? I'm sure Shemnara and the town would like to get back some of what he stole from them."

"I'll go check," the kender replied, his eyes once again alight with curiosity.

As Sindri moved off, Catriona wondered what time it was. From Elidor's description of the cave beyond the crack in the wall, Catriona was sure sunlight would never reach into the well chamber. As she thought of Elidor, she wondered if he and Davyn had made it past Gadion's men and the Beast to warn Shemnara of the imminent attack. If they made it, they might be fighting for their lives even now. Catriona smiled as she pictured the two.

Elidor was quiet and subdued, but Davyn definitely had potential. He reminded Catriona of a large puppy, eager to please, but hampered by his large paws and clumsiness. If Davyn managed to survive, Catriona reasoned, he'd make a strong leader and warrior some day.

The thought of Davyn as a man, as a seasoned warrior, made Catriona think. Davyn was handsome enough, she admitted, though in a country farm-boy way. Perhaps it would be in her best interest to be a little less argumentative the next time she saw him. As soon as the thought entered her mind, Catriona banished it. Nearra already had Davyn wrapped around her little finger, and Catriona, while not unattractive, couldn't compete with the girl's charms.

Maybe if Nearra doesn't wake up, Catriona started to think. Then she cursed herself for having such a thought.

As if in response, Nearra suddenly stirred. She sighed, almost contentedly, and then her eyes snapped open.

"Cat," she said weakly. "What happened. Where are we?"

"Still in the dragon well chamber," Catriona responded, helping the girl sit up. "The crack's too narrow to try and haul you through."

"Are you all right?" Catriona pressed as Nearra swayed and nearly lay down again.

"I'll be fine," she said at last, shaking her head to clear it.

"You said some strange things before you blacked out," Catriona said, passing Nearra her water bag.

"It was like all my nightmares, like I was living someone else's life," Nearra admitted, after taking a long pull from the water bag.

"Do you remember anything about it?" Catriona asked.

"Some things," Nearra said. "I remember that the people talked funny."

"How do you mean?" Catriona asked.

"Sort of old-fashioned, I guess," Nearra shrugged. "The last thing I saw was a warrior, yelling at me, or rather at whomever I was seeing through. He said I had to be destroyed so I couldn't hurt anyone again."

"What happened then?" Catriona asked.

"I'm not sure," Nearra admitted. "But I'm all right now." She shook her head. "Whoever it was, they're gone." Nearra forced a smile.

Catriona put a hand on Nearra's shoulder. "I want you to tell me if it ever comes back."

"I will," the girl promised.

"I mean it," Catriona pressed. "Whoever this was, or is, could be very dangerous."

"I promise," Nearra replied, a note of exasperation in her voice.

"Are you well enough to stand?" Catriona asked.

Nearra nodded, and Catriona stood to help her up. She wobbled for a moment as she got used to standing, then she seemed to be fine.

"Great." Catriona sighed. "Let's get Sindri and get out of here. It'll be dawn soon, if the sun's not up already."

"Where is Sindri?" Nearra asked, suddenly looking around.

Catriona peered around in the gloom. The light from the kender's torch glowed from beyond the ruins of the dragon well.

"Sindri," Catriona called into the darkness of the well chamber. "Nearra's awake. Let's go."

"Just a minute," Sindri's excited voice called back from beyond the dragon statues. "I found something really interesting."

"What?" Catriona muttered. "Did someone drop an old boot?"

Slowly, using the dim light of the lantern, Catriona and Nearra picked their way across the debris-strewn floor. Once they rounded the dragon statues and the ruins of the marble basin, they found Sindri standing on a large chunk of the shattered bowl, his torch stuck in one of the fallen dragon statues. He was reaching up, as high as he could go, prodding something on the wall with his hoopak staff.

"What are you doing?" Catriona chuckled, shaking her head.

"There's a seal up there, on the wall," Sindri replied, banging on something in the darkness. "It's really loose. I think I can knock it down."

Catriona held her lantern up high to illuminate the object of

Sindri's desire. Barely visible in the circle of light, Catriona could see a large, round object on the wall. There was an intricate design or carving on the surface, but the light was too dim to see it. She couldn't tell what it was made of, but parts of it glittered.

As Sindri pulled his staff back for another swing, Nearra gasped and grabbed Catriona's arm in a death grip.

"Sindri, no!" she shouted, her voice echoing in the vast, dark chamber.

Whatever spooked Nearra, her warning came too late. Sindri's staff shot forward before the words left her lips and slammed into the center of the carved circle. There was an explosive crack, and the seal crumbled away as if it had been made of clay.

"What's the matter?" Catriona asked Nearra once most of the seal had fallen in a cloud of dust.

Nearra didn't answer. She was standing still, staring up at the ceiling as if listening for something. Puzzled, Catriona listened too, but she didn't hear anything.

"Aw, it's just clay and paint," Sindri's voice came from where he'd crouched to examine what was left of the seal.

"Shush," Nearra and Catriona both hissed together.

Before Sindri could ask what the girls were listening for, he had his answer. A low rumbling suddenly shook the well chamber as dust and debris fell from the ceiling.

"Run!" Nearra shrieked, bolting for the crack in the wall. She'd barely taken three steps, however, when a violent tremor shook the tor, sending them all to their knees. "We've got to get out," she cried, leaping to her feet again.

Catriona wondered how Nearra had known what was going to happen, but this was not the time for such questions. She struggled to her feet and dashed after Nearra, Sindri right on her heels. When they reached the crack, they found Nearra standing in front of it.

"What are you waiting for?" Catriona demanded. "Go!"

Nearra stepped back, revealing what was left of the crack. The tremor had shaken rock loose in the cave beyond, and the way forward was blocked.

"Back up the stairs," Catriona insisted, "it's the only way out now."

"Uh, Cat," Sindri's voice called over the rumbling. "What's that?"

Catriona turned. The kender was staring at the wall where the seal had been. In the dim light of Sindri's torch, Catriona could see the black wall split apart. Light flowed from the space beyond, and Catriona could see a long crack running from just above where the seal had been down to the floor. A cold dread gripped Catriona. She was on the stair. If she ran she could be out of the chamber in a few seconds. But she couldn't. She'd been afraid before, but this fear was paralyzing. The last time she'd felt this kind of fear was when she met the green dragon, Slean.

Catriona couldn't move, she couldn't breathe, and she couldn't take her eyes off the crack that was growing ever larger as she watched.

The grinding sound continued, and the opening in the wall got bigger and bigger. A huge doorway appeared, light pouring from behind it and filling the well chamber. From the space beyond came a sound, a long, echoing hiss. The light suddenly moved and the head of an enormous dragon emerged. The head was massive. As big as he was, though, he was ethereal, transparent. To Catriona it looked as if the dragon's head was made of the same mist that had hovered over the liquid in the dragon well.

After the head came the body. The dragon floated silently into the room, his glowing body illuminating the floor. Catriona, Nearra, and Sindri stood absolutely still as the creature's white, glowing eyes swept the chamber, finally coming to rest on them.

"Who are you?" the dragon's voice boomed, full of anger and

malice. "Are you the best the brotherhood can send against me?"

"N-no," Catriona stammered, trying to control her tongue. "That is, what brotherhood?"

The dragon eyed them closely, bringing his head down to within feet of where they stood.

"Which of you set me free?" he asked, just as loud but with less malice.

Sindri tentatively raised his hand. "I did," he said. "I mean, I think I did. I broke that seal on the wall, if that's what you mean."

"Did you think to gain my power, kender?" the dragon hissed. "Did you think me all dried up and ready for the taking?"

"Oh, no," Sindri shook his head. He seemed to have an easier time overcoming the dragonfear. "We didn't even know you were in there. I was just looking for interesting things," he went on, holding up the gold buttons. "See what I found?"

"Silence," the dragon roared. "What brought you to this place?"

Sindri thought for a minute and then told the dragon their entire story, starting from when he first met Catriona. There were many wandering side trips, and Sindri's "magic" seemed to figure quite prominently in the story, but eventually he got through it all. When he was done, the mist-dragon began making a strange noise in his throat. With a chill, Catriona realized that he was laughing.

"Well, you are quite the adventurer, master kender," the dragon chuckled. "I am Theoran," he went on, the hard tone returning to his voice. "I was imprisoned here by the black brotherhood of the dragon," he growled. "For hundreds of years they kept me bound, a slave to their evil lusts for power."

Theoran's misty tail crashed down on the remains of the dragon well, shattering the statues with a blow that shook the tor.

"They took my blood and bound my body," Theoran said, "and

when they were done, they sealed me up in that prison of black stone to die."

"That's terrible," Sindri said, concern plain in his voice. "Are you free now?"

"Yes." The dragon's enormous head nodded. "But only for a little while. This form is what's left of the well's magic; my body died long ago. It rests in there." Theoran indicated the room from which he had emerged.

"I'm sorry," Nearra uttered, the first words she'd said since the dragon appeared.

Theoran turned to respond but something made him stop. He suddenly leaned down till his massive eye was only a yard from Nearra and looked her up and down.

"You bathed in the well," he gasped, anger creeping into his voice. "Do you take me for a fool? I know when someone has stolen my power."

Theoran reared his head, baring his teeth in anger.

"Stop it," Catriona shouted, stepping in front of Nearra. "You're scaring her. She was under the well when it broke; the liquid poured all over her."

The dragon considered this for a moment, then snorted.

"Very well. Since you have set me free, I will spare your lives. Before I leave this existence I will destroy this abominable place and all within. Flee now, while you can."

"I'm sorry," Sindri said. "I really am, but you see, we can't leave."

"What he means is that the way out is blocked," Catriona said, indicating the crack in the wall.

"In my cell, in the very back," the dragon said, towering over them, "you will find a hole that leads to the citadel's sewers. From there it joins an underground river. You can escape that way."

Catriona grabbed Nearra's arm and hustled her bodily across

the floor toward the opening of Theoran's cell. Sindri started after them but suddenly stopped and ran back.

"Thank you, Theoran. It was great to meet you," he said.

The dragon leaned down until his head was even with Sindri.

"It has been a long time since I looked on one of you two-legged ones with anything but contempt," he said. "I thank you for freeing me, little adventurer."

With that, the dragon blew a mist ring that washed over the kender. As it passed over him, it flashed with many colors, then disappeared.

"I have no doubt you'll be a great wizard," Theoran said, rising once again to hover in the center of the chamber. "Now go. I have delayed my revenge too long because of you, and my time grows short. Hurry."

Catriona didn't need any more encouragement. She charged into the dark room beyond, dragging Nearra after her. The light from Theoran's body shone into the cell brightly enough to see by. The room was large and round, but not high enough for a dragon to stretch its wings. Inside they saw the massive mound that had been the dragon's body. It lay curled up like a large, dark hill. Fallen scales were scattered across the floor. The scales looked black, but whether that was the dragon's original color, Catriona couldn't tell.

In the back of the room, just as Theoran had said, was a large, round hole. A set of rusted iron bars formed a cross over the top and were set deeply into an iron rim.

"What do we do now?" Nearra asked. Even Sindri wasn't small enough to squeeze through the narrow opening.

Catriona didn't answer. She lashed out with her booted foot and shattered one of the rust-decayed bars, then did the same to the next bar around.

"After you," Catriona gasped, motioning for Nearra to climb in.

"How deep is it?" she asked, staring down into the gaping black hole.

The echo of a distant roar reached them from somewhere far above.

"It doesn't matter, just go," Catriona commanded.

Nearra took a deep breath and jumped into the hole.

"Now you, Sindri," Catriona called, looking around.

The kender was staring sadly at the moldering mound of the dragon's body.

"There's not time for that," Catriona chastised. "Let's go."

Sindri stooped down and picked something off the ground, then he turned and leaped into the hole. Catriona gave him a few seconds to get out of the way before jumping herself. Just as she went, there was a thunderous boom and the sound of falling rock.

The drain went straight down a dozen feet, then began to angle, carrying Catriona along like a slide. It would have been fun had Catriona not feared it would fall in and crush her at any moment. Just as she was beginning to wonder how far this drain went, a foul odor assaulted her and she was pitched head first into knee-deep water.

Coughing and spluttering, Catriona struggled to her feet. Her lantern had gone out and the darkness was complete.

"Sindri?" she called. "Nearra? Where are you?"

"We're here," Sindri's voice called from somewhere to Catriona's left.

"I think I'm going to be sick," Nearra muttered weakly, her voice close to Sindri's.

"The sewers from the citadel must still be working," Catriona explained, trying not to breathe through her nose. "Don't think about it."

"I've got to get out of here," Nearra gasped.

"Which way?" Sindri asked, bumping into Catriona.

"Hold onto the back of my cloak," Catriona instructed. "Nearra, you hold onto Sindri."

"Got him," came Nearra's voice.

"We still don't know which way to go," Sindri pointed out.

"Downstream," Catriona explained, plunging her hand into the water to feel its direction. "This way."

Catriona started out as fast as she dared. She didn't know how high the passage was, so she crouched as she went. Occasionally roots and obstructions blocked their path, but Catriona just pushed through them and kept going. The stench was overwhelming, and Catriona was grateful there was no light. Just the thought of what was in the water turned her stomach.

"Do you think we're safe yet?" Sindri asked, holding onto Catriona tightly.

In answer to his question, there was a sudden rush of air down the tunnel and then the roar of rushing water.

"Run!" Catriona yelled, charging headlong down the dark passage.

24   Meetings, Pacts, and Partings

Despite the chill in the winter air, Davyn was sweating under his fur cloak. After a mile of walking, Set-ai collapsed, so Davyn and Elidor had rigged up a drag stretcher out of two small trees and a blanket. Elidor hadn't been much help as he couldn't move his right arm without excruciating pain. Set-ai agreed with Davyn that the elf's ribs were probably cracked. What all that meant was that through the waning hours of the night, and well into the dawn, Davyn had trudged through the woods dragging Set-ai's litter by himself.

"How much farther?" Davyn gasped, stopping to lean against a tree.

"I'm not sure," Elidor said with a shrug, wincing as his ribs reminded him not to move like that. "You're the one who always knows where he is in the woods."

"I haven't been paying attention," Davyn admitted. "I'm just trying to get one foot in front of the other."

"You're goin' the right way," Set-ai muttered from the stretcher. "It can't be much farther."

The big woodsman's voice was getting weary. Davyn knew he'd lost a lot of blood, and the effort of walking had taken a lot out of him. If they didn't reach town soon, Davyn worried that Set-ai might not make it at all.

"You're doin' fine, boy-o," Set-ai answered Davyn's thoughts. "Just keep goin'."

Davyn took a deep breath and hefted the stretcher again, pulling it slowly up a gentle slope to the top of a small hill.

"Are you sure my father's body will be all right till we get back?" Davyn puffed, trying to take his mind off the tremendous weight he was dragging.

"There are no predators for miles," Set-ai assured him weakly. "The Beast will have driven them off."

"We covered the body well," Elidor put in, trudging beside him. "It'll be safe till we come back."

"We?" Davyn raised his eyebrow. "I thought you weren't speaking to me."

Elidor smiled a weary smile. "I admit I was mad when I found out who you really are," he said, "but if you'd told us the truth any sooner, we probably would have driven you away. And then where would we be? If you hadn't been here, Slean would have killed us all. If not Slean, then the Scarlet Brethren, or the Beast. You were just a pawn in whatever twisted game Maddoc's playing, and you did your best to help us. Besides," the elf added with a wink, "I haven't even had a brother a full day yet. I'm not going to let a little thing like you lying about your past get in the way."

"Thanks," Davyn said, with a weary grin.

"So, what are you going to do now?" Elidor wondered, his expression turning serious.

"I'm going to take my father's advice," Davyn answered. "I'm going to get away from Maddoc and live my own life."

"And what will you tell the others?" Elidor prodded. "What will you tell Nearra?"

"The truth." Davyn sighed. "After all, it worked so well with you."

"Be careful," Elidor cautioned. "Cat is not as forgiving as I am, and she still has those dragon claws."

"I'll risk it," Davyn chuckled. "Seriously, though, if she wants to leave, I won't try to stop her—or any of them."

"They won't leave, boss," the elf stated plainly. "They may hate you for a while, but you've been too good a leader and too good a friend to abandon."

"Thanks, and don't call me boss," Davyn added absently.

"Sorry, boss," Elidor answered with a mischievous grin.

Davyn would've kicked snow at the elf if he'd had the energy. At the moment, however, it was all he could do to keep going. When he reached the crest of another little hill, Davyn called a halt. Set-ai seemed to be holding up all right, but Davyn was beginning to give out. He seriously doubted he could drag the stretcher much longer, and Set-ai was in no condition to walk the rest of the way.

"Maybe Set-ai could walk for a little while and let you rest," Elidor whispered so as not to be overheard by the woodsman.

Davyn was about to respond when a strange sound echoed over the forest. It was similar to the roar of the Beast, Davyn realized, a chill running up his spine. But it was strangely soft, as if heard from a great distance.

"What was that?" Davyn asked as the sound died away.

"You'd better have a look at this, lad," Set-ai said from behind him.

Davyn eased the stretcher down and turned. From his vantage point on the hill, Davyn could see the tops of the winter-bare trees stretching out behind them. In the distance was the black spire of Karoc-Tor. At first, Davyn wondered what Set-ai was talking about, but then the eerie wail broke across the forest again, and he saw it.

A white dragon swooped and circled around the tor, its body twisting and moving as if made of smoke. At this distance, Davyn couldn't hear what was happening, but what he could see made it plain enough.

As the dragon circled, it breathed great clouds of mist on the citadel and the tor. Everywhere the mist touched, the rock cracked and crumbled away as though aging thousands of years in seconds. As the rock crumbled, the dragon beat on the tor with its tail, shattering the rock and sending great chunks of the spire crashing down into the forest below. In minutes the citadel and the flat rocky top of the tor were gone. But the dragon's rage was not spent. It kept circling and smashing until a great cloud of dust raised by the falling debris obscured it. Finally the dragon emerged, circling high above the ruin of the tor as if looking for anything that might have escaped its wrath. After a moment of fruitless searching the dragon spread its wings to the sky. At that moment, whatever magic held its body together failed, and its smoky form silently drifted apart, leaving nothing but a vanishing trail of white mist.

"By the gods," Elidor swore.

"Nearra." Davyn's stomach lurched."Cat, Sindri."

Cold fear gripped Davyn as the dust settled around the wreckage of the tor. Only a pile of black rocks remained, barely high enough to rise above the trees. Every nerve in Davyn's body screamed for him to run and find Nearra, but in his heart he knew nothing could have survived the devastation of the dragon.

"Maybe they made it out in time," Elidor said. "It's been hours since we left them."

"We've got to go look for them," Davyn declared, not thinking clearly.

"Are you just goin' to leave me here, then?" Set-ai croaked.

"No," Davyn admitted after a long pause. "We've got to get you to Shemnara."

Davyn picked up the stretcher and began pulling desperately in the direction of town.

"Easy lad," Set-ai admonished. "If they're out there and they're all right, they'll come to town. If they're not all right, you'll need help from the town to find 'em—if we get there in one piece."

Davyn ground his teeth in frustration and strained to pull the heavy stretcher. He hadn't gone more than a few steps when the ground began shaking and a low rumble filled the air.

"The force of the mountain falling is catching up to us," Set-ai called. "Hold on to something."

Davyn clutched the stretcher tight and leaned against a good-sized tree. The trembling wasn't as bad as Set-ai had made it sound, and within a few minutes it had subsided. Davyn was about to push off the tree and continue toward town when suddenly a great geyser of dirt and snow erupted from the ground several hundred yards in front of him.

"What's that?" he yelled to Elidor over the noise.

"Must be a tunnel or something connected to the citadel," Set-ai said while Elidor shrugged and winced. "The force of the mountain coming down blew it out."

"I hear water," Elidor added as Davyn resumed trudging forward. "It must be an underground river. Let's check it out."

"You take a look," Davyn instructed, "I'm not taking one step I don't have to."

As it turned out, a thick stand of trees forced Davyn to go around them and that brought the group right to the scene of the eruption. Rocks, sand, and sludgy water had been expelled from a small hole in a hillside, where a little stream emerged, joining a larger one that cut through the countryside. Elidor wrinkled up his nose and tried vainly to wrap a handkerchief around his face with one hand. A moment later Davyn caught the odor of sewage.

Set-ai coughed. "Smells like the sewer outlet."

"Great," Davyn grunted. "Let's just get away from here as quickly as possible." The mass of debris expelled by the fall of the tor just reminded Davyn of Nearra. He wanted to believe she

DAN WILLIS

was all right, but not being able to go look for her was getting to him.

"Look," Elidor suddenly hissed in his ear, so loudly Davyn almost dropped the stretcher.

The elf was pointing to the area where the underground river exited the hillside. As Davyn watched, a muddy figure crawled free of the hole and stood up slowly.

"A survivor," Elidor stated the obvious, "one of Gadion's men."

"Not for long," Davyn growled, anger burning inside him. He quietly put the stretcher down and took hold of his bow. The thought that this vermin lived while his friends might be lying dead, crushed by thousands of tons of rocks, made Davyn tremble with rage.

Trying to hold his arrow steady, Davyn aimed at the muddy ruffian. Whoever he was, the force of the blast had obviously stunned him, for he seemed to be having trouble standing. Davyn held his breath to steady his aim.

He was just about to release when a second figure crawled from the hole and staggered to his feet. This person was wet but there was no mud on him at all. Davyn recognized him instantly.

"Sindri!" he shouted, lowering his bow.

The kender turned, startled, and broke into a wide grin, waving at them. Elidor dashed down the hill, groaning in pain every time his arm moved. Davyn was about to follow when he remembered Set-ai, who was demanding loudly to know what had happened.

By the time Davyn dragged the heavy stretcher down the hill, Elidor was helping Sindri pull Nearra, coughing, sputtering, and shivering, from the hole. Catriona, who had been the first one out, was covered in the muck from the sewer, and Davyn stepped back as she came to embrace him.

"We're glad to see you," she said as Nearra and the others joined them.

Davyn took off his cloak and threw it around Cat's shoulders while Elidor did the same thing for Nearra.

"We've got to get you out of this cold," Davyn observed, shivering a bit himself.

Everyone was glad to see Set-ai alive and, with Cat's help dragging the stretcher, the group made good time back to town. As she pulled, Catriona told Davyn, Elidor, and Set-ai about the fight with Gadion, the destruction of the dragon well, the appearance of Theoran, and their escape down through the sewers. No one could explain why Cat and Nearra had emerged covered in muck, but Sindri, while just as wet, was virtually spotless. The kender, of course, said his magic was responsible, which effectively ended speculation on the issue.

After Catriona finished, Elidor told them about finding Mudd and then Set-ai, and their fight with the Beast. To Davyn's relief, he left out the bit about the Beast being Davyn's father and Maddoc's part in the whole affair. The elf seemed to think that these were topics that Davyn should explain in his own time.

Despite Cat's help dragging the stretcher, it still took the little group over an hour to reach Potter's Mill. When they arrived in the town, they found Mudd leading a large posse of townspeople into the woods to look for them. Excitedly, Mudd told them how the townspeople had beat Gadion's bandits when they attacked at dawn.

Several burly men hoisted Set-ai's stretcher and took him straight to Shemnara's. Elidor trailed after them, but Nearra and Catriona demanded a bath first. Exhausted from the battle with the Beast, the ordeal of his father's death, and dragging Set-ai all the way to town, Davyn returned to the loft of Shemnara's house and went straight to sleep.

The steam from the bathhouse was warm and soothing, and Catriona let her mind drift as she soaked it in. It had taken her over an hour to scrub away the filth from Gadion's sewers but at last she felt clean. With fresh water in her tub and a fire in the room's hearth, Catriona was content to just lie there, suspended in the water, and let the world go away.

From somewhere to her left, Nearra's furious splashing disrupted Catriona's relaxation. Despite having washed her hair at least a dozen times, the girl was still rinsing it repeatedly with a pitcher.

Nearra had been a trooper about the whole sewer incident, right up until she saw herself in the bathhouse's mirror. Then she'd spent half an hour being sick in a bucket. After that she'd cleaned herself with a cake of lye soap until her skin was red. Catriona couldn't blame her, but there came a point when you had to admit that you were clean.

"You're clean already," Catriona admonished from her tub. "Soak a while. It'll make you feel better."

"I don't think I'll ever feel clean again," Nearra muttered miserably, from the tub next to Catriona's. "I can't believe Davyn saw me like that."

"Don't let it throw you," Catriona offered, philosophically. "Look on the bright side: he's seen you at your worst now, so nothing else is going to faze him."

"I suppose you're right," Nearra grumbled. "I did want to thank you," she continued, unexpectedly.

"For what?" Catriona yawned.

"Getting us out alive," the girl responded. "You kept your head and you beat Gadion. You're a hero."

"You want to know the truth?" Catriona said, sitting up. "I was scared to death. All I could think about was not letting you all down. It's what kept me going."

Nearra floated in her tub, as if considering this for a moment, then she sat up too.

"You once swore an oath to help me on my quest, to become my protector," Nearra said.

"I did," Catriona admitted.

"Well, I'm going to need your help," the girl went on, "now more than ever. I've decided I'm not going to run away anymore. I want my memories back. And I don't think I can do it alone."

"I don't know if you want to count on only me. I was so scared going up against Gadion that I could barely move. My fear got my aunt killed, remember? You need someone brave."

"Set-ai told me that bravery is doing what you have to, no matter what," Nearra said. "You and Davyn and Elidor, even Sindri, you're the bravest people I ever met. Promise you'll help me. Promise you'll help me even if it means your own death."

"Why are you saying this, Nearra? You know we'd do anything for you."

"Just promise me you'll do it."

"Of course I promise."

"Excellent," Nearra said, sinking back down in her tub.

Just for a second, Catriona thought she saw Nearra's eyes flash with a violet light, but after a moment she decided it must be her own exhausted brain playing tricks on her.

That evening, after Catriona and Nearra had returned to the loft to sleep, Davyn and Elidor set out from town alone. Set-ai wanted to go with them, but his healing was going slowly and Shemnara forbade him to make the trip. Elidor's ribs had been knitted back together by Shemnara, and now the elf admitted only to a little soreness if he moved too quickly.

Without the burden of injury or a heavily laden stretcher, the pair reached the spot where Senwyr's body lay covered by branches and snow. Davyn put down the bundle of wood he'd carried on his back, and Elidor handed him an axe from his own bundle. Wordlessly, the two set about chopping down several small trees and lashing the wood together into a raised platform.

Dan Willis

After an hour of work, they reverently lifted Senwyr's body onto the bier and covered it with wood. Davyn doused the wood with a flask of oil and struck a spark into it with his flint. The fire spread quickly, consuming the platform and Senwyr's body as Davyn and Elidor looked on.

"I never really knew my father," Elidor said at last. "I'm sorry you had to find your father like this, but I have to admit I'm jealous. After all he went through, his last thoughts were for you and your happiness."

"It makes me wonder if Maddoc ever did anything in my life that didn't have some benefit to him," Davyn said solemnly.

"Are you going after him then?" Elidor asked.

"No," Davyn said at last. "Senwyr was right. Trying to take revenge on Maddoc is only going to get a lot of people killed. Most likely people I care about."

"Then what are we going to do?" Elidor asked.

"As soon as everyone's recovered, I'm going to the coast," Davyn answered.

"Will you tell them the truth?" Elidor asked.

After a long moment, Davyn nodded. "I owe them that. I'll tell them as soon as we get back."

"Don't worry." Elidor smiled, putting his arm around Davyn's shoulders. "Even if they all hate you, you'll always have me."

Davyn grinned. "Gee, I feel so much better."

Davyn turned away as the bier began to burn down and started the long walk back to town.

25 REVELATIONS

By the time Davyn and Elidor made it back to Potter's Mill, night had fully fallen. Unlike the first time they saw the town, this time torches lit the streets, light poured from unshuttered windows, and the sounds of music and merriment were evident. Men, women, and even some children walked the streets without fear, and all of them welcomed Davyn and Elidor as if they were old friends.

After many thanks and slaps on the back, the pair finally managed to push through the crowds, and headed back toward Shemnara's house. They had barely taken a few steps, however, when a familiar voice called to them.

"There you are," Mudd puffed, running up to them. "I've been all over the place looking for you."

"We had some business," Elidor said.

"We burned the Beast's body." Davyn wasn't ready to talk about his father, but the simple truth would deflect most of the questions.

"Really?" Mudd seemed surprised. "The mayor will be sorry to hear that. He wanted its head for the town hall's hearth."

Davyn's jaw clenched and Elidor quickly put his arm around Mudd's shoulders, leading the young man on toward Shemnara's.

"The Beast was a creature born of foul magic," Elidor said, truthfully. "Its body had to be burned as a precaution."

"I see." Mudd nodded sagely. "I guess it couldn't be helped."

"If that's all," Davyn said, still angry at the thought of the Beast's head over a mantle somewhere, "we need to see our friends."

"I almost forgot," Mudd said, putting out his arm to stop the pair. "That's why I was looking for you. Everyone's gathering in the town hall. Your friends are there already."

The town hall was a large, barn-like building just off the central square. Normally it was used as a warehouse, but tonight the sacks of grain and barrels of molasses and ale were pushed aside and benches were laid down instead. At the back of the room was a raised stage where Davyn could see Cat, Sindri, and Nearra already seated. Next to them was an enormously fat man whom Davyn presumed was the mayor.

Mudd led the man and elf through the gathering throng of people up to the stage.

The fat man jumped up as they arrived, a move that defied his bulk. "Boys, I'm Mayor Shelton." He shook each of their hands in turn. "If you'll just have a seat with your friends, we're almost ready to begin."

"What's this all about?" Davyn whispered to Mudd as the mayor banged a gavel to settle the crowd down.

"You can't just save a town and not expect them to thank you." Mudd sounded as if Davyn's question were ludicrous.

Davyn didn't feel much like being thanked. On top of everything else, he'd been against going after Gadion from the start. If Nearra hadn't needed Shemnara's help so badly, he never would have gone in the first place. Davyn lowered his head—all this time he'd been thinking only of himself and Nearra. The plight of the people of Potter's Mill hadn't even crossed his mind when he'd made his decision to accept Shemnara's offer. His cheeks burned with shame as he realized what Set-ai would have done. The old woodsman would have gone after Gadion for the sheer pleasure of ridding the world of such an evil man. Set-ai had done just that when he'd saved Davyn and his friends in the mountains. Set-ai didn't know them. He just helped them because it was the right thing to do.

Mayor Shelton was talking, saying something about the courage and skill of Davyn and his friends. A great roar of approval from the crowd brought Davyn back from his reflections. The mayor was motioning for them to stand.

Apparently, Davyn thought, there's going to be some kind of presentation.

Much to Davyn's surprise, when Mayor Shelton called him forward, two men came up on the stage bearing a large bundle. Upon opening it, Davyn found a complete suit of hardened leather armor. Like Set-ai's, it was dyed green. Some of the pieces had been recently altered and none of them matched the style of the others. Davyn suspected they had been cobbled together from the armor worn by Gadion's men and cut down to more closely fit him.

"Thank you," Davyn stammered. Despite its rather dubious origin, the armor was an incredible gift and Davyn was grateful.

To Elidor, the town gave a similar suit of armor, this one dyed a darker shade of green. Catriona received a well-polished breastplate that had been obviously altered to fit a woman. Along with the breastplate were a steel helmet and leg guards as well as armored leather gauntlets. Nearra received an intricately carved staff capped with brass ends and three new suits of traveling clothes. A lady in the crowd was called forward and presented Nearra with a beautiful dress for special occasions, which had belonged to her daughter, one of the Beast's victims. Last, but not least, the mayor presented Sindri with several silk shirts, some new boots, a blank book, and some ink in a bronze inkwell shaped like a sunburst. Davyn suspected the inkwell to be of little worth, but Sindri immediately concluded that it was the ancient and lost emblem of the house of Suncatcher, and placed it reverently in his pocket as if it were worth a chest full of steel.

"Now, my fellow citizens," Mayor Shelton announced once the presentations were over. "This is a momentous night, one of celebration and merriment and thanksgiving for our deliverance. Let the feast begin."

Two burly men brought in a whole stag that had been roasted on a spit. Several trays of baked goods were brought out, and a keg of ale was tapped. It was, by all measure, a small feast, but to the free people of Potter's Mill, it was as good as a banquet.

Davyn accepted many thanks and many toasts. From the merriment going on in the hall, it seemed the citizens of Potter's Mill intended to revel all night. Finally, after yawning repeatedly, Davyn and the others were sent home to Shemnara's to get some rest.

Somewhere during the mayor's presentations and the festivities afterwards, Mudd had disappeared.

Davyn wasn't surprised to find him waiting for them in Shemnara's parlor.

"Shemnara wants to see you," he said. "She'll be ready in a few minutes."

Davyn nodded, shouldering the sack with his new armor in it.

"Give us a minute to put this stuff in the loft first," he said.

"Just leave it here," Mudd said. "The mayor's arranged for you to stay at the inn for as long as you're here. I'll take it over there for you. Right now your friend, Set-ai, wants to see you."

Davyn nodded and put his bundle down by the door; the others followed suit. They made their way back along the narrow hall to the sick room, where they found Set-ai sitting up in bed looking remarkably healthy.

"Well, it's about time you showed up, boy-o," he admonished Davyn as they gathered round his bed. "Everyone's been to see me but you and your elf-brother."

At this last comment, Catriona and Nearra looked at Davyn, but he pretended not to notice.

"We had to take care of the Beast's body," Davyn said.

Set-ai nodded sagely, and Catriona, Nearra, and Sindri all wore looks of desperate curiosity.

"Burned it, I suppose?" Set-ai asked.

Davyn nodded.

"That's right and proper, to be sure," the woodsman said. "You lot have certainly come a long way since I found you freezin' to death in the hills. A right fine bunch of adventurers you are."

"Because of you," Catriona pointed out. "If you hadn't come along we never would have made it."

"True," Set-ai admitted, "but if you lot hadn't learned all I tried to teach you, you never would have lived to see this day. You're heroes in your own right." He smiled.

"What are you going to do now?" Sindri asked.

"I'm gettin' a might old for huntin'," the woodsman said heavily. "I don't bounce back as well as I used to. I figure maybe I'll stay here for a while. That lad, Mudd, needs some lookin' after."

Davyn smiled at the thought of Set-ai training the gregarious youth. As if on cue, Mudd entered the sick room carrying a small bundle.

"Shemnara is ready for you," he said softly.

"Tell your mistress that I'll send 'em along in a minute, lad," Set-ai replied, taking the bundle from Mudd.

"And now, young lady," Set-ai said, turning to Cat. "I believe you have something of mine."

"Oh, right." Catriona blushed. She pulled the dragon claws from her belt and passed them, almost reluctantly, to Set-ai. "I've become so used to them being there, I almost forgot."

Set-ai accepted the dragon claws, holding them up for inspection.

"There's a bit of rust on these, my girl," he admonished, "and they're not as sharp as I'd like. Do you not have a whetstone?"

Catriona blushed furiously and stammered an apology, saying that there hadn't been much time in recent days for proper upkeep.

"You always have to maintain your weapons, lass," Set-ai scolded. "It's obvious to me that you need more practice. That's why I had the blacksmith make these."

Set-ai opened the bundle Mudd had handed him, revealing two new dragon claws. The design was slightly different but they appeared sturdy and well made. Set-ai held them out to Catriona, who received them reverently.

The woodsman grinned. "Take good care of 'em, lass. And just to be sure," he went on, handing Catriona a chunk of porous rock, "a whetstone to go with them."

Cat's eyes were brimming with tears and she threw her arms around the old woodsman, giving him a tremendous hug.

"Not so tight, child," Set-ai protested. "My ribs are still sore."

"I'm mighty proud of all of you," Set-ai said, once Catriona had released him. "You've all come a long way, especially you, boy-o. You've become a good woodsman and a fine leader."

Davyn blushed. Praise from someone as skilled as Set-ai was high praise indeed.

"Don't let this go to your heads, mind," he said, wagging his finger at them. "If even half of what I heard about your trip to Karoc-Tor is true, you're all lucky to be alive. Now get out of here and let an old man rest."

They each shook the woodsman's hand and thanked him as they left. Davyn went last of all. He knew that Set-ai would still be there in the morning but, for some reason, this felt like good-bye.

"You look after them kids, boy-o," the woodsman whispered, clutching Davyn's hand in a firm grip. "I'm relyin' on you to guide 'em right."

"I will, sir," Davyn promised.

The walk to Shemnara's room seemed longer than Davyn remembered it. This time when they entered, they found the seer sitting quietly on her overstuffed couch, the basin in front of her covered by its upholstered board.

"Please, sit," Shemnara said softly.

Davyn, who came in last, took the hard wooden chair to Shemnara's right. After everyone was seated there was a long pause before the seer spoke.

"I told you when we met that, if you went to Karoc-Tor, Gadion and the Beast would be defeated," she said at last. "As I recall, you didn't believe me."

"You also promised us that we'd each return with something priceless," Elidor interjected.

"So I did," Shemnara nodded. "Can you put a price on finding a brother, and the chance at a real family?"

Elidor looked shocked for a moment, then shook his head. "No," he admitted.

"Mudd tells me you've recently acquired some new weapons," Shemnara continued, turning to Cat. "Would you care to sell them to me?"

"No," Catriona replied, putting a protective hand on the bundle containing her dragon claws.

"Kender," the seer said, turning to face Sindri, "though you don't realize it yet, your quest has come to an end . . . and by so doing, it has only just begun."

Davyn had no idea what this meant, but Sindri nodded sagely as if it were the simplest thing in the world. Next Shemnara turned to him. How she knew where they were all sitting, Davyn had no idea.

"And what price for truth?" she asked Davyn. "Will you put a value on the knowledge you now possess?"

Davyn thought about all the years of lies, all the deceptions Maddoc had inflicted on him. He had to admit, no treasure would be more valuable than the truth of his past—than the chance to say good-bye to his real father.

"No," he admitted, "but the truth has cost me dearly."

"Truth always exacts a high price," Shemnara told him, "but truth makes us free—free to live our lives with honor, unencumbered by the burdens of deception."

"What about me?" Nearra asked as Shemnara turned to her. "The liquid from the dragon well spilled on me. It's the same stuff that's in your basin, isn't it? It's what blinded you. What did it do to me?"

"It replaced what you have lost," Shemnara said simply, "and it prepared your soul for what is to come."

With that, she leaned forward and took the upholstered board off the basin in front of her. Bluish light filled the room, and Davyn could see the strange pearlescent liquid moving unnaturally in the basin. Tendrils of mist rose and fell above the liquid, but they didn't venture outside the walls of the basin.

"When I was very young, just a girl in fact, I used to go exploring in the woods with my brothers." Shemnara smiled at the memory. "In those days, Karoc-Tor was abandoned, believed haunted. My brothers all dared each other to go explore it. I went with them. We found the stairs leading down and the room of bones. I thought the liquid in the well was the most beautiful thing I'd ever seen. To get a better look, I climbed up to the edge and looked in."

"What happened?" Sindri pressed, barely able to contain himself.

Shemnara removed the blindfold, revealing the white burn mark across her eyes. "My brother threw something into the well, and the liquid splashed across my face. It burned me and I fainted. When I woke up, I was blind."

"How did you get this?" Nearra asked, looking into the basin.

"My brother got it for me," Shemnara replied, putting her blindfold back on. "He'd travel to the tor and bring back a little at a time, until there was enough to fill this basin."

"Then he walled up the passage," Elidor guessed, "so no one else would get hurt?"

Shemnara nodded. "He blamed himself for the loss of my eyes. He was my guardian for the rest of his life."

"What happened to him?" Sindri asked.

"His name was Tully," Shemnara explained. "He was the man the Beast killed the first night you were here."

Davyn remembered the grizzled man with the crossbow who had greeted them when they arrived, wounded and hungry at Shemnara's door.

"I'm sorry," Nearra said after a strained silence. "I shouldn't have pried."

"You have a right to know," Shemnara stated. "You risked a great deal to learn about your past. The least I can do is tell you my part in all this."

"Can you tell me about my past, then?" Nearra asked, hope in her voice.

Shemnara nodded. "I said I would and I will. Your memories were taken from you by a wizard named Maddoc. He sought to use you as a vessel to further his knowledge of magic."

"But I don't know any magic," Nearra cried.

"An ancient power is upon you," Shemnara answered. "Where this power came from or how Maddoc knew of this, I cannot say, but his interest in you will be increased now. Your exposure to the liquid in the well has strengthened the bond between you and this power."

"How will Maddoc know about the well?" Nearra asked.

"He and his agents have observed you since the start of your journey," Shemnara answered simply.

The hair on the back of Davyn's neck was standing up.

"How is Maddoc watching us?" Catriona demanded.

"Perhaps you'd better ask his son," Shemnara answered, turning to Davyn.

All eyes turned to Davyn, who squirmed uncomfortably on the hard chair. Catriona had a look of murderous outrage on her face, but Nearra's look of hurt and betrayal cut Davyn to the quick.

"First of all, I'm not Maddoc's son," he said, holding up his hands for everyone to stay calm.

"You knew," Nearra gasped, the look of hurt turning to anger on her face. "You've been leading me around by the nose for all these months!"

Nearra's face was flushed with rage and she sprang to her feet. Without a pause, she said something—something guttural, as if in another language. The frail girl flung out her hand as if clutching something in the air, and suddenly Davyn felt himself gripped by a tremendous crushing power. The chair he was sitting on shattered, and he felt as if the Beast were back atop him, crushing the life out of him.

"What do you get out of all this?" Nearra shrieked. "Is he paying you?"

Davyn tried to speak, to explain, but he couldn't breathe.

"That's enough," Catriona shouted, the color gone from her face.

The shout seemed to startle Nearra, and she opened her hand. Immediately Davyn was released and fell gasping to the floor. Nearra clasped her hands to her mouth as if just realizing what she had done. There was fear in her eyes.

"I'm sorry," she cried, rushing to Davyn's side.

"Maddoc used you . . . ," Davyn gasped, "to try to revive a dead sorceress. Asvoria. That's where . . . your power comes from."

Davyn gulped a big breath of air and went on.

"I didn't know it would turn out like this. Once I realized that Maddoc was probably going to kill you, kill all of us, I tried to save you. I led us here, away from Maddoc."

"Why didn't you say something?" Nearra challenged him. "Why didn't you tell me?"

Davyn hung his head. "I was afraid you'd hate me," he admitted. "I'm so sorry."

Nearra's face softened, willing to believe him. But Catriona was not so easily convinced.

"You just expect us to trust you?" she said with a dangerous tone in her voice.

Davyn shook his head, struggling to know where to begin to explain.

"Let me tell them," Elidor said from his seat on the far side of the basin.

Davyn nodded as Catriona whirled on Elidor.

"You knew about this?" she challenged.

Elidor nodded. "I learned about it yesterday. I would have told you, but Davyn wanted to tell you himself. He hasn't had a moment alone with any of you until now."

"Convenient," Catriona spat. "But how can we believe a word that comes out of that . . . that traitor's mouth now?"

"Fine. If you'll sit down and listen," Elidor said. "I'll tell you everything."

Catriona grunted a response but she did at least sit down. Elidor told them the whole tale from the beginning. Davyn wasn't sure he wanted the others to know about his father, but now was the time for the truth—as Shemnara had told him. By the time Elidor was done, even Catriona was shocked.

"This wizard must pay for his crimes," she snarled, her fists clenching reflexively.

"No," Davyn interjected. "Maddoc's a powerful wizard. Believe me. If we challenge him, it will only get us killed."

"I have to confront him," Nearra said in a small voice. "It's the only way to get my memories back."

"We'll stand with you, Nearra," Sindri declared eagerly.

"That's right," Catriona said.

"I won't be a party to getting you killed," Davyn said. "I'm going to the coast. From there I'm getting the first ship south."

"What about your promise to Set-ai?" Shemnara said softly. "You promised to take care of your friends, to lead them right."

Davyn looked around the room at the faces of his friends. In all his life he'd never been as close to anyone as he was to these people. He knew going up against Maddoc was folly but he had promised Set-ai he'd take care of them. If he left them, they'd go get themselves killed fighting Maddoc. If he stayed, he'd at least have time to talk them out of it.

"I promised you I'd always be there for you," he told Nearra. "If you really want to take on Maddoc, I'll help you."

"Excellent," Shemnara declared with a strange, knowing smile. "I understand Mayor Shelton has arranged rooms for you at the inn. I suggest you get a good night's sleep and you can decide where to go from here in the morning."

"I thought we were going after the wizard?" Sindri said with a puzzled look on his face.

"The wizard is a formidable foe," Shemnara said, smiling. "You may want to consider what you will need to be ready for him."

"She's right," Elidor said. "We can't just go up to Maddoc's home and knock on the door. We need a plan."

All eyes turned to Davyn.

"Maddoc tried to teach me magic when I was younger," he said, putting up his hands defensively. "I was no good at it."

"What about you?" Catriona asked Shemnara.

The white-haired seer smiled. "I'm sorry. I have told you all my visions have shown me. Beyond that, I have very little knowledge that would be useful to you."

"Do we succeed?" Sindri asked suddenly.

"I don't know for sure," Shemnara admitted. "I have the feeling that you have yet many roads to travel and many hardships to endure before your journey's end."

With that, their interview was over. Shemnara rose and the companions filed quietly out.

Davyn held the door for Nearra, who smiled sweetly at him as she left. He was about to follow her out when Elidor grabbed his shoulder.

"Do me a favor, boss," he whispered, holding up a piece of the shattered chair Davyn had been sitting on. "Never lie to her again."

"Don't call me boss," Davyn replied automatically.

"Sorry, boss," the elf replied, slipping out the open door.

Grumbling, Davyn followed Elidor down the narrow hallway to the front parlor. Mudd was waiting for them, ready to conduct them to their rooms at the inn. As the others filed out after the lad, a hand gripped Davyn's arm, holding him back. Davyn turned to find Nearra confronting him.

"I was really trying to protect you," he said.

"I believe you." She stepped so close to him he could feel her breath on his cheeks. "But I need to know I can trust you now."

Davyn wanted to tell her that he'd do anything for her, but having her so close to him seemed to be interfering with his ability to speak.

"Uh," he managed.

"Maddoc will try to stop us," Nearra continued, still standing close. "We might even have to kill him."

There was a strange edge in Nearra's voice, and Davyn looked immediately to her eyes. Rather than being their normal blue, they were that strange deep violet. Davyn realized that those eyes must have something to do with Nearra's lost memories. He wondered for a moment if they were her original color.

"Do you think you could kill the man who raised you?" she continued, unfazed by Davyn's inspection of her eyes.

"I don't think we should risk confronting him," Davyn said, shaking off some of the paralysis he felt with Nearra so near. "If you want to face him, though," he conceded, "I'm with you to the end."

Nearra smiled a dazzling smile that made Davyn's knees wobbly.

"Good," she said. "That's what I wanted to hear." Then she did something totally unexpected—she reached up, put her arms around his neck and kissed him.

Davyn felt as if his body were so light that he was floating off the floor. Nearra held him tightly, pressing her lips to his for what seemed like an eternity.

Finally Nearra released him and stepped back, smiling up at Davyn.

"We'd better not keep the others waiting too long," she said shyly. "They'll get ideas."

With that Nearra turned and walked out the open door of the parlor. After a moment to catch his breath, Davyn followed her out into the winter night, closing the heavy door behind him.

26 SHAERA

Oddvar crouched against the sheltered side of the healer's house. The wind had picked up and the winter chill made his joints stiff. Inside the house, he knew, his young quarries were talking. If he pressed his ear to the frozen wall, he could just make out the sound of voices, but it wasn't loud enough to hear what they were saying.

The dwarf's keen sense of self-preservation had allowed him to escape the destruction of Karoc-Tor. After he left the weapons by the prison cell, he reasoned he ought to be away from Gadion as quickly as he could. He had hurried onto the path that wound around the tor and waited there, preparing to ambush the children as they made their escape. But what happened next, of course, was so astounding Oddvar wouldn't have believed it if he hadn't seen it with his own eyes. A great dragon made of mist had torn the citadel, and the entire tor, down. It was a disturbing display of power, and the dwarf wasn't entirely certain that the girl, Nearra, hadn't done it. Maddoc had said she possessed extraordinary magic and that stressful situations would release it.

On top of everything else, there was also the fact that Oddvar didn't know how the youths had survived the dragon's attack. He knew for a fact they didn't leave by way of the path that wound around the citadel. Imagine his surprise when he learned they'd been seen in the town. Now he stood crouched in the snow in an effort to hear anything that might shed some light on the mystery.

Taking up burgling? A distant, high-pitched voice suddenly sounded in his mind.

The dwarf started, half drawing his dagger before he saw Maddoc's black falcon, Shaera.

"Don't do that," Oddvar grumbled, knowing full well that Maddoc took great delight in startling him.

I expected to find you with Gadion, Maddoc said, *but instead I find Karoc-Tor in ruins.*

Oddvar quickly explained what happened at the tor. "Could it have been the girl?" he asked, still straining to listen to the conversation taking place inside the building.

I doubt she has any such power, Maddoc answered, though Oddvar was pleased to hear a tone of uncertainty in the voice. *How did they escape?* he pressed. *Were any of them hurt?*

"I haven't seen them yet," Oddvar whispered back. "As to how they got out, you're the wizard, you tell me."

Oddvar, I'm paying you . . .

The dwarf waved Maddoc silent and pressed his ear against the wall. The voices had died away.

"They're on the move," he hissed, moving around to the side of the building. "Someone said they're staying at the inn, so we should be able to get a good look at them when they leave."

Oddvar stole quickly behind a large tree as the door to the healer's house opened. The falcon soared into the branches over his head, and together they watched as four youths emerged and walked toward the inn.

"They don't look hurt," Oddvar observed.

Where's the girl, Maddoc asked, *and my son?*

231

"They haven't come out yet." Oddvar shrugged. "Maybe it wasn't wise to make your son the girl's protector."

What do you mean?

"Well," Oddvar said slyly, "he's a healthy young man, she's a healthy young girl . . . "

Oddvar left the thought hanging, not wanting to press Maddoc too hard. To the dwarf's immense satisfaction, there was a long pause from the falcon. Clearly Maddoc had not considered the dangers of putting two young people in such close proximity. Before he could answer, however, Nearra exited the house followed closely by Davyn.

You had me worried for a moment, Maddoc admitted. *My son knows his duty.*

"Can you tell if the girl's found her magic?" the dwarf asked.

Not from this distance, but I doubt it.

"Why?" Oddvar wondered.

Asvoria was not the kind of woman to have a quiet chat in a muddy little village, Maddoc explained. *If she'd resurfaced, she would have taken over by now.*

"What should I do, then?" Oddvar asked.

Keep following them for the moment. We'll arrange more challenges for them once they're back in civilized lands.

"Fine by me," Oddvar grumbled. "In that case, I'm going back to my campfire."

I think I'll go take a closer look, Maddoc said, as the falcon took off and glided easily toward the center of town.

Oddvar turned and trudged wearily back into the woods. He knew that five miles away Drefan, Fyren, and Gifre were roasting a pig. As he walked, he imagined he could smell it. It had been too long since Oddvar had eaten or slept and he was eager to be about it.

If Oddvar had just stayed in town a little longer, he would have seen Maddoc's falcon land on a windowsill, peering through the shutters.

He would have seen the bird suddenly seized by an invisible force and pulled right through the crack in the shutter.

There was nothing but a puff of feathers and a drop of blood left behind.

The adventure continues in

Return of the Sorceress

by Tim Waggoner

Armed with new weapons and a newfound confidence, Nearra and her friends plan to confront the wizard Maddoc. But before they can reach Cairngorn Keep, a skeletal griffin kidnaps Nearra and delivers her directly into the wizard's hands.

As Maddoc prepares the final spell to unleash the Emergence, Davyn and the others struggle to rescue Nearra. But in the confines of Maddoc's keep, appearances deceive. Friends become enemies. Dark dreams become reality. And naive Nearra may not be as innocent as she seems.

Available November 2004

ENTER A WORLD OF ADVENTURE

Do you want to learn more about the world of Krynn?
Look for these and other **Dragonlance®** books in the fantasy section
of your local bookstore or library.

TITLES BY MARGARET WEIS AND TRACY HICKMAN

Legends Trilogy
TIME OF THE TWINS, WAR OF THE TWINS,
AND TEST OF THE TWINS
A wizard weaves a plan to conquer darkness—
and bring it under his control.

THE SECOND GENERATION
The sword passes to a new generation of heroes—
the children of the Heroes of the Lance.

DRAGONS OF SUMMER FLAME
A young mage seeks to enter the Abyss in search of his lost uncle,
the infamous Raistlin.

The War of Souls Trilogy
DRAGONS OF A FALLEN STAR, DRAGONS OF A LOST STAR,
DRAGONS OF A VANISHED MOON
A new war begins, one more terrible than any in Krynn have ever known.

Want to know how it all began?

Want to know more about the Dragonlance® world?

Find out in this new boxed set of the first Dragonlance titles!

A Rumor of Dragons
Volume 1

Night of the Dragons
Volume 2

The Nightmare Lands
Volume 3

To the Gates of Palanthas
Volume 4

Hope's Flame
Volume 5

A Dawn of Dragons
Volume 6

Gift Set available September 2004
By Margaret Weis & Tracy Hickman
For ages 10 and up

THE NEW ADVENTURES

JOIN A GROUP OF FRIENDS AS THEY UNLOCK MYSTERIES OF THE DRAGONLANCE WORLD!

TEMPLE OF THE DRAGONSLAYER
Tim Waggoner

Nearra has lost all memory of who she is. With newfound friends, she ventures to an ancient temple where she may uncover her past. Visions of magic haunt her thoughts. And someone is watching.

July 2004

THE DYING KINGDOM
Stephen D. Sullivan

In a near-forgotten kingdom, an ancient evil lurks. As Nearra's dark visions grow stronger, her friends must fight for their lives.

July 2004

THE DRAGON WELL
Dan Willis

Battling a group of bandits, the heroes unleash the mystic power of a dragon well. And none of them will ever be the same.

September 2004

RETURN OF THE SORCERESS
Tim Waggoner

When Nearra and her friends confront the wizard who stole her memory, their faith in each other is put to the ultimate test.

November 2004

For ages 10 and up